# HER SECOND EARTH

## A SCI-FI ROMANCE OF

## ESCAPE, DISCOVERY, AND

## SECOND CHANCES

Amy L. Barrows

This novel contains depictions of relationship abuse. Reader discretion is advised.

ISBN-13: 979-8-9932204-0-6

Cover design by: 100covers

Printed in the United States of America

WASTLER PUBLISHING

# CHAPTER 1

From the outside world, it looked like I had a perfect life: a successful accountant husband, two adorable children, and the most beautiful house with a white picket fence and well-manicured lawn in the quaint waterfront town of Juno Bay, Maryland. Everyone thought I had it all. But looks can be deceiving. I learned early on in our marriage to put on a fake smile and pretend like everything was bliss. Behind closed doors, though, I was married to a narcissistic asshole named Griffin Cromwell. He micromanaged everything-from how I folded the laundry to how I cooked and cleaned. He even had to approve our weekly meals, and I couldn't deviate from it. Every dollar I spent had to be accounted for.

Griffin's emotional abuse made our home feel like a prison. He hurled insults, belittled me, frequently called me a terrible mother. One particularly heated argument occurred when I let our daughter, Autumn, visit a friend's house.

Griffin exploded in rage, shouting, "You're the stupidest motherfucker on the planet. I am amazed at your lack of brains."

Whenever Griffin exploded like that, I tried to shield the kids. I'd let Autumn visit friends and distract Dylan with a movie, keeping the volume high enough to drown out the yelling. I'd nod and agree to keep the peace.

Each morning, Griffin left for work around 6 a.m., claiming he wanted to avoid city traffic. I didn't care why, his absence was a relief. I'd get the kids ready, drop them at school, and head to my job as a Registered Xray Technologist at an outpatient clinic just ten minutes away. The hours fit perfectly, and I never missed a chance to tell the kids I loved them, something they never heard from their dad.

When the kids were younger, I paid an elderly neighbor, Mrs. Wilkinson, to watch them after school. Griffin was never home in time to help, so I handled everything. On a chilly evening, I'd quickly walk over in the brisk wind with the smell of winter in the air to pick them up.

"Hi, Mrs. Wilkinson. I hope the kids were good for you this afternoon."

"Hello, Faith dear. Yes indeed. They always are. I love talking to them both. And that Dylan sure does have some stories." Mrs. Wilkinson informed me.

"Oh, that he does. Always. Thanks again. See you tomorrow."

I always worried about all the stories Dylan shared. Was he telling people too much? What if he disclosed too much about what really goes on in the house?

That night, as we walked back, Dylan chattered happily while Autumn was unusually quiet.

"Autumn, honey, are you okay?"

"Yes, Mommy. I don't want Daddy to come home. He is so mean sometimes. I hate to see how he treats you."

I bent down and hugged her. "Oh, sweetheart, those are adult worries. Don't let it trouble you. Daddy is just stressed at work right now. He would never do anything to hurt you purposefully."

Even as I was saying it, I wasn't sure that was true. I hoped it was. It did seem to ease Autumn's fears some, though. Luckily, I sheltered Dylan enough that he did not know exactly how his dad acted. Just then, I got a text from Griffin.

Griffin: "Hey, sorry I'm going to be late. Going out for drinks with the guys from work."

I always had mixed emotions when he stayed out late. We got some peace, but I couldn't shake the feeling he was hiding something. Was he cheating? I was too scared to find out. I didn't think I could survive on my own as a single mother.

"Well, Daddy will be home late tonight."

Autumn perked up. "Oh, cool! Can I watch some TV then?"

"After you do your homework, you can."

With a smile, Autumn skipped into the house.

I still cooked the approved dinner, just in case Griffin came home and expected it. Then the kids and I cuddled on the couch under a thick blanket and watched a movie together which was a rare treat since Griffin monopolized the TV. It felt…peaceful.

When the movie ended, I announced, "OK, guys, time to get ready for bed."

"If you take your baths, I'll read you a book." I added.

"OK, Mommy," they said in unison.

And so, we launched into our nightly ritual. After their baths, we all cuddled up on Dylan's bed and read a chapter of The Magic Treehouse. Even as they got older, it stayed part of our routine. It was our way of bonding.

One evening, Autumn looked at me seriously, "Mommy, why don't you leave Daddy? He's so mean to you. You looked happy tonight without him being home calling you names."

My heart sank. I hadn't even realized Autumn knew how Griffin talked to me.

"Oh, honey, you shouldn't worry about things like that. We have a good life here."

"Yes, Mommy, a nice house in a nice neighbor-hood. But at what cost?"

I hugged her tightly, saying, "Oh, such a wise soul in a beautiful little girl."

And I left it at that, because honestly, I didn't know how to respond. I don't understand why I continue to endure all the things I did. Years have passed, and I was still going through life without genuine happiness. Griffin and I are more like roommates now. There's no longer any romantic love between us.

One morning, Dylan woke me up, looking pale and sick. "Mommy, I don't feel so good. I think I'm going to be sick."

Griffin and I both jumped up. Neither of us wanted Dylan to throw up in the bed. I carried him to the bathroom just in time. Poor thing looked green. I sat with him while I grabbed the thermometer.

I was shocked to see Griffin in the bathroom with us. He never helped when the kids were sick. I checked Dylan's temp—101°.

"He can't go to school," I said. "But Griffin, I'm the only mammography tech scheduled today. I can't call out."

Griffin looked at me, then at Dylan. "That's okay, buddy. I'll stay home and take care of you. But we'll have to go to the doctor."

"Okay, Daddy."

After settling Dylan in our bed, I got Autumn ready for school. I must've looked like a wreck when I arrived at work because my coworkers were visibly concerned.

Megan Lovelace, my work best friend, approached me. "Faith, are you okay? Griffin didn't do anything to you, did he?"

"No. Actually, he was helpful this morning. Dylan is sick, and Griffin offered to stay home and take him to the doctor."

"That's surprising."

"Yes. But he came home late and drunk last night. He probably just feels guilty. Something feels off. I can't figure it out."

"Oh, Faith, I'm sorry. He doesn't deserve you. You deserve better."

"Thanks, Megan. Right now, I'm just worried about Dylan."

I checked my phone all day, hoping for updates. Griffin hated when I texted too much, so I waited. Finally, at 1 p.m., I got a message:

"Hey, Dylan got the stomach flu going around. He needs to stay home tomorrow from school."

"Okay, thank you. I'll talk to Mrs. Wilkinson when I get home."

He replied quickly. "Don't. I already talked to her. She said she can watch Dylan all day for a small fee. Stupid old broad."

Griffin could be so inconsiderate. "Don't worry about it. I'll pay her. It's the least I can do."

No response. I finally focused on work, knowing Dylan was okay.

After my shift, I pulled into the driveway and saw Autumn coming from Mrs. Wilkinson's. A gust of wind hit me as I stepped out.

"Hey, sweetie, what were you doing over there?"

"I saw Dad was home, so I asked Mrs. Wilkinson if I could stay with her until you came. I helped her make cookies."

"Oh, that was nice of her."

Inside, Dylan was curled up on one couch. Griffin sat on the other, glued to the TV.

"Hey, buddy. How are you feeling?"

"A little better. The doctor gave me some medicine."

"I'll start dinner. Maybe just soup for you."

Griffin nodded but didn't say anything. As I turned to go, he called out:

"Faith?"

"Yes?" I asked cautiously.

"Pathetic. You call yourself a mother? You abandoned your son in his time of need. Good thing I was kind enough to stay with him."

Dylan glanced at me, embarrassed. I was furious. How dare he talk like that in front of our son?

"Griffin, I told you—I couldn't get off work. You know I would have if I could."

"Yeah, yeah. Always an excuse. Now go make dinner. You're already behind."

I rolled my eyes as I walked away. He could be such an asshole. While he laughed at whatever was on TV, I started cooking spaghetti—an easy meal that didn't take much thought. I had no energy left.

Dinner was quiet. Autumn did homework afterward. Dylan stayed on the couch. I cleaned up alone while Griffin watched TV.

My thoughts swirled. What am I doing? This isn't healthy—for me or the kids. But it's expensive out there. I can't live on my own. I stared out the kitchen window, imagining a better life. A loving husband. A warm embrace. Someone who helped, who cared. Then I jumped—pain shot through my side. Griffin had hit me. He stared, unapologetic, as I turned to face him.

"What are you doing?" he snapped.

I looked back at the overflowing sink. "Oh, shit. Sorry."

"Be more careful. We don't need a ruined floor from your stupidity."

Later that night, once the kids were asleep, I lay in bed staring at the ceiling. This wasn't the life I wanted. Not for me. Not for my kids.

Now, Autumn is 23 and away at college studying physical therapy. She barely comes home. Dylan, 21, lives with my parents and works maintenance at a small airport. Despite everything, they grew into kind, loving adults.

I miss them terribly. But I'm grateful they're no longer trapped here.

That night, I whispered a prayer to God:

*Help me. Please. This can't be all there is.*

I pulled the covers up to my chin, willing my mind to quiet as the house settled into stillness. Griffin's breathing had already deepened beside me, steady and oblivious. My eyes grew heavy as she stared at the ceiling, the soft glow of the streetlights filtering through the curtains.

I must have finally drifted off to sleep because I got startled awake by the loudest noise. At first, I thought it was Griffin downstairs, but when I looked over in bed, he was sound asleep. Listening more closely, there appeared to be a nasty storm going on. I could see flashes of lightning outside. Funny—I didn't think it was supposed to storm tonight. I remember hearing the weatherman say it would be clear skies to-night.

Lots of thunder and lightning, along with enough wind I thought we may be having a tornado. Surely any minute now the windows were going to shatter inward. I was seriously waiting for the roof to be ripped off. It sounded like the lightning hit something right outside our house. I don't know how my family was sleeping through all this racket.

There seemed to be a big explosion followed by a huge flash of light—then everything went black. It must have blown a transformer. The streetlights were out. That seemed to be the last of the storm because everything got quieter… then quiet. Almost too quiet.

Suddenly, I found myself getting super sleepy, almost like I was being drugged.

# CHAPTER 2

I woke with a start, heart pounding. Something felt...wrong

Usually, Griffin's clumsy morning routine would wake me, he was never quiet, always crashing around, caring only for himself. Or Dylan would be my wake-up call, running into my room and yanking open the blinds to shout in his cute little voice, "It's wake up time!"

But not today. Today was too quiet.

This morning felt eerie. It was too quiet. And something felt off. I can't quite put my finger on what it was, though. I sat up in bed and looked around. Everything looked like it was right, but at the same time, it didn't. Feeling nervous chills go down my spine, I started looking around. To my immediate right, I noticed the sun was shining in the window. Seeing that, I felt glad the storm had passed over us fairly quickly. Stormy days always make for busy days at the medical center. The pale blue window treatments were the same. Nothing had changed there. I slowly rotated my head to the left. In the corner of the room was our blue accent wingback chair with my favorite pale yellow chenille blanket draped over the back of the chair. OK, so that's the same. What is this feeling I have? I continued to survey my bedroom. My eyes went to my dresser that is across from our king-sized bed. That actually looks a little neater. I swore I went to bed with my dresser a mess. I meant to straighten it up last night, but with it having been such a busy day, I forgot. It still had the light blue accent lamps on either side of the dresser with the round mirrored glass tray I had my perfume and jewelry sitting on. That was still the same. The wall color was still the same pale yellow color I fell in love with when we first moved in. The door to our room was in between where my dresser and Griffin's dresser normally was, but while the door was in the same location, Griffin's dresser was gone. What the hell? That's very odd. Now I am really confused. But I continue my survey. An old Victorian vanity was in the place where Griffin's dresser should have been. Oh, I'm loving that. Great taste. Continuing on, I noticed double doors that are closed. I can only guess that it is our walk-in closet. I am curious about what's behind that door, but I've got more important things to worry about right now. Like what in the world is going on here. I prayed that God would help me out of this bad marriage. Was this the answer to my nightmare of a marriage? Did I do this?

On my far left, I saw the bathroom door, which was opened. There were no lights on inside, but it looked like it was as I remembered it. At least from where I was sitting, nothing in there had changed. I laid back in bed a minute to try and process what I had just seen. Looking up at the ceiling, I was overjoyed to see the canopy with the fairy lights I installed. I just love those. It adds a peaceful, romantic feel. But there was something definitely off. Mostly everything looked the same, but where was Griffin's dresser, and where were Griffin and the kids?

Stumbling out of bed, I put on my furry, cushioned flip-flop slippers and started off walking around upstairs first. All the rooms were where they were supposed to be, but the hallway looked smaller somehow. Stepping out of my room to the left was the kids' bathroom. Luckily, I guess, that looked the same. No change there. There was still a small linen closet across from that bathroom. Next to the linen closet was Autumn's room. Looking into what was supposed to be her room, I stopped dead in my tracks. I had to hold onto the doorframe. I felt faint. Nothing was like it was last night. It was like she had never lived here. Once I got up enough courage, I stepped inside. As soon as I stepped inside, the shades on the windows immediately opened, flooding the room with warm sunlight. It was like they were set on some motion sensor or something. OK, I'll admit, that made me jump a little, but it WAS very cool. The room was set up as an office. The room was minimalistic in design. The walls were a pretty antique white. A small white desk with two drawers was sitting across from the doorway. A fancy swivel chair was at the desk. In the middle of the desk sat a nice-looking laptop with rose gold accessories laying around the perimeter. Looking to my left, I noticed a decent-sized bookshelf with a few books and knick-knacks on different shelves. A comfy-looking hunter green armchair nestled in the corner next to the bookshelf with a white chenille blanket draped on the back. Damn, this version of me loved those chenille blankets. A small round wooden table sat next to the chair. On the opposite corner was a good-sized tall fig tree. I walked up to it. Yep, it was real. And this version of me apparently has a green thumb. Interesting. Well, I do like the way this room is decorated. My style indeed.

Once I had enough of Autumn's room, or well, I guess the office now, I gathered up my strength to walk over to Dylan's room.  If my firstborn child's room was

an office, what on earth was Dylan's room going to look like?  Walking across the hall, I closed my eyes, put out my hands to feel for the doorway, and stepped into his room.  I heard the shades on the windows opening themselves up again.  Slowly opening my eyes, my heart sank again.  My stomach felt like it was turning inside out.  Straight across from the door, there was a bed in his room, but it was definitely not his room any- more.  Where, oh, where was my baby?  A queen-sized bed with a tall beige fabric headboard was where Dyl-

an's bed used to be. The footboard and side rails were

also made of a beige fabric.  There was a beautiful sage green bedspread with sage green accent pillows on the bed.  The walls were painted with the same an- tique white as the office.  On either side of the bed, there were matching antique white nightstands with two drawers.  Small, elegant lamps adorned the nightstands.   On the far right wall underneath a win- dow was another accent chair.  This one was beige with a sage green chenille blanket draped over the

back.  Why am I not surprised it's another chenille

blanket?  On the same wall as the door, sat a dresser with a mirror attached that matched the nightstands. On either side of the dresser, there were sage green lamps with beige lampshades.  This was another well- decorated room.

So far I was impressed with the way the upstairs looked.  All the rooms seemed the same size, but over- all the whole second floor looked smaller than I re-

membered it.  My family couldn't have just disappeared

like that.  I did pray to God to help me the night before, but He would not have just taken my kids from me.  I mean, it's not like Griffin could have taken them while I was sleeping. It doesn't look like they have ever been here. Stepping out into the hall, I noticed for the first time that the hall was not carpeted like it had been last night. There were beautiful oak hardwood floors with a white and light blue rug runner going down the middle of the hall. I walked down the hall and stopped at the top of the stairs. Before I could get up enough courage to venture down to the first floor, I think I need to shower first. After all, I do have to get ready for work.

Making my way to the bathroom, I did a quick glance into the rooms as I passed by. This house doesn't seem like mine anymore. I really don't know what's going on. I gotta figure it out, but first, a shower. Hopefully, it'll wake me up, and I'll realize this is just a weird, bad dream. I want my precious kids back. Walking into the bath, the lights came on by themselves. Very futuristic. The bathroom, just like the rest of the upstairs, looked familiar but didn't. The shower looked like what I remember, with one expectation: there was an electrical panel where the shower knob should be. Oh boy, now how does this work? The panel was about a 1-foot square. I touched it, and the screen came to life.

"Good morning, Faith," a synthetic voice chimed.

My heart jumped. What the hell? Now it talks too.

I hope it can't see me naked, I thought.

"Hello," I said back.

"Would you like your usual shower this morning?"

I stared, stunned. "Yes, please."

Hot water streamed instantly. As soon as my hair was wet, a perfect amount of shampoo dispensed. Conditioner followed. Then body wash. I didn't lift a finger. It was luxurious. Creepy but luxurious.

When I stepped out, I realized there were no towels. A hidden panel popped open, revealing a robotic arm holding a heated towel. A gust of warm air from the ceiling dried me like a car wash.

"Okay, definitely in the future," I muttered, wrapping the towel around me.

I stepped into the closet. The lights blinded on, revealing rows of clothes and cabinets. A flat screen blinked to life.

"Good morning, Faith. Is it a work day or leisure day?"

"Hello, it's a work day," I cautiously replied.

Out of nowhere, the clothes rods started rotating like they were on a conveyor belt. It stopped at what looked like business attire. Those aren't scrubs. I started looking around. Come to think of it, I don't see any scrubs anywhere. I guess whatever I am, I'm not a Registered X-ray Technologist. I walked over and picked out a pencil skirt with a white button-down shirt and black heels. Man, I'm used to wearing scrubs and tennis shoes, not heels. I hope I can walk in these. Once I got dressed, I went back to the bathroom and finished getting ready by doing my hair and makeup. Walking into my bedroom, I took one last look in the full-length mirror that was on the bathroom door.

*Not bad for someone that never dresses up. Maybe that is part of my problem with my marriage. I let myself go. Wait, do I even still have a marriage? What crazy shit happened here? My thoughts were going a mile a minute, it seemed.*

Walking down the hall to the stairs, I started getting nervous. If the upstairs changed this much, I wondered what the main floor looked like. As I got to the top of the stairs, I noticed they too were hardwood with the same blue and white runner going down the center of the stairs.

"Interesting. I didn't notice that before my shower. I must be in shock or something."

As I descended the stairs, the blinds on all the windows started opening up. I'm glad it was still sunny out. I love the warm sun even in the winter. I stopped at the bottom of the stairs and took in what I saw. To my left were double front doors, now donned with elegant decorative glass with side glass panels on either side. At least they were pretty. To my far right was a hallway that looked like it led to the kitchen. I'll save that for last. I can look at that before I eat breakfast. Straight ahead was the living room. Might as well start there. I walked to the living room and stopped in the entranceway. I looked all around, taking everything in. It was very elegant in decor. The room itself was much bigger.   The walls were painting a light beige color. Straight ahead on the far wall was a huge fireplace with a white mantel and beige tile.  On the mantel sat a big mirror with a navy blue frame.  To the left of the mirror were three silver vases of varying sizes, and the right were two small picture frames with what looked like my parents and sister in them.  At least that didn't change.

The fireplace itself was a little futuristic looking.  It was just a big black box with an open space in the middle that looked empty.  I guess that is where you put the logs.  I'll have to figure that out later.  The wall to the left had two floor-to-ceiling windows with long navy blue drapes.  In between the windows was a long navy blue accent table.  In the middle of the room was a light blue and white rug that took up almost the whole room.  It looked like it matched the rug upstairs and the one on the stairs. There were two light beige couches and either side of the rug with two navy blue chairs up against the same wall  that the entrance to the living room was on.  Right in front of the fireplace was a beautiful chaise lounger.  I bet that's a good place to get toasty warm after a snowstorm.  In the middle of the furniture was an oval coffee table with a marble top and silver metal legs. In the center of the table was a black box.  I moved in to get a closer look.  It didn't look like it did anything. Out of nowhere, a voice spoke.

"Good morning, Faith." It said as I approached. "Would you like to watch a little TV?"

And with that being said, a big projection of a news channel appeared out of the black box.

"No, thank you."

A projection of a news channel briefly appeared, then vanished just as quickly.

Okay, TV cube. Got it.

On the wall opposite the windows was the entrance to the dining room. The blinds were also opened, revealing a big glass dining room table with seating for ten people. There were high leather-backed beige chairs around the table. Above the table was a modern-looking crystal chandelier. The walls were painted a light blue color. Straight across from the entrance was another floor-to-ceiling window with the same drapes as in the living room. It tied everything together. To the left of the window was a long beige buffet cabinet that matched the table. The opposite wall was the entrance into the kitchen. This is the room I need. All this touring of the house, well, I guess my house, was making me hungry.

Walking into the kitchen was like stepping into the future. Everything looked so high-tech. It was so very open and white. There was a white table with a hole in the middle and matching chairs off to one side of the room. No cabinets or appliances were in the so-called kitchen. Just a long countertop on one wall with two bar stools and a touchscreen pad.

A voice announced, "Good morning, Faith. What would you like for breakfast?"

"Oh, hi. Um, I guess I'll just have a hard-boiled egg and fruit."

"I am forever at your service. I will get it for you. Have a seat at the counter. It will come up in just a minute."

I looked over to the counter. I grabbed the first bar stool and sat down. Once I sat down, I just realized I had not sat down since I woke up. I was tired and I hadn't even gotten to work yet. I don't even know what I do for a career. Hopefully, I can figure it out once I get to wherever I need to go. I'll figure that out later. All of a sudden, I heard a low humming noise and out of the middle of the countertop came a robotic arm with a tray holding my breakfast.

"Wow, thank you."

"You're welcome, ma'am. Can I get you any-thing else?"

"Yes, please, some coffee would be nice."

"Right away, ma'am."

"Oh, wait. I need...."

"Yes, we know all your preferences. Black and decaf. Always. Ma'am"

Just then a tall cup of black coffee appeared on the tray next to my breakfast. As I sat eating my break-fast, a small screen popped up from the middle of the countertop and the news started playing. "Oh, I didn't push any buttons to watch TV. I like to eat my break-fast in peace and quiet."

"Ma'am. Don't you remember? It's mandatory viewing first thing in the morning."

"Oh, I'm sorry.  I don't know what's wrong with me.  I forgot"

"Ma'am, are you feeling okay?  You seem a little off this morning. I can have a doctor come and give you a physical. "

"No, that's alright.  I'm fine, thank you.  Just didn't get enough sleep last night."

While I was eating, I started watching the news. After all, maybe it'll clue me in on what's going on.  A female voice spoke up on the TV

"Good morning city residents.  Today is Thursday, February 18th, in the year 2036. Hope all is well…"

*Wait, 2036?  The date was right, but with all this futuristic bullshit, I was sure that maybe I time traveled somehow.  Even though that's impossible.  Confusion filled my mind.*

The female news anchor continued "As you know, the Space Fleet set out to orbit our planet to protect us against the upcoming invasion of the Cordelia tribe.  As we have recently found out, their home is on the moon of Uranus.  Their technology is much more advanced than ours."

"Great," I muttered. "I escaped a narcissistic husband somehow just to come to a world that is getting ready to be invaded by aliens."

Luckily, I was done with breakfast. Time to brush my teeth so I can leave for work. However, I'm not sure where to go for that. As I was walking up the stairs to my bathroom, I thought "Maybe the car's GPS will give some clues". Once in the bathroom, I realized my toothbrush was not in the holder like it normally was. Actually, there was no toothbrush holder. OK, now I know damn well that dental health is still important. I opened up the medicine cabinet to see my toothbrush on the middle shelf. Oh, thank God. Well, damn, I hope there is still a God. Everything here is making me second-guess everything I have ever known. Surveying the cabinet, I noticed there was no toothpaste.

"UGH!! Now where is the toothpaste?"

Just then, a long tube came out of a hole on the side of the medicine cabinet. At the end of the tube was a little valve. Reluctantly, I held my toothbrush up to the valve. To my surprise, it squirted just the right amount of toothpaste. Looking at the faucet, I saw there were no knobs to turn on the water. This house can be very frustrating when you don't know how to use anything. I guess once I get used to it, it'll be great. I waved my hand under the faucet, and water started to come out. I placed my toothbrush under the water to wet it a little, then began brushing my teeth. Once finished, I started looking around.

"Now where do I find mouthwash? This is all too much."

Just as I was getting frustrated again, a little cup came out of a small opening in the tile by the counter. I grabbed the cup and saw my minty mouthwash. It's weird. It's like this house is reading my mind. No, it can't be. I am a person of routine. I'm sure this version of me is too. After I spit out the mouthwash, I looked up into the mirror.

"Damn, I clean up nice. Now to find out where I work."

I headed downstairs and approached the coat closet.

"Can I help you, ma'am?" The house computer asked.

"Jeez, that damn voice is everywhere. Oh, I was just going to get my coat."

"Your coat, ma'am? I am confused."

"Well, it is February. I can't exactly go outside without a coat on. It's freezing out."

Confused myself, I started opening the closet door.

"But ma'am. You don't need a coat. It's a balmy 72 degrees out."

With a puzzled look on my face, I said "But, how can that be? It's never that warm in February."

If it was at all possible, the computer voice spoke up again, sounding confused. I didn't realize a computer could sound confused, but I managed to confuse it. "But ma'am, it hasn't been cold in decades.

Don't you remember, the Earth was covered with greenhouse gas emissions, causing the temperature to slowly climb?"

Well, damn. I do remember the scientists on the Earth I came from saying something about that. I guess they were right.

"OK, well, thank you. Goodbye, I'm off to work."

"Goodbye, ma'am. Your car is all ready for you."

"Thank you. That was kind of you"

"It is always my pleasure to serve you."

I turned around and headed toward the kitchen. Once in the kitchen, I turned right and saw the door that led into the garage. I was a little apprehensive after all the garage I knew was a mess. It had everything from yard tools, golf clubs, shelves full of canned goods and cleaning supplies, a deep freezer, yard equipment, and let's not forget Griffin's gym equipment. Everything but cars. Thinking about what that garage looked like, apprehensively I slowly opened the door. It took me a minute to register what I was seeing. This is not a garage I was used to. For one, this was immaculate. The floor was a shiny gray concrete. NO stains or anything. My car was in the middle of the two-car garage. The car was beautiful. Can a car even be beautiful? I guess to a car geek, it can. I am not a car person by any means, but even I think this is cool. I started walking around the car. It was sleek in body with shiny gray paint. All the windows were tinted. Curves everywhere. It appeared to have a back seat. I'm not exactly sure how the car doors opened up or where the doors even were. And another important thing was missing. No wheels. There was a bright neon blue strip of light shining out from just under the bottom edge of the car. I walked up to the driver's side and started feeling around.

*How the hell am I supposed to get in? I thought.*

Just then, as my hand was feeling the smooth exterior, the whole driver's side opened up like on a hinge that was mounted on the roof of the car.

"OK, that was nifty."

Looking inside, everything was black leather. The seats looked like sleek black leather recliners. There was still a dashboard, but nothing was on it except the steering wheel, and that looked weird. It was just two crescent moon-shaped bars with a bigger solid bar in the middle.

Just as I was getting ready to get in the car, the garage doors opened up, but not the way I knew them to open. They slid open like if you were walking into a store. With them opened, I was finally able to get a good view of the street. I walked out onto the driveway and looked around. It was a beautiful sunny day, and I noticed a slight warm breeze in the air. Breathing in the air, I noticed a scent of fresh-cut grass and daffodils.

"These are smells of spring for sure. Not February winter smells."

The sun felt so good on my skin. I was glad to see there was still green grass and big mature trees lining the street. Walking a little further down the driveway, I noticed my picket fence.

"OH, thank God that's still here. I love that fence. Griffin always thought I was stupid for wanting a fence just for decorative purposes."

I walked to the end of the driveway to get a good look at the other houses on the street. Everybody's yard was so pristine. The exterior of all the houses looked the same. It was a sleek white exterior like maybe stucco with black trim. The windows on all the houses looked like they were all in the same exact places. I turned around to get a good look at my house. It used to be a brick house, but not anymore. It was the same sleek white exterior with black trim. Other than that, it looked like the exact same house. I heard a low rumble and looked toward the garage. The car started moving forward on its own. I was scared at first, but then realized that if my house can make me breakfast, I guess the car moving itself out of the garage should not be weird. The door to the car opened back up, and a voice from inside started speaking.

"Ma'am, we better get going. You are going to be late for work."

"Yes, I suppose you are right," I said as I was walking up to the car. I gently put my hand on the roof and took one more look around. Everything just seemed so clean and sterile. I wondered what work would be like.

"Here goes nothing."

I got into the car. As soon as my ass hit the seat, a seatbelt automatically fastened on my chest and waist.

"Oh, damn. That's a little tight. So, now what do I do?"

"Ma'am, you don't do anything. I will drive you to work."

"Right, of course, you can do that too. Good thing too because I don't know where I work."

After getting settled in my seat, I started feeling a little apprehensive. Even though this dimension's Faith had been working at this company, I had not. What if people can tell I have no idea what I'm doing? Will they call the cops and report me for being a fraud?

# CHAPTER 3

The car hummed softly as it navigated itself through the pristine neighborhood. A GPS of sorts popped up on the windshield like a hologram. I was glad to see it. I could watch where we were going. Driving downtown, I leaned back, taking in the sleek skyline. No cars had wheels. They were all hovering above the road. Looking around, I noticed everything seemed to have changed. I saw no fast food restaurants or coffee shops. Not even a Starbucks or a Dunkin'. Damn, I'm going to miss that coffee. The closer we got to the city, the more new-world the houses and buildings looked. Some structures even looked like they were hovering above the ground without anything anchoring them to the ground. There were no more bypasses anymore. Exit signs were just hovering in mid-air with yellow and white lights lighting up the roadway. Cars would go off their exit, ascending like an airplane. I looked up and saw cars whizzing by us in the air. I was stunned at what I saw. I've only ever seen this stuff in the movies. Before I knew it, my car was getting off one of those exits, and I could feel myself going further and further up in the air.

"Oh boy, I don't like heights."

With a queasy stomach, I felt myself holding on-to the seat for dear life. Once up in the air, we went faster than I've ever been in a car before. Now I see why these cars drive themselves these days. They almost have to. This could be very deadly. I felt myself getting nauseated, so I rolled down the window a little to get some fresh air, and the smell of the hot asphalt with an oily chemical odor came flooding in.

"Big mistake. That smell made me even more nauseous."

The closer I got to the city, I couldn't help but wonder how the roadways worked there. With the tall buildings, the roads can't be in the air like this can they? But my question was quickly answered not a minute later. I reached the city with all its labyrinth of tall buildings. Indeed, I did see cars coming and going in all directions on the ground and in the air. I don't know if I'll ever get used to seeing that. My car finally came to a stop at the famous 50-story Lowe building. Which is kind of weird. This is a financial building. I am horrible at math. Well, at least in my dimension, I am.

"Here we are, Ma'am. Your office building."

"Oh, why, thank you. I guess I'll be off then."

"Have a good day, Ma'am."

"Thank you."

"And Ma'am, your office is suite 3208. I thought I would remind you. You seem a little out of sorts today."

"Yes, I'm not feeling all that well. Thank you."

"Should I contact a doctor for you?"

"NO, that won't be necessary."

Stepping out of the car, I looked up and saw this building that at least looked like I remembered it in my world. Nothing too futuristic-looking. I slowly started walking toward the entrance while enjoying the gentle morning breeze. I was awestruck as I walked into the building. The floors were a shiny gray marble. There were magnificent floor-to-ceiling windows letting an abundance of light into the massive entryway. Everything else was white from the walls to the security desk that was in the middle of the room, to the elevator doors. I walked slowly past the guards. I wasn't sure if they would stop me or not.

"Good morning, Ms. Faith." A deep, masculine voice said as I walked past.

"Good morning." I wasn't sure of his name, so I left it at that.

There were ten elevators, five on each side. I was wondering which one mine was when Megan walked up to me.

"Hey, you. You didn't wait for me outside like normal."

"Oh, Megan. Am I glad to see you? I'm sorry. I'm not feeling particularly well today. It's been a strange morning."

"Oh, really? Are you okay?"

"Well, actually…." Just as I was getting up enough nerve to tell Megan everything, someone walked up behind us waiting on the elevator. I glanced over my shoulder and told Megan, "I'll talk to you later."

Megan glanced back and replied, "Oh, okay."

A ding sounded and the elevator doors opened up. We all stepped in and I noticed the elevator looked the same as before.

I was thinking, "Thank God this hasn't changed." All of an sudden the elevator whizzed sideways faster than a train. "Holy moly, I was not expecting that. NOW I'm dizzy."

Megan must have noticed my worried look because with a concerned voice she said,

"Hey, Faith, you okay?"

"Yeah, I'm fine. It's just been an interesting morning."

The elevator came to a sudden stop.

"*Oh,* thank God. We are done.*"* Or so I thought. But nope, the elevator, like a bolt of lightning, went up. "Great, here we go again."

Luckily that didn't take as long. Before I knew it we had stopped at the 32nd floor and the doors slid open. I stepped out and stopped. I had no idea where I was going.

"Faith, what are you doing? Our offices are this way." Megan explained as she was gesturing to the left.

"Oh, right. Sorry."

Megan glanced at my direction with a puzzled look. "Seriously, Faith. What's going on? You really are starting to worry me."

I looked around. Nobody was close to us, but I did notice we were walking toward a big, long desk with an older lady sitting down.

"Oh boy, you are going to think I've lost my mind." I glanced at her with a concerned look.

"I'm here for you. Nothing you can say will scare me."

"OK, but maybe someplace more private. Too many ears here."

"Well, let's go to your office." We started walking hastily down the hall to the right of the reception desk.

I stopped at the office door that said Faith Cromwell, Accounting Manager.

*That's funny. I guess in this world I'm actually good at math. I thought*

"Faith??"

"Oh, sorry. The title on the door just surprised me."

"Really?!? It shouldn't. You have always been a math wizard."

At that, I laughed, and Megan looked at me funny again. "Well, that's what I need to tell you."

"OK, you are kind of worrying me." Megan expressed.

I quickly opened the door and stepped inside. The décor inside was so white and sterile. Very minimalist. There was a white, small buffet-type cabinet on one wall with a nice green plant on top. Across from that sat my white desk with silver metal legs and a big-backed white leather executive chair. We walked inside. I glanced around out in the hall, then closed and locked the door.

Turning to Megan, I started explaining, "So what would you say if I told you I was from another time or place or universe? Honestly, I don't really know where to say I came from, but it's definitely not this time and place."

"I'd say, did you bump your head? I've known you since grade school. Faith, I swear, you have always been here."

"Yes, a version of me has, but Megan, something weird happened last night."

And with that, I started explaining everything. From my bad marriage to Griffin to my wonderful, loving kids to what my world looked like and how futuristic this world looks to the strange, bad storm that brought me here to this dimension.

All of a sudden, I screamed, "That's it. I'm in a different dimension."

"Faith, WHAT!!"

"Do you believe me? I just don't understand what else it could be."

"OK, I'll admit it. It's too much detail to be just a dream. And you never had a very good imagination. But honey, you are single, and I've never heard of anyone named Griffin. Which is a good thing because that guy sounds like an ass."

"Oh, you don't know the half of it. I remember praying to God to help me out of that bad marriage. Did I somehow cause this? If I knew I'd lose my kids, I would never have prayed that. I would have worded it differently. I just don't know what I'm supposed to do. Stay here or try to figure out a way to get back to my dimension."

"I don't think you caused this to happen to you. Would it be so bad for you to stay here? I mean, what life did you have there? You were in a bad marriage."

"Yes, I was, but I miss my kids. If I stay here, what does it mean for them? Does that time even exist? Are my kids wondering what happened to their mother?"

"Faith, honey, I know you have a lot of questions. I'll nonchalantly ask around to see if I can find someone who can answer some of your questions. In the meantime, why don't you try to get some work done?"

"Megan, I have no clue what I'm doing when it comes to math."

"Well, you might surprise yourself. Look at it this way. You are in THIS Faith's dimension. Maybe you have THIS Faith's brain. You know the smart one."

"Funny, really funny, Megan."

"Just trying to lighten the mood. Seriously, sweetie. Don't worry, we will figure this out." Megan moved closer to me and gave me a hug. I probably hugged a little too long, but I was lonely and needed someone. I'm just glad she didn't change.

As Megan turned to walk out of my office, I went over to the desk. Glancing around, I didn't see any computers, laptops, or printers for that matter. "Hey, Megan." Megan stopped in the doorway and turned back around to look at me.

"Hey, girl, what's up?"

"Um, where is the computer?"

"Oh, right, new dimension or whatever for you. So the computers that you had became nonexistent about 10 years ago. There is a microchip in the top of your desk. Once you sit down, just wave your hand over the desk, and a holographic image will pop up at an angle over the desk. Then a keyboard will appear on the desk."

"OK, does it speak too? My whole house seems to talk to me. Everything here is just so weird. I feel like I'm in a sci-fi movie."

"Well, you do love sci-fi. Sci-fi movies aren't really around these days. I mean, we are kind of living it now. And no, your computer does not talk to you randomly, but it is an option for certain things you may need." Megan explained to me.

"Gotcha. Thank you. I guess I should get to work then."

"Faith, don't worry. Our accounting software is AI-driven. So it should be super easy for you."

"Artificial Intelligence, really? I never thought that was a good idea when they were excited about trying it in my dimension. I mean, letting computers run things seems like a recipe for disaster. What will stop AI from taking over?"

"I agree. I was really worried at first. The government has protocols in place to prevent that kind of thing from happening. So far, it's been working fine. Try not to stress too much. Maybe working will get your mind off things. I'll come by at lunch to walk you to the cafeteria."

"That sounds good. Thank you, Megan. I'm so glad you are here."

Megan took one last look at me, waved, and went to her office. I walked across my office and sat down at the desk. As soon as I sat, the computer came to life and popped up out of nowhere just like Megan said it would. The Crimson Financial logo came on first, then a second later, a bunch of icons popped up as if they were floating in the air. I sat studying them for what felt like a lifetime. I eventually found one that read "Accounting". I touched it, hoping that was the one I needed. The next image that opened up showed what must be 50 folders. It took me a good 10 minutes to look through them all. I finally saw one that read my name, so I touched that one. It must be where I go to do my work. A screen with tons of folders with different years on them came up next. I touched the folder that read 2036. Once I opened up that folder, another folder opened up simultaneously that revealed a bunch of financial information from various companies. I'm assuming this is where the accountant part of my job comes in. I spent the majority of the morning figuring out how to input all the information into the correct folders under the 2036 tab. As soon as I got the hang of this accounting work, it was actually fairly easy, which was weird since I was never good at math. Maybe part of this dimension's Faith resides in me somehow. I wonder what else is different about us. Or for that matter, the same. I'm sure, in time, I will find out.

Before I could even think about it, it was lunchtime. How did I know this? Well, at precisely 12:00, my computer screen turned red and displayed a message that read, "LUNCHTIME." I attempted to touch the screen, but it buzzed and refused to open my work. Just then, Megan entered my office.

"Hey, girl. It won't let you work through lunch. Break times are very important in this dimension. We get an hour for lunch. Come on. I'll walk you to the lunchroom. You'll love this."

"Oh, crap, Megan. I didn't bring anything for lunch."

"Girl, you don't need to. We get lunch for free. I can't wait to show you."

"OK, that is cool of them. I may like it here after all."

As we walked to the lunchroom, Megan asked about my morning. I told her how it took forever to even find what I was supposed to do, but touching almost every tab, I eventually found what I was looking for.

"It took me a while, but once I figured it out, it was actually fairly easy. I guess I still have some of the other Faith's memories."

"That's cool. I knew it would work out."

"Oh, really? Like you've been through this before, right?"

"Well, No. But it had to work out. Doesn't it always?"

"I guess things always do have a way of working out in the end. I just hope this whole adventure has a way of working out."

"Oh, Faith, I'm sure it will. It's got to be hard and weird for you."

As we were talking and since I was following Megan, I didn't realize we had just stepped out of the elevator into the basement of the Lowe Building.

"Where are we?" I was puzzled.

"I guess I should have told you. Sorry. The lunchroom is in the basement. "

The elevator was at the end of a long, dark hallway.

"It's a little spooky down here," I observed.

"Oh, yes, it is. The lights will come on as we walk. We must be the first ones down here. Usually, it's already lit by the time I come down here."

"We are the first ones? Who all comes down here to lunch?"

"Oh, everyone does. Since lunch is free here, no one really brings their lunch or goes out to lunch."

"I guess that makes sense."

As we walked, the lights came on and brightened up the hall. At the end of the hall were two big, double doors on the right side. We stepped inside the room, and I stopped dead in my tracks.

"This is the lunchroom? It's as big as a warehouse."

"Yeah, it's big. But it is for everyone in the building."

The room did not look like we were in the basement but outside. The lights mimicked the sun. They even left a warm sensation on my skin. There were big, beautiful trees in the middle of the room, and where there should be a hard floor was thick, lush grass. The air down here even smelled of the fresh outdoors. I looked around, taking in everything I saw. There were round metal tables scattered around all the trees.

"There must be at least 100 tables in here," I said in wonder.

"Megan, it looks like we just stepped outside. This is probably the coolest thing I've ever seen."

"I know. They renovated the lunchroom about 5 years ago. I don't know how they did it, but everyone loves it. Before the renovation, people would come down to get their lunch but just leave and go back to their office or outside in the courtyard."

"The courtyard?" I questioned.

"Oh, yeah, I have to show you that after work. It's really pretty."

On all four walls surrounding the tables were rows and rows of tall monitors with what looked like mail slots that you would see in doors.

"So Megan, where do we get the food?"

"This is the cool part. We go up to any one of those monitors, the AI recognizes us, it can sense what nutrients we are lacking and recommend proper foods."

"Wow, that's pretty cool."

We walked up to the monitors and took two side by side to each other.

As soon as I walked up it came on. "Good afternoon, Faith. It seems you are low in vitamin D and iron. I would recommend a spinach salad with tuna steak."

"OK, that sounds really good. I'll have that. Can I also have some fruit with my salad?"

Turning to Megan I said, "I like fruit with my lunch."

"Yeah, I remember that. The Faith in this dimension does as well."

The monitor spoke up "Yes Faith, I will get you your usual yogurt and water to go with that."

"Thank you."

And just like that my food appeared in the slot below the monitor.

"Damn, Megan, that is cool."

"I told you."

I grabbed the tray from the slot and followed Megan to a table. We sat and ate our lunch while we talked about our morning. As we ate, I took off my shoes and put my bare feet in the grass. I just love connecting to the earth this way. Touching the earth with my bare feet always makes me feel refreshed.

Before long, a couple of Megan's friends came up to sit with us.

"Hey guys," her friend Alena said in a very chipper voice.

"Oh, hey, Alena," Megan joyfully replied.

Megan later told me that along with being an impressive executive assistant that knows everything about the company, Alena was also a gardening genius. I made a mental note to ask her over to my house later to help out with my flower beds. I noticed this morning they were in desperate need of some TLC.

"Did y'all hear on the news this morning that the Cordelia Tribe is getting closer to us? I'm scared. I hope our government finds a way to prevent them from entering our orbit." Alena worriedly admitted.

"Oh yeah, I meant to talk to Faith about that earlier this morning, but more important things came up."

"Oh, really? Like what, Faith?" Alena questioned.

"I just woke up not feeling myself this morning. Something just seems off." Faith admitted.

"Oh no, I hope you aren't coming down with something. Why don't you go to the infirmary here? I'm sure they can give you something to help. Nowadays, they have miracle pills for everything, you know." Alena said enthusiastically.

"Oh, well, I guess I didn't think of that. I'm sure I am not sick. Just didn't sleep very well, I guess," I confessed.

"Didn't sleep very well? Why? Didn't you take the Inactive pill?" Alena said, puzzled.

I glanced at Megan with a bewildered look. She just shook her head.

"Oh, I guess I forgot," I admitted. I made a mental note that I would need to ask Megan what the hell an Inactive Pill was.

"Well, that is something to worry about. The government does not like people accidentally forgetting to take their pills," she said.

"Don't worry, Alena. I'll take her after work to get checked out. I'm sure she just has the flu or something," Megan quickly interjected.

*Thank God for Megan. What freaky world did I come into? I thought.*

"OK, Megan. That's a good idea. I'm just worried about Faith. She isn't acting normally."

"I agree," Megan said.

"OK, guys. I'm okay. I'm sure it's just a cold. I would, however, feel better if Megan went with me this afternoon to the infirmary."

"Yeah, Faith, I don't mind. I can go."

"Thanks, girlie."

Megan and Alena both looked at me weirdly. "*I guess they don't say girlie in this dimension. Jeez. I don't know if I will ever get used to this place.*" I thought.

"Sorry, guys, it's just this sickness talking."

"Oh, okay. I guess I better go back to work. Thanks for letting me join you two."

"Oh, you are so welcome, Alena." Megan proudly said.

"Bye, Alena. Have a good afternoon."

"Bye, Faith. You too."

"We better go back to work," Megan sadly admitted as we both got up to go.

Walking into the hallway, I took one look back at the lunchroom. "Megan, will I ever get used to this place? I really don't know what I'm doing here. Will I ever be able to go home and see my kids again?"

"Faith, sweetie, I know it must be so confusing to you. How about I come over tonight with a bottle of wine, and I explain everything to you?"

"Oh, wine still exists. Thank God. And that would be lovely. Thank you so much."

We slowly followed the crowd to the elevator. Surprisingly, the elevator fit about 25 people. Which was a bit too many people for my liking. I carefully stepped in behind Megan. I was so worried the elevator would not hold all of us. Like this is the first time all these people got onto the elevator. I need to start calming down and just going with the flow. Alena looked suspicious earlier. I really don't want anyone to know I'm from another dimension. They will surely ship me off to the loony bin.

# CHAPTER 4

Walking into my sunny office, I went straight up to my desk and powered up the computer. To my left was my water bottle. I never went anywhere without it. To my right was a cup of tea, my favorite after lunch. I focused on work when my tall, dark, and handsome boss popped his head into my office.

"Hey Darren, what can I do for you?" I asked, surprised the name came to me so easily. *How do I know his name? That was weird,I thought.*

"I want to make sure you have that project done. It's one of our biggest clients. I can't tell you how important this is. You've been known to drag your feet, so I'll need you to work late tonight to make sure it's finished."

"Darren, it's almost done. I was just putting on the finishing touches. You have nothing to worry about."

"Good. I'm glad. I'm leaving now. See you tomorrow."

"Bye, Darren."

He left without a second glance. *Why does Mister Tall, Dark, and Handsome have such an attitude? I need to ask Megan about that later,* I thought.

I spent the remainder of the afternoon reviewing the project. *After all, I don't want Mister Attitude to get his panties in a bunch.* I was so focused I didn't notice the time until Megan popped her head in.

"Hey, Faith, are you ready to go home?"

"Wow, is it that time already? Yeah, give me a second."

"Cool. Do you really want to go to the infirmary?" Megan asked.

"No, I'm not sick. I just said that to appease Alena."

I quickly closed things up for the night. "Let me just grab my things and we can leave."

I reached into the desk drawer for my purse and work bag, then jointed Megan at the door. We chatted as we walked toward the building's entrance when all of a sudden it dawned on me.

"Wait, what about my car? I don't even know where it is. It left me at the front of the building this morning."

"Don't worry, Faith. Your car will be there. Everything's AI now, remember? It knows when you leave the office and drives itself to the front of the building to wait for you."

"Oh damn, that is cool but also feels like an invasion of privacy." I commented.

"Yeah, that's what I thought at first too.  You get used to it." Megan reassured me. "But before we head out front, let me show you the courtyard."

Instead of walking to the front doors, Megan turned and led me past the elevators.

"The courtyard is this way.  This building is a giant square with a beautiful garden in the center.  People sometimes have their morning coffee out here or private meetings."

We stopped at a set of glass double doors. Megan opened open and ushered me through.  I stepped onto a stunning stone patio surrounding a man-made pond.  Off to the right was a small bridge leading to a gazebo.  Small bistro-style tables were scattered around the pond, with benches in between.  Enormous trees looking centuries old, provided ample shade. There was an unusual scent in the air, not what I expected outdoors and a sudden feeling of peace wash over me.

"Megan, this place is lovely.  So peaceful. I suddenly feel calm and relaxed."

"Yes, it is.  The company tries to give its employees incentives. They pump something in the air to help calm the employees. Now are you ready to go home?"

I nodded as we exited the courtyard and headed to the front of the building.

Stepping outside into the bright sunshine, I saw a line of identical cars waiting by the curb. Back home, there were hundreds of car models, but here they all looked the same—only the colors varied. I froze, unsure which one was mine, just as a neon red projection of my name hovered above a car like a spotlight. Looking down the row, I saw similar projections above each car. Megan's car was parked right behind mine.

I stood there staring until Megan quietly said, "People are watching."

Feeling eyes on me, I quickly walked toward my car.

Turning to Megan, I asked, "Hey, Megan, do you want to come over tonight? You can help me with this project of mine."

Megan knew full well it wasn't about a project, but there were too many people around listening.

"Oh yeah, I sure can. Let me just go home, change, and let the dog out," Megan said.

*Aww, I forgot she had a Cavalier King Charles Spaniel. They are so stinking cute, I remembered.*

"Sounds great. Thanks, Megan."

"No problem. Want me to bring Chinese for dinner?"

"Oh yes, that sounds yummy."

I hopped in my car and immediately heard that all-too-familiar AI voice.

"Good afternoon, Ms. Faith. How was your day?"

"Very well. Thank you."

"If I may say so, Ms. Faith, you must be feeling better. You sound much better compared to this morning."

"Oh, actually, I am. Thank you for noticing."

With that, the car quickly took off. I expected it to drive forward like a normal car but nope. Without warning, it lifted vertically fifty feet into the air. My head felt like it was in the spin cycle of a washing machine.

*Will I ever get used to this new way of life?*

# CHAPTER 5

Walking into the house, I noticed the setting sun glowing in through the windows. The decor gave off a tranquil vibe, peaceful after a long hard day at work. Setting my things down in the coat closet, I hurried upstairs to get comfortable before Megan arrived. Stepping into my walk-in closet, I went over to the flat-screen.

"Good evening, Faith. What would you like to wear tonight?"

"Something casual and relaxing. A friend is coming over."

Just like that, the clothes spun around and stopped at t-shirts and yoga pants. After changing my clothes, I wandered downstairs to the kitchen.

The kitchen AI immediately spoke up. "Hello, Ms. Faith. What would you like for dinner?"

"Hello there. I actually have a friend coming over tonight for dinner, so I'm good. But we could use a good bottle or two of wine?"

"Yes, ma'am. What kind of wine would you like?"

"How about a Pinot Gris and a Malbec?"

"Sure thing, Ma'am. Here you go."

Before I knew it, two bottles of wine rose from the countertop. The white wine was perfectly chilled in a metal wine caddy. I got out two wine glasses and sat them next to the wine. "All ready for Megan."

I walked into the living room to peek out the window and see if Megan was here yet. Nope, no sign yet. Looking down the street, I noticed a really cute neighbor taking a brisk walk.

*Mental note…I've got to find out who that is and get to know him. He's HOT. Oops, I've stared too long.*

Just then, the hottie turned and looked in my direction, waving a hello. I turned five shades of red and waved back, then spun around a little too quickly. Taking a deep breath, I walked over to the couch and grabbed what I assumed was a computer tablet off the coffee table. It was a thick 8x10 glass plate of sorts. Looking at it, it powered up immediately. There were all sorts of weird symbol applications on the screen. Finding one I recognized as Google, I tapped it, and up popped the internet.

Just for fun, I started randomly searching different kinds of things. I started Googling food because I was hungry. Like that's going to satisfy me. Nope, it just made me hungrier, but still scrolling away, I looked to see what was around the area. Before I knew it, there was a knock on the front door.

"Oh, cool, Megan is here."

Walking to the door, I opened it to see Megan standing there with her arms full of food bags.

"Hey, girl, these bags are getting heavy. Can you grab one, please?" Megan asked politely.

I didn't realize I had been standing there staring outside, probably looking for Mister Hottie.

"Oh, shoot, sorry Megan. Here, let me take that bag." I said while reaching for the one she was barely holding onto.

"Thanks, Faith. That's the most important bag. It's got the wine in it. I wasn't sure how much you had stocked, so I picked up a couple just in case."

"Oh, thanks. That's nice of you. I did find some with the little computer voice's help." I laughed

"I know, Faith. This all must be so weird for you. We'll talk more later, but first, let's eat. I'm starving."

Just then, as if the computer was listening, two plates and silverware rose from the center of the island.

"Is that computer always listening?" I questioned.

"It's programmed to listen and help when need-ed. I know it takes a bit of getting used to, but you can turn off that feature. I turn it off when I have company." Megan advised.

"You'll have to show me how to do that later. But first, I agree with you, we need to eat. I didn't realize how hungry I was until I smelled that food."

Megan grabbed the food and plates while I grabbed the wine and glasses. Walking over to the table.

"Oh, I was caught staring at the cute neighbor walking before you got here. He looked right at me and waved. Talk about embarrassing." I said.

Megan started laughing and said "That would be Keith. You two had a brief thing last year."

"That would make sense why he noticed me noticing him and waved. But how much of a thing are we talking about?" I asked.

Now it was Megan's turn to go red. "It was pretty hot and heavy with a lot of tumbling around between the sheets for a good couple of months. But you broke it off when you found out he was using you for sex because his fiancé was still living out of town."

"A player I see. What a dick. I'm sure that really pissed me off. Great, now he thinks I'm interested again."

"No, I doubt that. He probably thought you were just mad at him. You kind of have a resting bitch face when you're concentrating." Megan teased.

I started laughing. " You are right about that."

We each filled our plates with Chinese food.

"I feel like I haven't had Chinese in so long." I said as I looked at my plate. "I definitely think my eyes are bigger than my stomach."

"A Chinese meal wouldn't be complete without an egg roll." Megan said as she handing me one.

"Megan, thank you for getting dinner. I'm so glad this dimension of me likes the same things."

"Yeah, I am too. I didn't think of asking before I started ordering the food."

I got the wine opened and poured us each a big glass. "Thanks, Faith. I need this after today. It was a busy day."

"Yeah, me too. I'm still confused. I'm just glad I

survived the day."

We talked as we were enjoying our dinner and wine.

"So, Megan, can you explain the whole medical situation here?"

"Oh, yes, it's different now. First off, they give everyone the Inactive Pill to help sleep. They have found that if you have a good night's sleep, you're more productive and healthier. So they give it free to everyone. It's like melatonin but with a little extra to help you fall asleep faster without side effects. Plus, they add something else, but we don't know what. I've been taking them for years and I'm fine."

I listened intently. "Well, hopefully, I can find some here. I sure could use a good night's sleep."

"The other Faith, always had her medicines and supplements in her medicine cabinet."

"Oh, I didn't see them there this morning."

"The cabinet isn't old-fashioned. There's a little button on the right side that moves the front shelves to the back and brings up the shelves that were in the back."

"That's cool. I can't wait to try that out tonight."

"Yeah, the improvements are pretty cool. People can see where you itch, hurt, and even tingle. If you are in pain, a red mark appears in the area of pain. If you itch or have nerve problems, a lightning bolt appears in the area of the itch. If you injure a bone, a blue mark appears in that area as well. It's really helpful for the doctors."

Up until now, I thought everything was pretty cool, but this felt too invasive. "Megan, that's strange. I don't know if I want everyone to know what's wrong with me."

"I know it is a little weird at first, but it helps the Doctors, Nurses, X-ray Technologists and Physical Therapists diagnose what's wrong with their patients."

"I guess I can see how it could be helpful."

Once we finished eating, I took the plates to the sink while Megan cleaned up. "Hey, Megan, do you want to take some wine to the living room?"

"Sounds like a plan."

We grabbed our glasses, a new bottle of wine since we'd finished the first, and headed to the living room. Sitting down, Megan began telling me about this new world.

"So what else is different in the medical field?" I questioned.

"Oh, well, when people need an ambulance. Say if they are sick or hurt, a big medical drone comes and picks them up to take them to the hospital. We no longer have ambulances."

"I could see how that would be a good thing. There must be so many medical drones then."

"There are thousands," Megan said.

"WOW, that's crazy."

"Oh, and the medical community can pretty much grow any organ that you need. So there really is no more kidney failure, heart disease, and so on. No matter what your illness, they can fix it."

"That's a great improvement. More help for the people," I admitted.

"All the medical improvements really are for the better."

"Do they still do diagnostic imaging the same way?"

"Oh no. They have a machine that scans your whole body and highlights anything suspicious. Kind of like a panoramic scan. It also uses AI to help with the scanning procedure and results. X-ray technologists mostly work remotely now."

"That's a great idea. I always said they needed something like that. But it must've put techs out of work."

"It really is. X-ray departments are not as busy as they used to be. There is only a front desk person and one or two tech aides that position the patient. It's an easier, streamlined process. The government stepped up and helped the ones who lost their jobs find other work." Megan explained.

"Wow, that is surprising and very nice of them."

Since I was a Registered X-ray Technologist in my other dimension, I found it interesting. All the advancements really are for the better of the people. If only they could do it without the use of Artificial Intelligence, it would be so much better.

"So, Megan, do you have any idea what brought me here? I mean, it seems better. My abusive husband is gone, but so are my kids. I miss them, something fierce."

"I don't know. It is strange. You said there was a bad storm that brought you here."

"That's my thinking." I admitted.

"You know, I know a brilliant professor at a college that's about an hour from here. We used to date. He'll do anything for me. Want me to give him a call?"

"Yes, please. That would be great. I guess I just want to know I'm not going crazy." I exclaimed.

"You aren't. Time travel can happen. I just have never known anyone that it has happened to. His name is Bert. He's a physics teacher and he loves this kind of stuff. I'll call him in the morning." Megan said with a helpful voice.

"Thank you so much."

"So, what else is bugging you about this futuristic place."

I thought for a moment. "What's up with these computer voices being everywhere? I mean it's in my car, living room, kitchen, and even my bathroom. Is there any privacy? Should I be worried?"

Megan smiled at me. "A.I. was first developed for the medical field, but the government soon discovered how helpful and important it was becoming and used it for the military. They used AI for everything, even in times of war. Once the general public saw how great AI was becoming, they wanted it for their homes. The public had rallies and petitions going demanding that the government make AI available to everyone. So eventually, they made civilian grade along with military grade AI software. And before we knew it, AI was literally everywhere. People found out how much easier it made their lives at home, at work, and even in the car. There have been fewer accidents since AI has started driving."

I listened intently to Megan explaining about AI. "That sounds interesting. But I am still worried about AI overtaking everything."

"Some people were extra worried about that and made their concerns known. The government made sure there was a protocol to prevent a takeover from happening. I was one of them. We went to Congress and everything."

"Good for you. I'm glad you helped make sure everything was thought of."

"Faith, let me show you the basement. There are some important things down there you need to see."

Megan took me downstairs to show me the storage and equipment room. As we descended the steps, I noticed a panel the size of a door on the wall to our right.

Megan saw my gaze and mentioned, "That's the controls for the house computer. "

I shook my head. "Good to know."

Further in, I noticed big five-gallon drums sitting neatly on metal shelves.

Megan motioned toward the shelves. " That is where all your toiletries are kept. A company comes out and fills them once a month for free."

I got wide-eyed and said, "So, we don't pay for the product they put in."

"Nope. That is all included with the taxes you pay. You can choose from different options." Megan said enthusiastically.

At the end of the room was a big, thick metal door.

"That is where the food magic happens." Megan pointed to the door as she explained the room.

Shaking my head, I said, "Oh, I see.  Can we go in?"

"Yes, we can." Megan walked up to the door and pulled on the long lever handle. A hissing sound could be heard as air escaped the enormous sealed room.

Inside, I could see robotic arms everywhere. Two by a huge refrigerator, two by a stove, two by a wall oven, and four over a long metal table all hanging from the ceiling.  I stood at the doorway taking it all in. "This is impressive."

"Every six months, there is maintenance on the equipment to keep it in tiptop shape."

Shaking my head, I said, "OK, I'll have to remember that."

Once back in the living room, Megan finished her glass of wine and glanced over at me.  "Faith, sweetie, this has been lots of fun, but I should go home. It's getting late.  I'll call Bert in the morning and let you know what he says at lunch."

"That sounds great.  Thank you so much."

Getting up from the couch, I walked Megan over to the front door.

"Megan, I really appreciate you coming over and explaining things.  I feel a little better."

"Anything for you, Faith. Hope you get a good night's sleep. See you in the morning."

"Drive safe, Megan."

"Don't need to. My car drives for me. Remember."

"Yep. See you."

"Bye."

Oops, I may have said that a little too loudly for this time of night. I think we drank a little too much wine. Shutting the door, I watched to make sure Megan got into her car okay before locking up for the night. I sure do appreciate Megan's friendship. Having someone that believes me makes this transition that much better.

# CHAPTER 6

I woke up the next morning feeling happy and refreshed. This might not be the world I am used to, but I was determined to make the best of it. First, I need to get ready for work. Today went much more smoothly than yesterday. Before long, I was showered, dressed, with makeup and hair done. I was actually excited to start the day.

Walking into the kitchen, I headed over to the screen, which lit up immediately.

"Good morning, Faith. What would you like for breakfast this morning?" That oh-so-familiar and confusing voice asked.

"Good morning, I think I will have my usual. A hard-boiled egg, some fruit, and black coffee."

"Coming right up, ma'am."

As I sat down at the kitchen island, the mandatory news flash appeared.

Loud instrumental music played followed by a bright red screen appearing on the TV monitor with white letters reading **NEWS FLASH**. The red screen only stays up for about 30 seconds, then disappears, and a blond woman in a navyblue suit sits behind a news desk.

"Good morning, city residents. Today is Friday, February 19th, in the year 2036. Hope all is well. Alien spacecraft from the Cordelia Tribe have been spotted in our solar system, but have no fear, Space Fleet is sending up armed drones to protect our Earth's atmosphere."

"Wonderful." I muttered, "First, I have to figure out this different dimension, now I have to worry about aliens too."

An image of Earth appeared on the screen with four hexagon-shaped spacecraft hovering near the planet. I started getting a little warm and anxious while watching this scary newscast.

"As you can see here, this satellite image shows four alien spacecraft just outside our atmosphere. Zooming in, you can see in great detail that the ship is indeed hexagonal in shape with lights underneath in the same hexagon pattern. There are no signs of doors or windows. There is some strange writing on the side as you see here when we zoom further in. We are unable to decipher it. The military is theorizing it says where they are from or their federation name. So far, they don't appear hostile, but our drones are not up there yet. We will pass along any important information we receive to you as soon as possible."

Loud instrumental music played again, followed by a bright red screen appearing on the TV monitor with white letters reading **NEWS FLASH**.

"Well, that's just great." I said aloud. "So much for having a good day. Might as well go brush my teeth and leave for work. Now I really have to talk to Megan."

"Ms. Faith, are you alright? You seem troubled." The voce asked.

"Yes, I'm fine. It's just the news. I'm going to be leaving for work soon. Would you please get the car ready?"

"Yes, ma'am."

Not only was I running upstairs, but my mind was running as well. Between this high-tech world, multi-dimensional crap, and now aliens invading Earth, I was starting to feel overwhelmed. Hopefully, Megan's friend Bert can help me. I must have been moving on autopilot because before I knew it, I was walking to the car. As I approached, the door automatically opened. Sliding into the seat, I took a deep breath, trying to calm my worries before another workday.

"Good morning, Ms. Faith. Where to today?"

"Hello, you can take me to work."

"Would you like to stop at your favorite coffee shop today? We always stop there on Fridays. You say it's your end-of-week treat."

"Oh, yeah, I forgot it's Friday. Coffee sounds wonderful. Do we have time?"

"Yes, ma'am, I can make time."

I was surprised when the car took the normal aerial route rather than driving on the roads.

*Now how am I going to get coffee in the air? I thought*

Before entering the city, the car drove into a floating restaurant mall in the sky. The same restaurants that existed on the ground in the area were connected to their sky counterpart by big metal tubes.

*"Oh, this is neat. I wonder how we get food from these places. It's not like we can get out of the car and walk in." I found myself thinking.*

The car pulled up to a coffee shop called Cosmic Coffee. I didn't see any drive-thru windows but just when I was wondering how this worked, a big screen lit up next to my parked car.

"Good morning, ma'am. Please select the type of coffee and size."

A touchscreen lit up with ten different kinds of coffee. Quickly scrolled the options, I decided on a large Galaxy Mocha Latte. Within seconds, a metal arm popped up from the bottom of the screen and gently rose up to the car window with a piping hot cup of coffee. Reaching out, I took a hold of the coffee and quickly tasted it. I couldn't wait to see how good it was. Immediately and very carefully putting the coffee to my lips while the car drove off, I tasted the piping hot liquid.

"WOW, that's probably the best coffee I have ever had."

"Yes, Ms., Cosmic Coffee is the best in town. Are you ready to head to work?"

"Yes, I guess I better.  Thank you for stopping."

Work was only fifteen minutes away from the coffee shop, but somehow the car got me there in seven.

"Wow, thanks for getting me here so fast."

"Always at your service, ma'am.  Have a good day."  "Thank you."

Grabbing my work bag and purse, I headed into the building, looking for Megan, but she was nowhere in sight.

*"Oh well, maybe she got here earlier.  I'll see her at lunch, I'm sure. Luckily, I remember how to get to my office." I thought.*

Walking into my office, I looked around and let out a big sigh.  *"OK, let's do this thing."* I put my things away.  Before I had any time to bring up my computer, my boss, Darren, walked in.

"So, do you have that project ready for me?" He demanded in a sarcastically.

"Well, Good morning to you too, Darren. Yes, it's right here." I declared while I reached over and grabbed the all-too-important project off the file cabinet.

"Here you go, Darren."

"Thank you," he said, turning to leave before pausing at the doorway. "Good morning, by the way. I don't mean to be rude, but the big man is on my back about this."

"No problem, I understand."

Once Darren was out the door, I felt relieved and got to work. Accounting was starting to get easier, or maybe Faith's memories from this di-mension were finally surfacing. I was so bust that I lost track of time until there was a light knock on the door.

"Hey, Faith, are you ready for lunch?" Megan asked.

"Oh, hey Megan. Yeah, now that you mention it, I'm starving. Let me put my work away real quick."

I quickly tidied up, then hurried out the door with Megan. I'm a neat freak. I don't like leaving things a mess.

"I missed you this morning," I said with concern.

"Yeah, I didn't see you when I got to work. The higher-ups don't like us waiting around. They think it's a waste of production time, so I had to go straight to my office," Megan explained.

"Oh, okay. That makes sense. I stopped to grab a latte."

"Yummy. You stopped at Cosmic Coffee? Isn't that the best coffee in the world? I used to go too much, so I'm limiting myself."

"OH, it's SO good. I can see how going there could get out of hand."

Walking into the elevator, Megan asked, "So how was your morning? Better than yesterday?"

"It was much better. I'm starting to feel like myself again. I handed in that project to Darren, so that was a huge weight lifted off my shoulders. How was your morning?"

"Busy and productive. It sure did make the morning fly by. By the way, I called that my friend for you."

"Oh, wow, Megan. Thank you. What did he say?"

"We will talk about it at lunch. We're here now."

We exited the elevator with other employees and headed to the lunchroom. After ordering our food from the big screens, we sat at our usual table.

"So, Bert was very excited to hear about you. He wants to meet tomorrow morning if you're able. The only catch is we have to meet him at the college, but I'll drive."

"Awesome. I have no plans, so that works great. I can't wait to hear what he has to say."

"How about I meet you at your house at seven tomorrow morning? Is that too early?"

"Nope, that's perfect. I'm an early riser anyway." I declared.

We continued to talk until Alena approached.

"Oh boy," I said to Megan.

"Faith, she really is nice, just overly concerned."

"Yeah, it seems that way. She did seem nice when I met her yesterday."

Alena came up to them and helped herself to a chair next to Megan. Looking over at me, she asked, "Hey Faith, how are you feeling? You look better to-day."

"Oh, did I look that bad yesterday? I feel better, thank you. I remembered to take my Inactive Pill and slept so much better."

"That's wonderful. See how much better you feel with a good night's sleep? The government sure does know what they are doing."

"Yeah, they do. I appreciate your concern."

"Anytime. I want all my gal pals to be in great health. It's for all our best interests." Alena said enthusiastically. "Well, I better be heading back to work. Y'all have a great afternoon."

"See you later, Alena. Thanks for caring." I yelled as Alena walked away.

Megan yelled right after. "See ya, Alena."

After lunch, as we headed to work, I found myself in deep thought about tomorrow's meeting with Bert and didn't realize we were already on our floor until Megan spoke.

"Hey, Earth to Faith. We are here."

"Oh, damn, sorry. I was just thinking about tomorrow."

"Yeah, I figured. You've got a lot going on. I'll try to catch up with you after work so we can talk more."

"OK, see you in a few hours. Have a good afternoon."

Megan yelled to me as she walked away. "Yeah, you too."

Back at my desk, I got back into the groove of work, though my mind kept drifting to thoughts of Bert and hopefully finding answers. Maybe I'd figure out how to get back home to my kids. God, I missed them so much.

I was lost in work when a loud knock startled me. Darren walked in.

"Good afternoon, Faith. I just wanted to say thank you. I went over your project and it was superb. Great work. I knew I could trust you. You may see more responsibilities coming your way,"

"OK, great. I'm glad it was what you wanted."

While I didn't start the project, I sure did finish it, and knowing I did it right was a relief. That sure did make my day. I found myself smiling when Megan knocked on my office door.

"Hey, you look happy." Megan noticed.

"Oh, hey, Darren just paid me a compliment. It just feels good to know I am doing something right in this weird, different world I'm finding myself in."

"I'm sure it does. I can't imagine how you must feel. It's a lot to deal with. Are you ready to go home?"

"Yes, I am. The sooner I get home, the sooner tomorrow comes and I get answers."

"I have to admit, I am curious as to what Bert has to say." Megan said as they walked to the elevator.

Like before, our cars were parked next to each other. We said our goodbyes, and I hopped in my car. As it pulled away, I realized how tired I was. Between work and adjusting to this new life, it was starting to take a toll on me.

# CHAPTER 7

Early to bed meant sooner to finding out what the heck was happening. Climbing into my big, soft bed felt like snuggling into a cloud. As I lay on my pillow, exhaustion took over, and I quickly started yawning.

*Wow, I really am tired. Hopefully, my excitement for tomorrow won't keep me awake.*

But instead of sleeping well, I tossed and turned all night. Closing my eyes, I focused on something soothing, but nothing worked. Midnight passed, then 1 a.m., 2 am and finally 3 a.m. before I decided to get out of bed. Going downstairs, I grabbed a quick snack and a glass of water, hoping it would help. I managed to fall back asleep but woke up again at 5 a.m.

Deciding to start my day, I went into the bathroom and took a long shower. Since I woke up so early, I had plenty of time to get ready without rushing. As I showered and did my makeup, my mind wandered.

*How exactly is Bert going to help me?*

Once I was ready, I sat down in my bedroom chair for what felt like only thirty minutes before the doorbell rang. Grabbing my shoes, I ran downstairs to answer it. Bad idea because as I was running down the stairs, my socked feet slipped on the carpet runner and I slid down the stairs. As soon as my butt hit the hardwood floor, I didn't miss a beat and quickly recovered to answer the door. Breathing heavily, I opened the door to find Megan standing there with a huge smile.

"Good morning, girlie, you ready to get some answers?"

I replied enthusiastically, "Yes, so ready. I couldn't sleep last night thinking about it, even with the Inactive Pill I took." I wasn't about to tell her I just fallen down the stairs. No need to if she didn't bring it up. It was too embarrassing.

"How about we stop at Cosmic Coffee for a caffeine boost?" Megan suggested.

"Yes, please, that's exactly what I need." I admitted.

On our way to the college, we swung by the coffee shop.

"Faith, what would you like? Do you want anything to eat?" Megan asked.

"Oh, yes, I'll have a pastry and a Galaxy Mocha Latte."

Megan put in my order, then her order of a pastry and a Milky Way Macchiato. "I sure do love their macchiatos here. They're the best."

"I'll have to try that next time. I seem to be loving their lattes."

"Yeah, that was your other favorite as well."

Once caffeinated, we headed to the college about an hour away. The campus, looked over a hundred years old, with stone exteriors on every building. The main building where Bert worked looked like an old castle with towers on each side, perched on a hill overlooking the bay.

Getting out of the car, Megan turned to me. "Bert said there are benches out front. He'll meet us there."

Walking up to the building, I admired the scenery - big trees, benches and tables scattered around. The shade was inviting and I could picture students studying under the trees. As my eyes wandered, they landed on a very handsome man. When I thought of a physics professor, I pictured an old gray-haired guy with glasses, not someone gorgeous like him.

"Oh, there he is," Megan said, waving.

"That guy?" I put a hand on Megan's arm. "Girl, you didn't say he was gorgeous." I blurted out with wide eyes.

Megan smiled. "Surprise. I didn't want to spoil the fun. Your reaction is priceless."

"Damn, when I think of a professor, I expect an old guy with glasses. He is hot."

Megan added, "And he is your age. I thought it would be nice for you to meet someone your age since technically you are new here in this dimension."

"Thank you. That was nice of you."

Bert stood up and walked toward us. "Hey, Megan. And you must be Faith. Nice to meet you."

"Hey, nice to meet you too." I managed to say, my voice a little nervous. Megan gave me a reassuring look and smile.

"Do you ladies mind if we go to my office? It'll be more private for what we need to discuss."

Together we said "Yep, that's fine."

Bert held open the massive front door. I stopped dead in my tracks, staring at the ornate ceiling and furniture.

"Wow, this place is amazing. Hard to believe it is a college."

"It was a castle a hundred years ago before becoming a college. The family that owned it actually founded the school." Bert explained as he led them up a massive wooden staircase. "My office is just up here. First door on the right."

He unlocked his office door and gestured for us to enter first. "Have a seat, ladies," he politely said.

His office was spacious, with a mahogany desk and big leather chair behind it. Two smaller leather chairs faced the desk, where Megan and I sat.

"So, Faith, Megan tells me you're from another dimension."

"Yes, I went to bed in my normal life. I remember a bad storm that night. When I woke up the next day, I was here. I don't really understand it. Luckily, Megan believed me. I was afraid she'd think I'd lost my mind."

"No, girl, you aren't crazy. I got your back." Megan said, giving me a side hug.

Bert leaned forward. "I did some research. Time travel through multi-dimensions is possible."

Instant relief washed over me. "That does make me feel a little better."

"I'm glad. You ladies have heard of a wormhole, right?" We nodded. "Well, no one goes near them because they're too scared of what will happen if they get sucked in. Scientists have researched them for years. When someone goes through a wormhole, they're transported to another universe. All the universes look similar, with the same people, but there are little differences, like what you are dealing with here. When a person travels through a wormhole, it's almost like a thunder and lightning storm, with electric flashes everywhere." He paused. "Are y'all with me so far?"

Megan shook her head.

It all started to make sense to me, almost. "Yeah, but I am still confused. This happened in my bedroom."

"I believe during that bad storm, the heavy thunder and lightning caused a wormhole to form in your room. You didn't notice because you were sleeping so still that the electric activity didn't detect you. The wormhole formed and swallowed you up, so to speak. This is all very exciting. You could be famous, but don't worry. I won't tell anyone. I can only imagine how disorienting this is for you."

"This is a lot to take in. It's still confusing and hard to believe." I said, feeling overwhelmed. Megan placed a comforting hand on my back.

"Give it time to sink in. I'd love to talk more, but I have a meeting with a student I must get to."

"On a Saturday?" I asked.

"Yep, a professor's work is never done," He laughed. "Hey, Faith, why don't we meet tomorrow and talk some more? I'm sure you'll have questions after thinking about today."

I looked at Megan with a questioningly.

"He asked you, not me," Megan teased with a smile.

"Yeah, sorry, Megan. Since this happened to Faith, I figured she and I could talk some more. I want to think about it more tonight and pick her brain tomorrow. This is really fascinating."

I was still surprised, "Sure, that sounds great. I would love to talk to you some more." I told him as I was thinking, *But I hope this stays as just a friend thing. I don't think I want to try a relationship right now.*

"Great. Why don't we meet for breakfast at Astra Diner? It's about thirty

minutes from here."

Catching myself staring at him, I quickly said, "Ok, sounds great. I'm sure my car will know where it is."

"That's a great plus for this dimension, isn't it? See you there, say at 9 a.m."

"9 a.m. it is."

We stood up and said our goodbyes. Bert walked us outside, then gently pulled me in for a hug and whispered in a soft, sexy voice, "It was great meeting you." I was sure Bert was just being polite, but his warm breath whispering in my ear sent chills down my spine.

Feeling my cheeks burn, I thought, *OH BOY, that's so going to be noticeable. Just friends, Faith. Friends.*

Waving goodbye, we walked to the car. I could feel his eyes were on us as we left. Once the car doors shut, I immediately blurted out, "What was that?"

"Girl, you were so red when he leaned in. He likes you," Megan commented.

"Yeah, but he's your friend. A woman never steals a man from her BFF."

"Faith, please don't worry. We grew up together. He's more like a brother. It never worked out when we dated. Our mothers are best friends. So, are you excited for tomorrow?"

"Man, I'm all over the place. I felt down while talking to him because it doesn't seem like there's anything I can do about going back to my dimension. Then I was like, okay, so make the best of it. I'm lonely without my kids but meeting someone and having someone to go out with would help."

"Girl, you've only been here for a few days, and someone already likes you. I can't wait to hear how tomorrow goes."

"Oh, Megan, I'm nervous. But I can't wait either. I do want to be friends with him for now."

"I'm sure you are nervous, but Faith, he really is a great guy. Just go with the flow and see what happens."

"Good plan. He really does seem to be a great guy. "

We talked about everything on the way home, from Bert the handsome bachelor to everything that he said about wormholes and dimensions. Before I knew it, we were back at my house.

"Hey, thanks for driving today. Want to come in for a glass of wine or something?"

"You're welcome. Sorry, sweetie, I can't. I've got some work to catch up on. Call me tomorrow after your breakfast date."

"Oh, Megan. It's not a date. Well, I don't think it is. Is it?"

"Seemed like it to me. After all, he just asked you out. It's in the morning, so it's nothing serious. Just a get-to-know-you type of thing."

"Wow, okay. I'm glad you told me. There is no way I am sleeping tonight."

"Yeah, I wouldn't either. Talk to you tomorrow."

Megan hugged me then walked to her car. I shut the door and stood there for who knows how long. There was so much to think about. It didn't seem like there was anything I could do to get back home. This was my home now, so I might as well make the best of it. I had a sick and sad feeling in the pit of my stomach because that means I would never see my kids again, and that just breaks my heart.

# CHAPTER 8

I felt light on my feet Sunday morning. I had a date today well, was it a date? I still had no idea. It was just breakfast to discuss my situation further. Just a friend thing. There was after all nothing remotely romantic about this hang out. Hopefully, this will allow me to get to know Bert better.

After my showered and fresh makeup, I stood in the closet wondering what to wear?

"It's been decades since I've gone out with another man. What do I wear?" I said aloud.

Walking up to the monitor in the closet, I heard that oh-so-familiar voice say, "Good morning. What would you like to wear today?"

"Well, now that's a good question. I'm meeting a guy friend for breakfast."

The picture on the monitor scrolled rapidly, going through rows and rows of clothes. It landed on a couple of options. This definitely made it easier to decide what to wear. I finally decided on skinny blue jeans with a nice hunter green blouse and tan ankle boots.

Getting into the car, I heard, "Good morning, ma'am. Where are we headed today?"

"Good morning, the Astra Diner, please."

"Yes, ma'am, nice choice."

The car pulled up to the diner, but it didn't look like any diner I had ever been to. The restaurant was in the shape of a flying saucer. The building was completely made up of metal and glass with windows all around. It was the neatest thing I had ever seen. I couldn't quite figure out where the door was located. Just then, Bert pulled up. My heart started racing, and my palms went sweaty. Boy, was I nervous. It had been forever since I'd been on a date or a friend thing with the opposite sex. Plus, I hadn't had much luck picking men. Hopefully, he was nothing like my husband. He must have seen me sitting in my car because he gave a big, cheery wave and smile. Bert got out of the car the same time I did.

"Good morning, Faith"

"Good morning, Bert."

"You look a little puzzled. Let me guess, trying to figure out how to get into the diner?"

"Yes, there is a sidewalk leading to nothing." I sounded mystified as I spoke.

I felt Bert's warm hand link with my cold hand. He had such strong hands.

"Damn woman, your hand is cold."

"Yeah, they always are. I have Raynaud's Disease. It makes my hands and feet cold. My husband used to get so mad at me when I put my cold feet on his warm legs at night. He would fiercely yell at me in the morning. Like I can control what I do when I sleep."

Bert inspected my hands. "Do they hurt? They have red marks on them "

I looked down at my hands. "They do hurt when they are cold or warm up after being cold. They have a tendency to hurt. They even get red. It's weird seeing them with red marks like that though. I don't know if I'll ever get used to people knowing where my ailments are."

Bert gently touched my arm. "You'll get used to it. You see the big rectangular concrete paver?"

I nodded.

"Step on it and keep your eyes on the building as you do."

I reluctantly but carefully stepped on the concrete with Bert standing behind me. Looking at the building, I saw what I thought was initially a glass window transform into a metal panel and started moving slowly, lowering down to the ground, making a ramp to walk right up into the diner. The expression on my face made Bert laugh.

"Come on, beautiful. Breakfast awaits."

I was pretty sure I turned red when he called me beautiful. Bert placed his hand on my back as he led me into the restaurant. The instant I stepped foot inside, the aroma of grease and burnt coffee hit me in the face. A woman in a short fuchsia dress with a black collar, sleeves, and apron greeted us at the door. Looking around, I noticed all the employees had the same out-fits on. There were booths along the outside windows. In the middle was a big circular bar with the kitchen in the direct center of the building.

The woman led them to a booth on the right side of the door. Placing 2 menus on the table, she said, "Please be seated. Your server, Babette, will be right with you."

"I'm glad you could make it," Bert admitted.

"I'm glad too. It's nice to have someone else that knows my situation that I can trust." I replied.

"You are definitely unique in that aspect. Be careful telling anyone else about it, though. The wrong people hear about it, and you could become a test sub-ject." He warned.

"Oh, I don't plan on telling anyone else."

We concentrated on our menus, then ordered when Babette, the waitress, came over. I noticed the entire time I was ordering that Bert did not take his eyes off me. It was a little uncomfortable but nice at the same time.

"So, Faith, continue. You were married in your dimension?"

"Yeah, to a real asshole." I confessed, going into great detail about my bad marriage and everything that had happened in my other life. I even told him about my two kids and how much I missed them.

"It sounds like you are safer in this dimension away from that narcissist. But I'm sad for you that your kids couldn't somehow come here. How was their relationship with their dad?"

"Well, he yelled a lot, but deep down, he really did love those kids. I think if he had to, he would be a great dad to them. I believe a lot of his problem was because he wasn't happy in our marriage."

"You said he would come home late a lot. I hate to put this out there, but did you ever think he was having an affair?"

"That thought has crossed my mind a lot. I've even confronted him before, but everything I questioned, he had a good answer for. He would just tell me I was crazy or that I imagined it or am just overreacting. I went snooping and saw his dress clothes that he had stashed in a big tote in the garage. I saw a receipt for 2 to a hotel room. Oh, I also saw an expensive dinner and breakfast receipt from the same area as the hotel. I even saw pictures of the woman he was having an affair with on his old phone. All of those things he had a good reason for or would just say I did see them. He would make me think I was crazy. I needed solid proof that he could not dispute, like a picture of him and his mistress."

"I get that, but it sounds like you had enough proof that he was cheating. Not to mention, he was verbally and emotionally abusive. An even better reason for you to be over here. I'm so sorry you've had to go through all that."

"I was afraid to tell anyone how I failed in my marriage. Afraid I could not make it on my own with kids."

"Faith, you didn't fail. Marriage takes two people committed to each other. You tried your hardest."

"Thank you, Bert. You're sweet."

"So now that you've had a night to think about what we talked about yesterday, do you have anything else you need to ask me?"

"I keep thinking about how stuck I am here, and there doesn't seem to be any way out. Is that right?"

"Unfortunately, from what I can tell, yes, that's correct. I am sorry."

"You apologize too much for things that aren't in your control. That's OK. I'm slowly getting used to the idea that I'm going to have to call this place my home. And now that I've met you, things are looking up." I said in a flirtatious tone.

"I know we just met yesterday, but I can't imagine my life without you in it now. You're so easy to talk to." Bert nervously admitted.

"Awe, thanks. I find it really easy to talk to you as well. But I do have one kind of personal question for you."

"OK, shoot." Bert said with a puzzled expression.

"Well, Bert's not a very common name, at least not where I'm from.  So why'd your mom decide on Bert? Is it a family name?"

Bert laughed. "Nope, not a family name. It's funny actually, especially considering what I do for a living. Believe it or not, my mom named me after Albert Einstein. She's somewhat of a science fanatic."

"That's fitting, especially considering you are a physicist. At least you're named after a genius."

"Yes, there is that."

Just then, Babette arrived with our breakfast and coffees.

"Thank you," they both said simultaneously, then looked at each other and smiled.

We stared into each other's eyes at the same time. I thought that stare lasted a little too long. There was that warm feeling in my chest again.

*How can I like a guy I just met? He's so great.* Thinking to myself as I picked up my coffee and took a big sip.

"You like your coffee black, I see." Bert observed.

"Yes, I do. I mean, I like the foo-foo drinks too, but when it comes to places like this, I just like a regular cup of black coffee."

"A woman after my own heart. I drink mine black as well." He said winking at me.

I felt my cheeks turning red again. *Jeez, he's going to think I embarrass easily.*

"Sorry, did I embarrass you?" Bert asked.

"No, not at all. I'm just not used to men being nice to me and giving me nice compliments."

"That's a real shame. Stick with me, baby, and I'll treat you like a queen." Bert declared.

I smiled big as I gazed at my breakfast. "Maybe we should eat while it's still hot."

"Right. Yes, we did come here to eat. Not flirt. Let's eat."     While we ate, we continued getting to know each other. I was surprised at how comfortable I felt around him. Bert seemed to really be enjoying himself too.

The busboy came by to clear the empty dishes. Once he left, Babette came over.

"Can I get you guys anything else?"

Bert spoke up immediately. " Maybe some more coffee." He chimed in, glancing over at me.

"Yes, please, more coffee would be great."

"You know, Faith, I'm enjoying talking to you. Why don't we finish our coffee and go someplace else? Unless you have plans today?"

I was a little shocked. "No, I have no plans."

"Great. I know a little park nearby."

"Sounds great. I'm so glad to hear parks are still a thing. I love being out in nature."

"OK, wonderful. That's something we have in common. I love anything outdoors."

Babette came over with the coffee. "Can I get you guys anything else?"

"Just the check, please."

"Sure thing. I'll be right back."

*Oh crap. I forgot about the check. I should have asked for separate checks. I don't have cash. Maybe he'll let me pick up the bill. It's the least I can do.*

Babette laid the check on the edge of the table. We both reached for it, but Bert was a little faster. "Please. My treat. You've been through enough this week."

"That's very nice of you. Thank you."

As we finished our coffee, I found myself looking at Bert on occasion. *How could this perfect man be single? Why is he interested in me?*

"Should we go now?" He interrupted her thoughts.

"Yes. We shall."

Bert got up from the table first and put his hand out to help me up.

"You are such a gentleman. Thank you."

"I believe that ladies should be treated with re-spect."

Walking side by side, I could feel Bert's warm hand on the small of my back again. He had such a tenderness about the way he treated me.

*I'm reading way too much into this whole situation. Don't be ridiculous. He's just being nice.*

He stopped me before I could get to the entrance.

"Um, Bert, how do we get out?"

I was puzzled and looked around, seeing no way to open the hatch. Bert put his hand on my shoulder as he pointed to round metal discs on the floor.

"You see those metal discs on the floor?" I shook my head yes. "They sense when we get near them and start opening the door hatch. See, watch."

We slowly stepped up to where the metal discs were, and just then the door hatch started to open.

I got a big smile on my face. "How cool is that? I'm starting to love this new world I'm in."

A couple walked in right as I said that to Bert. They glanced over at me with a strange look on their faces.

I whispered, "Oops, I guess I need to be careful how loud and where I talk."

Bert gave a playful smirk and shook his head yes. He took a hold of my hand and guided me out the door.

"I'd say you can ride with me, but I don't think your car is allowed to stay here."

I turned to Bert, "That's okay. I'd prefer to have my car with me anyway."

Bert got a worried look on his face. I put a hand on Bert's arm. "It's not that I don't trust you, I do. It's just I always prefer to have my car. You never know what may happen."

Bert gave a sigh of relief, "Very true. Good thinking. You can follow me. It's not far away. Just about 10 minutes." Bert looked at me in the eyes and leaned down. I thought for a second he was going to kiss me, but it was way too soon for him to attempt a kiss. He must have thought the same thing, either that or he read my mind, because he immediately straightened up. "OK, I'll see you there."

Bert watched me get into my car, then he did the same. I glanced over at him, and he waved at me. He smiled and waved back before backing out to leave.

"Hello, ma'am, are you going home now?"

"No, not yet. We are going to a park. Oh, crap. I didn't get the name of the park. He said it was 10 minutes away. I'm supposed to follow him."

"OK, ma'am, I know which park you are referring to, but we will follow him anyway." And just then, my car backed out and followed Bert.

My head was spinning with everything that had happened at breakfast. Bert was a great guy. So attentive, nice, and intelligent. But it seemed to me that he had other things in mind than just friends, and I don't know if I am ready for that. I may not be married in this dimension, but I was married where I came from, and it was too soon to get involved with anyone. But I really do like Bert. Oh boy, what was I going to do?

Before long, we had arrived at the park. It wasn't too big, but it looked like there were a few hiking trails, some picnic tables, and a lake with a trail around it.

"Wow, this place looks really peaceful. Just what I need."

After parking our cars, Bert hurried out of his and ran over to open my car door for me. "Thank you. You really are such a gentleman."

"Is that a new concept for you?"

"Well, actually, yes. My husband hasn't been very gentlemanly in a long, long while."

"I am sorry. That's so sad you had to live like that, but no more. He's not here with you. Remember that. You can start fresh and have a new life you deserve."

"Yes, I can. It's a habit. I keep calling him my husband. I thank God every day he is not here with me. I didn't know how to leave him, especially having the kids." I admitted.

"I'm sure it's harder with kids involved."

I followed Bert to a small path. "There is a nice lake with a trail around it just up ahead. I thought we could walk off some of that breakfast. Is that okay?"

"That sounds perfect. I love going for walks."

While walking, I took in the surroundings. I could feel the unseasonably warm breeze whipping through my hair. I just loved the fresh smell of the outdoors. The warm sun felt so good on my skin. We walked through a canopy of maple trees. It was like we were in a tree tunnel. It was so beautiful.

"It's beautiful here. Thank you for suggesting it."

Bert took my hand in his. "You are so welcome. I just knew you would like It."

We had finally made it to the lake. I noticed there were nice teak wooden benches all along the lake's edge. "Hey, Bert, do you mind if we sit down for a little bit?"

"No, not at all. I was going to suggest that my-self."

The wooden teak benches had a lumbar support curve which made it quite comfortable. We sat down facing each other simultaneously.

"So, Bert, you know a lot about me, but I know nothing about you except that you are a physics professor. Do you mind telling me a little about you?"

"Sure thing! I've been here my whole life. I've never been married, but I've had a few serious relationships. A while back, I dated someone who I thought was serious about me, but it turned out she was cheating on me. That pretty much turned me off on dating."

"I'm sorry. That sucks. Now I get it. You had experience with cheaters. That's why you brought it up."

"Yes, I did. And I know how much it hurts. You put all your trust and love into someone just for them to rip your heart out and stomp on it."

"Yes, that's exactly how it felt. But I could never get proof."

"Well, I'm sure we both have learned a lesson as far as that's concerned."

"Yes, I have. Have you ever decided to start dating again?"

"No, I haven't. At least not until recently." Bert admitted while winking at me.

*Oh boy, what am I going to do about Bert?* I thought. I decided to just smile at him.

We sat on the bench and talked for what seemed like an hour, then Bert said, "Hey, do you want to go walk around the trail now?"

"Sure thing."

Getting up from the bench, Bert held his hand out to me. Taking Bert's hand, I wondered if that meant anything to Bert. I needed to tell him I just wanted to be friends for now but I need to make sure he wants more than friendship. That would be embarrassing.

We started walking along the lake trail. The warm breeze tousled my hair. Just as I was about to look at Bert, he reached for my hand. We walked hand in hand, chatting about our pasts. Holding hands sent shivers down my spine, which was a bit scary because it felt peaceful for the first time in ages. But I can't have a relationship right now. I was having a great time, but I felt like I needed to break free from this 'get-to-know-you' conversation.

"So, Bert, what do you think about the Cordelia tribe entering our atmosphere? I'm a little worried about it."

"I'm sure you are. As far as I know, aliens don't exist in your dimension. We have known about the existence of aliens for decades. They have always been able to keep them at bay. This is not the first time they have entered our atmosphere. Don't worry. The government is on top of everything. They used to never tell us about aliens, but about 10 years ago, there was a huge uproar when they had gotten closer than they ever had been. Government workers told their families, and the news spread like wildfire, which caused riots and protests."

"Damn, I had no idea. I just figured it was a new thing the way it was all over the news. Does anyone know what they want?"

"NO, at least not that the government is sharing with the general public."

"Just my luck, I escaped a narcissist just to come to a world where aliens are trying to invade."

"Try not to let it bother you too much, Faith. We don't know what they want. No need to worry until we know what to worry about."

"OK, I will try not to worry. But that's what I do, I worry about things. Too often, my therapist tells me." I tried sounding reassuring but was failing. I was nervous as hell.

We continued to stroll the trail when I glanced at my phone for the time. "Wow, Bert, it's mid-afternoon. I hate to say it, but I'm going to have to be leaving. I have stuff to do for work tomorrow."

"Time flies when you're with good company. I'll walk you back to your car."

We took our time strolling the trail to the cars while chit-chatting about our work days tomorrow. Back at our cars, Bert turned to me, "I had fun today. I'd like to see you again."

"I had fun too. I really needed this relaxing time today."

"I'm glad you were able to relax some. So are you busy next weekend?"

"Oh, no, I'm not busy."

Bert gazed into my eyes. He leaned in. "What about we go out to dinner Friday night?"

"That sounds lovely."

Leaning in further, I saw Bert going for a kiss. Gently, I put a hand on his chest to stop him.

"Look, Bert, I really like you, but I always rush into things when it comes to dating. With everything going on right now, I want to take it slow. If that's okay with you, I'd love to go out with you Friday night but just as a friend. I could use more friends here."

"I can totally respect that. I understand. I would love to be your friend. And if you want things to progress further, I'll be here. Can I get a hug?"

"Now, a hug I could definitely use."

Bert leaned down for a hug. He was probably a head and a half taller than I was. He wrapped his strong arms around me. I immediately felt at ease and safe in his arms. Releasing his hold on me, Bert gazed into my eyes again. For a brief moment, I thought he was going to try and kiss me again, but he was a gentleman and just smiled at me before saying his goodbyes. I got in my car and waved goodbye to Bert as he got in his car.

"Good afternoon, ma'am. Where would you like to go?" The friendly car voice asked.

"Just home. Thank you. I'm tired now."

As the car drove off, I was thankful that I didn't have to drive because I couldn't get today out of my head. I was completely distracted.

"WOW, that was unexpected."

"Ma'am. Are you okay?"

"Oops, I didn't realize I spoke out loud." I said to myself.

"Yes, sorry. Didn't mean to speak out loud."

Sooner than expected, I arrived home. I thought of Bert the whole way home. Megan was awaiting my call. I barely had the door shut when I got my phone out and rang Megan.

Megan didn't even wait for me to say anything. She answered the phone with, "Girl, where have you been? I was getting worried. You guys could not have been at breakfast this long."

"Oh, no, we weren't. Although breakfast was longer than I was anticipating. We were at the diner for 2 hours. Which, by the way, is the coolest little restaurant."

"Yeah, I thought you might like it. Well, what happened?"

With a big smile, I responded, "He asked if I wanted to walk off breakfast at the park that was 10 minutes away. It had really nice trails with a lake. Very pretty and relaxing. We had a great conversation. I really enjoyed getting to know him."

Megan was listening intently, "And… What happened next?"

"And nothing. That was it. He hugged me and then left."

"Really?? Well, that's disappointing. I was hoping for some spark between you two."

"Oh, there was a spark or two. He kept staring into my eyes. Although it felt like he was staring into my soul. I really do like him. We are going out this Friday night."

"EEKK, that's awesome. So did he kiss you?" Megan cheered.

"He tried, but I stopped him."

"WHAT!! Why?" Megan asked.

"Every relationship I have had starts out getting really intense really fast. If I have a chance to start over, I want to do it right and take my time getting to know him and build a friendship first. I made it clear that I really did like him and would maybe be interested in furthering our relationship later after we get to know each other first. We are just going out this Friday as friends."

"I guess that is a smart move. But typically Friday nights are for dates. Aren't they?" Megan asked.

"Yes, but it can also be for friends to hang out."

"True. I'm excited for you." Megan admitted.

"I am too. But I picked the wrong man to marry. What if I make the same mistake again?" I admitted.

"You aren't marrying the man. You are just going out on a first date. Taking things slow and getting to know him is a good idea." Megan commented.

"True, just a first date. But now I'm tired. Today was fun but mentally and physically exhausting."

"I'm sure it was. Your poor brain has had a lot to think about these past few days."

Before I got off the phone, I added, "Have a good night. See you tomorrow."

"You too. See ya. Have good dreams." Megan remarked back.

"Oh, I hope I do."

Once off the phone, I went into the kitchen for a snack. It was too late for a full meal, but some apple and peanut butter sounded good. Walking up to the monitor in the kitchen, I asked for the snack. Taking a seat at the kitchen island, my food popped up just in time. Robotically eating my snack, I thought of nothing but Bert the whole time. I really wanted to start slowly with him and build a meaningful relationship, but it would take a lot of willpower. Deciding it was time for bed, I got up and headed upstairs.

Curling into bed, I thought how nice it would be to share a bed with a man that truly loves and cares for me. Talk about putting the cart before the horse. Even my brain had a habit of moving too fast.

# CHAPTER 9

As soon as my head hit the pillow, it seemed like my alarm was going off. It couldn't be time to get up already, but sure enough, it was. I quickly got ready for work. The sooner I got to work, the sooner this week would end. Friday couldn't get here fast enough. I had just seen Bert yesterday, but I wanted to see him again.

On the way to work, I stopped by my favorite coffee shop, Cosmic Coffee. It was becoming part of my routine and made my mornings so much better. As my car pulled up to the building, I saw Megan getting out of her car. She turned and waved.

"Hey, girl,"

"Hey, Megan."

"Did you sleep at all?" Megan inquired.

"Yeah, I guess, but it didn't seem like I slept at all. It went too fast."

"Did you have any hot dreams?"

"No, not that I remember. I wish I could, though."

We continued talking as we walked up to the offices.

"See you at lunch," Megan called as I went into my office.

"Yep, see you,"

My morning flew by, which I was thankful for. Lunch with Megan and Alena was always nice and relaxing way to break up the day. The lunchroom itself was relaxing, but the conversation made it that much better. After lunch, I was in my office organizing files at my desk. I didn't hear or see Darren walk in as I was not facing the door.

In a soft voice, he spoke close to my ear. "Good afternoon, Faith."

Startled, I jumped about a foot into the air and turned around, hitting my butt on the desk. I was surprised to see Darren standing just a couple of inches away from me.

"Oh, I didn't see you come in. How long were you standing there?"

"Long enough to observe your fit body diligently at work," Darren said as he rested his hand on the desk right next to my butt. Feeling uncomfortable, I stepped away from him.

*Mental note: Don't wear tight skirts to work anymore, I thought.*

"What can I do for you this morning, Darren?" I asked, trying to steer the conversation away from the inappropriate interaction we were having.

"Oh, there is plenty I'd love for you to do with me... I mean, for me. But if you are talking work-related, I have a bigger project from a new client I'd like you to start working on. I emailed you the details."

I had moved to the other side of my desk to put some distance between us.

"OK, but you could've just called me and waited for a response."

He placed his hand on the desk, leaned in closely and whispered, "Well, then, I wouldn't be able to feast my eyes on this beauty before me."

"Can you give me some time to look over it?" I said, hoping he'd take the hint and leave.

Putting on his best business voice, Darren replied, "Since you did such a great job last time, I wanted to give you the opportunity, but I need to go over it with you first. Why don't you stay late tonight? I can order us some dinner, and we will review it together."

*Where is all this coming from? I've got to talk to Megan about all this. I thought.*

"I can't tonight. I have plans." I lied. "Can we go over it tomorrow?"

"Sure thing. I've got a meeting in the morning, but we can go over it after lunch."

*Oh, thank God. Darren is a real creep. I thought.* "OK, great. That'll work." I responded a little too loudly.

Darren gave a little wink before leaving the office.

"That was creepy." I mumbled to myself.

The rest of the day went by fairly quickly. Later, I heard a knock at my door and jumped up.

"Sorry, sweetie. I didn't mean to scare you. Are you ready to go?" Megan apologetically asked.

"Sorry, I didn't realize I was so jumpy. Yeah, give me a sec."

I shut down my computer and grabbed my things before heading out with Megan. I was quiet as we hurriedly walked to the elevator.

Megan started to ask, "What's..."

Just then, Darren popped out of his office and yelled down the hall. "Good night, Faith. Don't forget about our meeting tomorrow afternoon."

I nervously waved at him as an acknowledgment. Feeling a little creeped out, I turned my attention back to Megan.

Megan gave me a worried look. "What was that all about?"

"Ugh, I guess there is another big-deal project he wants me to do."

Looking worriedly at me, Megan asked, "Are you okay? You seem kinda on edge."

I glanced over my shoulder and replied, "Yeah, something weird happened today. I'll tell you later. Not here."

Megan looked at me with concern and nodded yes to show she understood.

We didn't say anything else until we got to our cars. Megan was the first to speak up.

"Hey, you've been quiet. Thinking about Bert?"

"No. Well, yeah, he has been on my mind a lot today. But..." I glanced over my shoulder to make sure no one was around. There were people all around, but no one of importance within earshot. "Darren made a pass at me. He was being really inappropriate. It made me feel really uncomfortable."

"Oh, girl. I should have warned you about him. He's a player. He's slept around with a lot of women in this building."

I was shocked, " No one has thought of turning him in? I can't be the first person to find him repulsive."

"Oh no, you aren't. But he's a smooth talker and a manipulator. He bribes the women to keep their mouths shut."

"What an asshole. Now I don't know what to do. He wants to meet me to go over the project. He actually asked me to stay late tonight. I didn't think that was very appropriate, though."

"Oh, girl, just be careful. Try to keep it as professional as you can." Megan warned.

"I'm going to try. That's why I pushed the meeting to during the day when there are people around."

Megan leaned in and gave me a hug. "Try not to worry about it tonight. Think about your hottie new boyfriend." Megan winked.

"Oh, please. He's not my boyfriend...yet. But I hope one day he will be."

I said goodbye and got into the car.

That oh-too-familiar voice spoke up, "Good evening, ma'am. Where to this evening?"

"Just home, please. Thank you."

"As you wish."

I leaned back in the seat, grateful for self-driving cars in this dimension. Watching the world go by, I thought of the past couple of days. I could feel my anxiety rising. My heart rate was increasing, breathing was becoming more rapid, and I felt like pulling my skin off. I was having a panic attack.

Trying to calm myself down, I thought how much of a wonderful surprise Bert had turned out to be. But Darren was a real creep. I was going to have to deal with him soon.

Finally home, I quickly ate dinner and got ready for bed. I grabbed a book to read to relax. As my eyes grew heavy, the book fell onto my chest.

"Nope, I gotta finish this chapter first. It's getting good."

Picking the book up, I started reading again, but before I knew it, I was drifting off to slumber. Panic attacks sometimes had a way of wiping me out. It can take a lot to calm myself down. While falling asleep, I made a mental note to check and see if there is anything in this dimension to help with them.

# CHAPTER 10

Waking up, I felt something heavy on my chest. Lifting my head up from the pillow, I looked down and noticed the book lying on my chest.

"Wow, I don't even remember falling asleep while reading."

Setting the book on the nightstand, I gradually got out of bed to get ready for work. I was not looking forward to my meeting with Darren. Maybe if I just kept my mind on Bert, the day or rather the week, would go better.

"Thinking of Bert, he never called me last night. I wonder if I should call him tonight. I don't want him to forget about me."

I was pretty much on autopilot all morning. Between Creepy Darren and Hottie Bert, my mind was preoccupied with everything except work. Still, the day seemed to fly by. Before I knew it, it was time for my meeting with Darren. We were supposed to meet in my office, but the scheduled time came and went with no sign of him. I certainly wasn't going to go searching for him. I had enough work to do without his interruptions.

While I was diligently working, there was a knock at my door. Looking up, I saw Darren peeking his head in. Glancing at the clock on my computer, I noticed it was thirty minutes until clock-out time.

"Hey, Darren. What can I do for you?"

"I got hung up with work. Sorry I missed our meeting. How about tomorrow morning? I promise I won't disappoint you this time." Darren said with a wink.

"That's okay. I was busy all day anyway. I didn't even notice what time it was. Yes, tomorrow morning will be fine."

"Great. I look forward to it. Have a great night."

"See ya."

And with that, Darren turned to leave. *Thank God. That wasn't too bad. Now I just have to fret and worry until tomorrow. He probably did that on purpose.*

Megan peeked her head in. "Hey girl, how was your meeting with Mister Creepy?"

"Oh, we didn't have it. He was busy. It got pushed to tomorrow morning." I said rolling my eyes as I was explaining it to Megan.

"Well, at least you got a reprieve for today."

Gathering my things, I followed Megan out to the cars. We talked about Bert the whole way. Megan gave me a hug and advised "Just give him a call. You know he likes you. He'll no doubt love that you called him first."

"OK, I guess I'll put my big girl panties on and give him a call after I eat dinner. See you tomorrow." Waving at Megan, I got into my car.

"Good evening, ma'am. Where to this evening?"

"Good evening. Home, please. Thank you."

"Right away, ma'am."

Looking out the window, I watched the cars flying by in the sky. It was mesmerizing until my car began to descend to the road below, which made me dizzy watching it. Leaning back in my seat, I closed my eyes to try and calm down the nausea. Bert's big smile was the first thing I pictured. His big blue eyes were looking down at me when he attempted his kiss. I could still feel his strong, muscular chest as I put my hand out to stop him. *Oh, why did I stop him?* I tried imagining his soft lips gently gliding over my soft, plump lips.

"Ma'am, you are home."

"Oh, thank you."

I hurried into the kitchen to grab dinner before calling Bert. Just thinking about talking to him got my heart pounding and palms all sweaty. The way Bert got me so nervous must be a good sign. I never remember feeling like this with Griffin. Picking up my phone with a shaky hand, I took a deep breath and dialed Bert's number. Oh my, it felt like my heart was in my throat because it was beating so hard. Bert picked up on the first ring.

"Hey there, Beautiful. How are you this evening?"

"Hey, I'm good. And how are you?"

"Better now that I am hearing your gorgeous voice. So tell me, how has your

week been so far?"

"Ugh, it's been okay I guess. My boss was acting a little inappropriate towards me. Made me feel really uncomfortable."

"Well, don't let him get to you. Report him to HR if you have to."

"If it gets too far I will."

I proceeded to explain everything that took place that week between Darren and myself. I could hear the anger in Bert's voice.

"I'm sorry. I don't mean to upset you. It just feels good to get it off my chest. I'm glad I'm not the only one who thinks it's uncalled for behavior."

"It pisses me off when men use their authority to abuse women or anyone for that matter."

I walked into the living room to continue my conversation with Bert in comfort. We must have been on the phone for an hour talking about everything from work to our hopes for the future. A knock on the front door startled me.

"Shit, there's someone at the door."

"Be careful. Are you expecting anyone? Megan perhaps?"

"NO, not expecting anyone. Megan was busy tonight. Can you hold on a minute? I'm sorry."

"Sure thing."

I got up to go answer the front door. Walking up, I peeked out the peephole.

*Shit, what the hell is he doing here?* I said loud enough for Bert to hear, "It's Darren."

Reluctantly, I opened the door an inch to peek out at Darren. "Oh, hey, what are you doing here? I didn't know you knew where I lived."

Placing his strong, big hand on the door, Darren pushed his way in. I gasped and backed up screaming. "Hey, what the hell, Darren?"

"Sorry, sweetie. I need to talk to you. And I am your boss, I can look at your personal file whenever I want."

"Darren, I'm not at work. That doesn't give you the right to just show up here."

"Oh, come on, Sexy. I just want to go over the project with you. It can't wait anymore."

"We are scheduled to go over it tomorrow morning. This isn't appropriate for you to be here. I need you to leave."

"I see the way you look at me. We can't be alone at work, but here we can."

Darren was gradually getting closer to me as he was talking. I was getting nervous that he was going to try something. The look in his eyes was like a piercing intensity. It was an evil look. Like he was on the prowl. I started backing up into the living room as I needed to try and turn this situation around.

"OK, Darren, if you insist. Why don't we go into the kitchen? We can use the table there."

"NO, I want to be comfortable. Sitting here on the couch will work best."

Darren declared as he was getting closer, forcing me to back up even further into the living room. I glanced at my phone on the coffee table. Hopefully, Bert could hear the interaction between me and Darren. It looked like my phone had gone to sleep.

"Come over to the couch, Faith. Sit here next to me," Darren gestured as he took a seat on the couch.

I was surveying the area and my options. The car was already put away. So a quick escape, if need be, was not an option. I could run out the door, but where would I go? It's not like I know any neighbors. So running to them was out of the question.

*Oh, great, I'm still wearing the dress I wore to work, I thought.*

That wasn't good because Darren could have easy access to my goodies. I was hoping to save those for Bert. Walking over, I sat on the opposite end of the couch.

Darren looked puzzled at me. "Oh, no, sweetie. That's too far." He quickly slid over next to me and placed one hand on my left thigh. "So shall we get started?"

"I didn't see you carry anything in with you," I observed.

"Oh, I figured we could use your laptop. I emailed you a copy of the file," Darren stated.

"OK, I'll go get it. It's in my bag in the kitchen. I'll be right back." I leaned forward to grab my phone. Maybe I could talk to Bert and ask for help.

"Oh, no, sweetie. You don't need your phone just to walk into the kitchen. Leave that here," Darren demanded with an authoritative voice.

I rose to my feet. While I did so, Darren put a hand on my thigh and slid it upward close to my butt. I instinctively smacked his hand away.

"Darren, I did not give you permission to touch me like that," I was hoping by verbally saying what he did that Bert could hear. If he was even still on the phone. I had no idea. Maybe I'm just all alone in this situation that can go horribly wrong very fast. Glancing back at Darren as I smacked his hand away, I saw him wink and smile at me.

*Damn, he really gives me the creeps. He thinks he's God's gift to women. I thought.*

Walking into the kitchen, I took a deep breath trying to stop a panic attack that was coming. That's the last thing I need right now. Placing one hand on my work bag, I wondered how I could get him out of my house. I would just try to be professional and get work done as quickly as possible. Taking another deep breath, I picked up my bag and slowly walked back into the living room.

"There you are, sweetie."

*Ugh, I wish he would stop calling me sweetie. I'm not his sweetie. Gross.*

Placing my bag on the coffee table, I took a seat again on the other side of the couch.

"Why are you so far away? We can't work together with you all the way over there." Darren got up and moved closer to me. Placing a hand on my right thigh, he continued, "You ready to get started?"

The way he talked sent shivers down my spine. Brushing his hand off my thigh, I got the laptop out and turned it on.   Ignoring where his hand was, I said, "So,

I'll just pull up my work email." Placing the laptop on
the coffee table, I got to work getting into my email.

Darren put an arm around me while I leaned
forward.  Shivering, I tried moving it off my shoulders,
but he only kept moving it further down until it rested on
the small of my back. Darren positioned himself so he
was only mere centimeters away from my ear.

"Why don't you let me help you take off that
dress and slip into something more comfortable first?
You aren't looking cozy over there at all."

"That's because you are making me feel uncomfortable.  Can we please just concentrate on work? I'm
not interested in you."

"Oh sweetie, I know you want some of this.  Every woman at work does. You'd be the envy of everyone." Darren then tried leaning in for a kiss.

I pushed Darren out of the way and got up to my
feet, "Darren, please. You are my boss, and I am not
interested in you like that.  Besides, I'm dating someone."

He stood up beside me. "I'm sorry.  You're right.
I am your boss.  It would not be right to get into a relationship with you.  Let's get to work."

*Oh, thank God. He is finally seeing reason. Persistence is key, I thought.* "OK, here I have my email up. Let me open the attachment you sent."

We spent the next hour reviewing work and what needed to be done for the new project.

"OK, Darren. I understand what needs to be done. I will get to work on it first thing in the morning."

"Great. Thank you for letting me come over."

"Well, I didn't really invite you, but you are welcome, I guess."

As I leaned forward to put my laptop away. In what seemed like a split second, I was thrown back against the couch, and Darren was on top of me. He had his hands on both of my shoulders, holding me down. I tried getting out from under him, but he was strong, and I couldn't budge him. No amount of strength was working. My breathing quickened in panic. I hated not being in control of a situation.

Looking Darren in the eyes, I screamed, "WHY ARE YOU DOING THIS?"

In a calm voice, he said, "Oh, sweetie, no one turns me down. I always get what I want."

Crying, I pleaded, "PLEASE."

"Oh, you want it, baby? Coming right up."

I have to get a hold of myself. "NO, PLEASE, STOP." I started crying because I was so scared. My heart was racing so fast. Trying to calm myself down, I started rationally thinking what I could do to get away. Just then it dawned on me. I lifted my knees up really hard into his crotch. At the same time, Darren was trying to kiss me. As soon as my knee made contact with his body, he released my shoulders to grab himself. This was my chance. I pushed him backwards with my hands then kicked him with both feet. Quickly getting off the couch, I moved to the opposite wall.

"You bitch." Darren yelled. "No one rejects me."

Darren was pissed. He ran up to me and slapped my cheek so hard it knocked me down on the ground. Pushing myself up against the window, I curled into a ball as Darren continued to kick my side.

"Shh, sweetie, there is no one here. Just relax." Darren said in such a calm voice it scared me even more. "If you behave, I'll give you a treat."

Crying even louder, I screamed, "The only treat I want from you is for you to leave me alone. PLEASE JUST GO."

"Sorry sweetie, I'm not going anywhere until I get what I want." Darren said. "I've gotta get my endorphins somehow." He stopped kicking me in the side only to kick me in the head.

I sobbed really hard, screaming, "STOP. STOP. PLEASE STOP." I pictured myself dying right there while I was being attacked.  I would never know the love of Bert.

Just then I heard a loud bang.  Darren was too busy trying to get his endorphins that he didn't notice anything happening. Without warning, Darren was lifted up and thrown across the room.

I heard Bert's voice and boy was he angry, "SHE SAID STOP ASSHOLE."

In a calm voice Darren replied, "Who the hell are you?  We were just having a little fun."

"NO, ASSHOLE. YOU WANTED TO HAVE SEX WITH HER, AND WHEN SHE SAID NO, YOU TOOK YOUR FRUSTRATIONS OUT ON HER." Bert yelled. He pushed Darren to the door with one hand behind his back.

Megan ran over to me, tears in her eyes. "Oh, Faith, are you okay?  That asshole hurt you." She gently examined my face.  "You've got a red mark on your forehead and cheek."

"I'm not surprised.  He kicked me there. Also on my left side.  And held me down really hard on my shoulders. Those areas probably have a red mark as well.  I'm sore, but I'm okay."  Megan helped me up from the floor. I went over to Bert. "Where is Darren?"

"Oh, that asshole is already gone.  I scared him. But we need to call the police."

"NO, I don't want to. Thanks to you, I'm okay now."

Megan spoke up, "Honey, it was still assault. The police need to know."

"Not now, please."

"OK, can we at least take you to the hospital?" Bert asked her.

"Thank you, but I think I'm okay." I turned to Bert. "I don't know how to thank you. You saved me. Did you hear the whole thing?"

"No, as soon as I heard it was going south, I immediately got off the phone and called Megan. I needed her to tell me where you lived, and she insisted on meeting me over here."

Megan gave me a hug while glancing over at Bert. "Yeah, girl, I was worried about you."

I started crying again. "I don't know how to thank you guys. I was so scared. He was so strong. I couldn't stop him. I didn't even invite him over here." I started shaking uncomfortably.

Bert put his arm around me. "Yeah, I heard that part. I heard him insist on sitting in the living room. I figured that didn't sound good, so I decided to come over and help out with this asshole."

I was crying even harder now. "What am I going to do about work? I can't see him now. I don't want to?"

"Faith, sweetie, just take off for the rest of the week or at least work from home. I'm pretty sure Darren won't say anything." Bert advised.

Bert put both arms around me and held me while I sobbed into his arms. Megan was rubbing my back.

"Faith, honey, it looks like you are in good hands here. I am going to leave, but please call me if you need anything."

I let go of Bert for a minute to say goodbye. "Megan, I can't say thank you enough. I really appreciate you coming over and helping to save me."

"Anything for you, honey." Megan hugged me then left.

"Thank you for helping, Megan. Drive safe." Bert added.

We three walked to the door. Once Megan was gone, Bert closed and locked the front door. I had held Bert's hand the whole time, too afraid to let go.

Bert gently led me over to the couch. "Let's sit down. Do you need anything?"

"Honestly, I could use a glass of wine." I admitted.

"Sure thing, I will go get you one. Hold tight."

Bert got up and went into the kitchen. I just sat there and went over the events that had happened that evening. Thinking of everything that Darren had done had tears falling down my cheeks. Leaning forward, I put my elbows on my knees and started quietly sobbing into my hands. All of a sudden, I felt Bert sit down next to me and put his hand on my back. Sitting the wine glass on the coffee table, Bert gave me a hug. I leaned into him and sobbed into his shoulder. Time passed without either one of us realizing it.

Eventually, I stopped crying and apologized. "Bert, I am so sorry. I'm embarrassed I keep crying."

"Babe, you went through something very traumatic. You have every right to cry. Don't feel like you have to hold your emotions in for me."

"Thank you so much for being here for me."

"You are very welcome. Anything for you."

Bert leaned back against the couch and opened up his arm for me to cuddle into. We sat like that for a while before I said, "Do you mind if I go upstairs? I need to get washed up and changed."

"Of course. I can leave. I think a bath or shower will make you feel so much better."

"Oh, please, don't leave. I don't want to be alone right now. Can you stay?"

"Of course. Let's go get you into the shower."

Bert got up and held out a hand to help me up off the couch. Before we got to the stairs, there was a knock on the front door. I looked at Bert with a worried expression on her face.

"Don't worry, babe. I'll get it." Bert opened the door and came face to face with a Department of Citizen Safety or DCS drone.

The DCS drone projected a hologram of a DCS officer who immediately spoke up, "Good evening, sir and madame. We got a call of a domestic disturbance."

I looked shocked at Bert. "Babe, I didn't call anyone." He admitted.

The DCS officer hologram spoke again, "No, sir. It was a neighbor. They called when they heard screaming and cries for help."

I looked relieved and explained, "Oh, thank you for responding. I did have an issue with my boss, but I don't want to press any charges at this time."

"OK, ma'am, but please give us a call if you change your mind. If a crime was committed, it's your civic duty to report it."

"Yes, sir, I will. Thanks again."

The hologram quickly disappeared at the same time the drone sped off at the speed of light. Bert shut the door, took me by the hand, leading me upstairs.

"So that's how they do police here? That was interesting." I questioned.

"Yeah, the government changed the police force around about the same time as AI came about. It took some getting used to, but it is so much easier to get an officer when needed. And they are able to shoot if need be." Bert explained.

"That's good to know, especially since if they were a little earlier, they may have needed to shoot Darren. I was afraid he wouldn't stop."

Bert guided me upstairs while he was explaining the DCS.

"My room is straight ahead at the end of the hall."

Walking in, Bert stopped at the doorway and took in all that he saw. "This is nicely decorated. I love it."

"Thank you."

"I didn't think I'd be seeing your room this early in our relationship, though."

"I'm sorry. I didn't either, but I didn't want to be alone, and I've got to get out of these clothes and wash off the bad night."

"That is perfectly understandable. Why don't you relax, and I can get your shower or bath ready?"

"Oh, thanks. A shower would be wonderful."

"Coming right up," Bert declared as he went into the bathroom.

I sat on the bed while waiting for Bert. Just staring off into space, I couldn't help but think about how things went down tonight. I was exhausted from crying so much, and not to mention a little embarrassed to cry that much in front of Bert. Not hearing Bert walk in, I jumped when he spoke up.

"Hey, beautiful, sorry, didn't mean to scare you. Your shower awaits."

"Oh, thank you." Getting up, I walked up to Bert. "I appreciate it." Reaching up, I gave him a kiss on the cheek.

"Anything for you, beautiful. I'll wait out here for you."

As I walked by Bert into the bathroom, he put a hand on my arm and gently caressed it as I walked by. I smiled at him when I walked by.

I walked up to the bathroom mirror and just stared at myself. I indeed had a red mark on my cheek on the top of my head. It looked like my hair was dyed bright red. "OK, that's weird." That would be too noticeable. Taking off my shirt, I glanced at the reflection in the mirror. There were sizable bruises starting to form on my side, stomach, and both my shoulders along with bright red marks showing the pain. Luckily, nothing to indicate injury to bones. I must have made a loud gasping sound because Bert called, "Hey, everything okay in there?"

Calling back to him, I said "Yeah, I'm fine."

I didn't want to tell him about the bruises right now for fear that he would take me to the hospital. All I wanted was to wash this horrible night away and lie down in bed. Stepping into the shower, I stood under the water and let it wash away all my worries. I couldn't help but think of what Darren did. He had no right. I fell to the shower floor, curled into a ball and cried my eyes out. Maybe I should have turned him in, but I didn't feel like getting into all that. I just wanted this to go away. Turning the hot water all the way up made my skin turn bright red. Maybe the hot water would wash everything away. I kept scrubbing and scrubbing away at my skin, hoping to wash away the feeling of Darren's hands and feet kicking my body. The thought made me nauseous. But I needed to finish up and get to my savior who was waiting in the bedroom.

Stepping out of the shower, I looked in the mirror. The bruises were getting bigger and more purple. Great. Bert was eventually going to see them. I was worried about his reaction. Grabbing a camisole and pants set,

I quickly got dressed as excitement started to fill me. Bert definitely turned this day around. Heading for the door, I stopped dead in my tracks. Nervous that he was going to see the bruises and red marks through my camisole, I reached out for my silk robe that was hanging on the back of the door. Putting my hand on the door, I took a deep breath. This would be the first time Bert saw me like this. Maybe it was too soon, but I could not be alone tonight. Opening the door, I stood there for a second just staring at Bert lying on my bed. He looked so comfortable. His head was resting on my pillow. He had his hands folded over his chest with his legs crossed. Gently shutting the bathroom door, he opened his eyes and turned in my direction.

"Hey there, beautiful. You look so much better. How are you feeling?"

"Honestly, I'm a little sore and tired." I admitted.

"I'm sure you are. He was really rough with you. Why don't you come lay down?"

I walked over and climbed into bed. Bert opened up his arm so I could lay on his shoulder. Snuggling into Bert felt so right. Like I was home. Resting my right hand on his chest, I started gently rubbing his chest.

"Bert, I can't thank you enough for everything you did for me tonight."

"Faith, I really like you. I would do anything for you. Do you want to get under the covers?"

"Yes, actually I do."

We got up and reached down to move the comforter back. Sitting down on the bed, I started moving my legs under the covers. Bert put a hand on my shoulder and I winced.

"Hey, I'm sorry. Did I hurt you? Why don't you take off your robe?"

I just looked at him and took a deep breath. "Because I didn't want you to see this." Just then I removed the robe to reveal the bruises and bright red marks on both my shoulders.

Bert's face got really red. "That asshole. He hurt you. Do you have bruises and red marks anywhere else?"

"Yes, on my side and stomach from where he kicked me. It's okay. I'll be okay."

"NO, honey. It's not okay. Can I do anything for you?"

"Just hold me under the covers, please."

"Are you sure? I don't want to make you feel uncomfortable."

"Yes, I am sure. And I just want you to hold me while I sleep. That's it."

"Yes, of course."

We both got into bed and pulled the comforter up to cover ourselves.

Bert leaned into my ear and whispered, "Good night, beautiful."

"Good night, my knight."

That put a big smile on Bert's face.

As I snuggled into my hero, I felt torn. I was really starting to like living here because I meant a great kind man. On the other hand, if I was never in this dimension, Darren would have never attacked me, but I would still be in a loveless marriage. Which world is better for me is the real question.

# CHAPTER 11

The sun shining brightly into the bedroom window startled me awake.

"Shhh…" Bert whispered. "It's okay."

"Good morning, my knight. What time is it?"

"It's after 8."

Jumping up to a seated position, I started panicking. "Crap, I've got to call work."

Patting me on the back, Bert reassured me, "Megan texted me. She figured you'd still be sleeping. She told Darren you wouldn't be in today. He didn't say much. He didn't seem surprised."

"Remind me to thank her. I was not looking forward to talking to the asshole."

"Yeah, she figured you wouldn't want to."

"Oh damn. Are you late for work?"

"No, I'm good. I don't have a class till 11 today. I just need to be in by 10:45. Would you like me to get you some breakfast?"

"Coffee sounds good right now."

Bert stood up and bent down to kiss me on the forehead, "Coming right up."

I sat up in bed and watched him leave the room.

"Damn, he looks good from behind." I thought. Or rather I thought I said it in my head. Bert quickly turned around after I apparently spoke out loud.

Looking over his shoulder, Bert replied, "Thanks Beautiful." Then he continued to walk down the hallway.

I proceeded to turn five shades of red.

While he was gone, I smoothed my hair and adjusted my shirt so it covered where it was supposed to. I was fluffing the pillows and comforter when Bert walked back in with a tray of coffee, pastries, and fruit for the both of us.

"Oh, Bert, that looks lovely. Thank you. I didn't realize I was hungry until I saw all that."

"I thought you might be. I hope it's okay that I brought it up here."

"That's perfectly fine by me."

He sat the tray down on the nightstand, then crawled into bed. Reaching over, Bert handed me a coffee mug.

I smiled and suggested, "Hey, just sit the tray here on the bed. We're adults. We'll be careful."

Bert placed the tray down between us.

"Here you go, beautiful."

I grabbed a pastry and started to chow down.

As we were eating breakfast, a TV monitor dropped down from the ceiling with the loud music of a **NEWS FLASH** playing simultaneously. I jumped several inches off the bed, not expecting it. Bert looked at me, alarmed.

"Hey, you okay?"

"Yes, sorry. I've just never seen that monitor appearing in here like that. I guess it startled me."

Bert patted my back reassuringly.

The red screen with white letters indicating **NEWS FLASH** appeared on the monitor. The same news anchor appeared on the screen.

"Do they have anyone else that does the news? I've only ever seen her." I questioned.

"Yes, but she's the only one that does the important news flashes." Bert explained.

The news anchor smiled brightly. "Good morning, city residents. Today is Wednesday, February 23rd, in the year 2036. We have breaking news coming in from our west coast affiliate. It appears that the Cordelia tribe's spacecraft has landed in Death Valley National Park in California. As of right now, no one has made contact with us from their spacecraft. The marines are heading there now to set up a barrier to keep our citizens safe. Do not fear. We see no threat as of now. We will keep you updated as we know more." As she was talking, a picture of the hexagon-shaped spacecraft sitting in the desert of Death Valley appeared on the screen.

"Well, this is just great. What are we going to do now?" I stuttered, turning to Bert.

Bert, trying to comfort me, responded, "I guess there is not much we can do right now. Just go about our daily lives and stay alert. Are you still interested in going out Friday night?"

"Oh, yes. I'm looking forward to it."

"OK. Awesome. So am I". Bert glanced at his watch. "Beautiful. I'm going to have to go. I need to swing by the house first. I probably shouldn't show up for class in the same clothes I was wearing yesterday. The students will talk." He was trying to lighten the mood.

I chuckled, " Well, we can't have that."

Bert stood up from the bed and leaned down to kiss my forehead. "Try to get some rest. I'll check in on you later."

"OK. I'll try. And thanks again for coming to my rescue last night. I don't know what I would have done without you there."

"Anytime. I'm always here for you."

Walking toward the door, he turned and looked me dead in the eyes. winked, and waved, before walking down the hall.

Moving the tray back to the nightstand, I decided to lie back down. But every time I closed my eyes, I kept thinking of what Darren did last night. Somehow, when Bert was here comforting me, it wasn't on my mind. Now, all alone with just my thoughts, I couldn't shut my mind off.

"Well, I might as well get up and get some work done. But first, I've got to shower. Hopefully, that'll make me feel better."

Maybe I should have gotten out of bed when Bert was still here. The second I stood up, dizziness hit me. The room felt like it was spinning, which only made me nauseated. Sitting back down on the bed, I gave myself a few extra minutes to regain composure.

"Maybe I just got up too fast. Let's try this again." Slowly standing, I waited a moment before moving. *"OK, I think I'm OK."*

The reflection in the mirror scared me. My shoulders were badly bruised and oh so sore. Lifting up my camisole, I looked at my side and stomach.

"Shit. Maybe I should have gone to the hospital. That looks really bad." I slowly moved my shoulders all around. "I can move them all around with little effort. Maybe they're just sore from the big bruises."

Once the water was nice and steamy hot, I stepped into the shower but winced as the water hit my skin. "Oh boy, that hurts. Maybe a hot shower isn't the best idea." Sitting on the shower stool just out of the water, I finished up real quickly.

After getting dressed, I decided to grab some more coffee and head into the home office. Even if I wasn't going into work, I could still be productive today. Getting the laptop out of my bag, I booted it up and went right to my work email.

"Of course, that asshole would email me. Wonder what he wants."

Seeing Darren's name in my inbox had my heart racing. I started to break out in a panicky sweat. Was he going to fire me now that I wouldn't sleep with him? I hovered over the new email for a few seconds before eventually clicking to open it.

**From:** Darren Miller

**To:** Faith Cromwell

**Sent:** Today, 7:48 a.m.

Good morning, Ms. Cromwell.

I hear you won't be in today. Please understand this project is from a very big and important
client. I expect you to work on it while you are
home. Rest and recover from whatever ails you, but
don't neglect your job. Email me if you have any
questions.

Thank you in advance,

Darren

" 'From whatever ails me.' Asshole. You did this to me. On that note, I'm really about to piss you off."

I started to construct my own email to him.

**From:** Faith Cromwell

**To:** Darren Miller

**Sent:** Today, 10:20 a.m.

Good morning, Mr. Miller.

I plan on working on the project today. It will be done on time. Do not worry.

I won't be in the rest of the week. I seem to have injured my back, shoulders, and stomach in an assault. My doctor thinks I need to stay home and rest. Hopefully, I'll feel better by Monday.

Sincerely,

Faith

"So it's a little white lie. But the asshole deserves it, and my back really is hurting."

Taking one last look at the email, I was satisfied with how it read and hit send.

Working diligently, I hadn't realized several hours had passed until Bert called to check up on me.

"Hey there, beautiful. How are you feeling? " Bert eagerly questioned.

"Oh, hey. I'm sore. My shoulders and back are the main problem. Shouldn't you be in class? " I wondered.

"Sweetie, it's almost two o'clock. I've been out of class for a while now. I just finished lunch. I was thinking of you, so I thought I'd give you a call."

"Damn, Is It really that late? I decided to get my laptop out and get some work done. It's nice not getting interrupted. I can get so much more work done here at home. I could definitely get used to working from home. " I said, mostly thinking out loud.

"You know, right now might be a good time to ask Darren for anything you want. I'm sure he'll say yes just to keep you from going to the police. He did pay off those other women you know." advised Bert.

"That's a good point. I already emailed and told him I wouldn't be in the rest of the week. He emailed me first thing this morning and acted like nothing happened, being a professional and not so understanding boss. He said 'rest and recover from whatever ails me', like he has no clue what he did to me. That asshole pissed me off, so I told him I wouldn't be in the rest of the week."

"Well, good for you." I could tell Bert had a big smile when he said that. "Beautiful, I hate to cut this short but I've gotta go. I have student meetings this afternoon. I'll call you on my way home. Unless you'd like me to come over tonight? ".

"That's OK. I really appreciate it but you've been here all night and I'm sure you didn't get much rest.

"Actually, no, I didn't. Truthfully, I'm really tired," Bert admitted.

"Go home and get some rest tonight. I need you feeling well for Friday night."

"Oh, nothing will stop me from going out with you Friday night." "

"That's awesome to hear."

"Goodbye, Faith."

"Bye, Bert. Talk to you later."

I almost said "I love you," which shocked me, but it was probably just out of habit.

The rest of the week went smoothly, except for Darren's daily emails. I managed to stay focused on my work and even submitted everything early. I'm hoping that by being extra diligent and going above and beyond my usual stellar work ethic, Darren might approve of me working from home when I finally ask him. Fingers crossed! The project was wrapped up before the deadline.

After submitting it, Darren was quick to respond to her email.

"Thank you, Faith, for your hard, diligent work. After reviewing it quickly, everything seems to be in order. I will look over it more closely and let you know what I think."

"EEWW, everything from him now gives me the creeps. I can't stand him. I wish he would get fired or worse."

I considered replying but decided against it. I needed to start building boundaries with him and keep them. For now on, I'd have as little contact with this asshole as possible.

The week finally came to an end. Aside from when I first arrived in this dimension, it had been the longest week of my life thanks to that awful incident with Darren. Finally, the day of my date with Bert had arrived. I just had to get through the afternoon which was a hard task given the fact that my mind kept wandering to the evening upcoming events.

# CHAPTER 12

The master bathroom was all steamy from the hot shower. As soon as I stepped out of the shower, my cell phone started ringing. I rushed over to answer it before whoever it was hung up. Forgetting that I was still wet, my right foot slipped and I felt myself slowly falling forward toward the edge of the countertop. Just in time, I held out my hands to brace myself. Wet hands came slamming down on the countertop. Luckily, it was enough to keep me off the floor.

"Phew, that was a close one. I'm such a klutz."

Picking up my cell phone, I saw it was Bert.

"Oh, I hope he's not calling to cancel. I've been looking forward to this all week."

Hitting the answer button, I responded enthusiastically, "Hey there, Bert. I just got out of the shower."

"Hey, Beautiful. I was calling to make sure you were still on for tonight. I'm guessing that since you just got out of the shower, your answer is yes."

"Oh, most definitely. Looking forward to tonight is the only thing that has kept me going all week," I admitted.

"OK, that's great to hear. I'm on my way home from work. I should be heading over in about an hour."

"Sounds perfect. One quick question. What are we doing tonight? I'm trying to decide what to wear."

"Well, I'm taking you out to dinner at a nice restaurant. Then I thought I'd show you my favorite spot."

"Oh boy, this isn't an old teenage boy's favorite spot, is it?"

"No, nothing like that. Well, at least it wasn't mine."

"OK. Well, that's good, I guess. See you soon."

As I was hanging up with Bert, I stared at the mirror in the bathroom. "Oh. Now I'm getting nervous. And what the heck am I going to wear?" My heart started beating fast, not because of panic but because of sheer nerves.

Slipping on my robe, I went into the closet. The overhead light as well as the computer monitor came to life as soon as I stepped inside. Immediately turning towards the monitor, I heard that familiar voice.

"Good evening, ma'am. May I please help you find something?"

"Oh, yes, please. I'm going on a dinner date."

"Several options are coming on the screen now, ma'am."

"Awesome, thank you."

" My pleasure."

The screen started scrolling through various options. The first outfit I saw was jeans, a black tube top, and heels.

"Nope, not jeans. But I do like the nice outfit, though."

Swiping to the left past that outfit, the next was a teal slip dress with a slit on the side.

90"That's a really nice dress, but too much for a first date, I feel. Sorry, but no. Not yet."

Swiping to the left a little too quickly, I finally stumbled upon the outfit for me. It was a wrap dress which was a little bit below the knee in navy blue.  It was shown with beige heeled sandals.

"Now that's the dress. Not too fancy, but just enough, I think."

Touching the outfit on the screen, her dress all of a sudden appeared on a rack to the right of the screen.

"Yay. It's beautiful in person. Thank you."

"I'm glad you are pleased, ma'am. Do you need assistance with anything else?"

"No, I'm good. "

Once the outfit was decided, I went back into the bathroom to finish getting ready before getting dressed. The closer the time came, the more I glanced at my phone, checking the time. The more nervous I became. I could feel my heart start to race, my hands were sweaty and shaking.

"Oh, this is ridiculous. It's not like I've never been out with him before." But maybe I was nervous because it was the first official date I had been on in over a decade.

Once my makeup and hair were done, I made my way into the bedroom.   With shaky hands, I reached for the dress.  Slipping one arm in the dress at a time, I could still feel myself shaking.

"I only hope once I see Bert, I start to calm down. I don't want him to think I'm some inexperienced fool."

Reaching my arms around the back of the dress, I tried pulling the zipper up but was not able to reach it.

"Oh, good grief. I hate living alone.  How am I supposed to get this zipper up?"

"Ma'am, do you require assistance?"

"Only if you can somehow grow arms and help me pull up this zipper?" I questioned as I kept trying to reach the zipper with no avail.  All I managed to do was spin around in circles like a dog chasing its tail.

"I must really look ridiculous."

I jumped about a foot in the air as I felt a cold hand on my back. Turning around defensively, I noticed a robotic arm had appeared out of nowhere. As I turned back around, the arm pulled the zipper up and disappeared as quickly as it had appeared.

"Oh, wow, that's cool. Thank you."

"You are welcome, ma'am. Do you require any further assistance?"

"No, I don't think so. That will do."

Sitting down on the bedroom chair, I slipped on my beige heeled sandals that came with the dress. Standing up, I walked over to the full-length mirror. As I stared at the reflection, I heard the doorbell ringing.

"Oh crap, it's that time already. Time flies when you are having a panic attack."

In a panicked voice, I yelled, "I'll be right there."

Taking one last look in the full-length mirror, I gave myself a thumbs up then ran out of the bedroom and down the stairs.

I stopped at the front door. Taking a deep breath, I placed my hand on the door knob.

"Well, I better open the door. I'm pretty sure he can see me through the frosted glass." I thought.

Taking air in deeply through my nose, I slowly twisted the knob and opened the front door to see Bert standing there in dark jeans, a navy dress shirt, and a sports jacket. I always thought he was handsome, but this man standing in front of me was even more good-looking than I could ever imagine. Oh, and he smelled so good too. I could feel heat radiating up from my toes into my cheeks. I'm pretty sure my cheeks were five shades of red now.

"Hello." I managed to softly speak.

"Well, hello there. You look amazing." Bert said in a soft, sexy voice.

Feeling myself blush even more, if that was possible, I replied, "You are looking very handsome."

"Come on in. I just have to grab my purse." I held the door as Bert stepped into the foyer.

"OK, No hurry. I'll just wait right here."

As I went into the kitchen to grab my purse, I could feel Bert's eyes on me as I walked away. Turning the corner, I took a quick glance at Bert propped up against the front door. He wasn't just staring in my general direction but following my every move with his piercing eyes. Wide-eyed, I mouthed "WOW" as I put my hands on the counter and grabbed my purse.

Quickly walking back to Bert, I blurted out, "OK, you are perfect." Blushing, I suddenly followed, "I meant to say, I'm perfect. We can go now."

Shaking my head, I lowered my eyes to my feet and stepped toward the door, reaching for the handle. I could sense Bert standing right behind me. He placed a warm hand on my shoulder and gently turned me around. Resting one hand on the door just to the left of my head, he reassured me.

"Faith, no need to be embarrassed. You just said what's on your mind. I love that in a woman. Always speaking her mind. I just want to tell you, you are perfect in every way. You look great. I just want to do one thing before we leave. I know it is usually done at the end of the date, but I've been wanting to do this since the last time I was here, but that wasn't the right time."

My heart stopped for just a second, then sped up faster than I had ever felt it before. With his left hand on the door, Bert placed his other hand on my left cheek, then leaned forward and gave me the softest kiss I had ever felt. It wasn't much, just a little kiss with the tip of his tongue quickly invading my mouth before retreating. The kiss was over as fast as it had started. We both stared at each other with heat radiating between the two of us.

Finally, Bert spoke up, "Ready for some dinner?" He whispered.

I could not yet find my voice, so I just shook my head yes. I stepped aside, and with a grin, Bert opened the front door. As I stepped outside, Bert placed his hand gently on the small of my back. He guided me to the passenger side of his candy apple red Mustang convertible.

"Wow, Bert, this is a really nice car. I've always wanted one just like this."

"This has been my pride and joy for many years. I only drive it on the weekends and for special occasions." Bert explained as he opened the car door for me.

Bert held my hand as I sat down. Once he was assured I was in the car, he shut the car door and walked over to the driver's side. I followed his every move. I couldn't help it. There was an attraction with him that I had never felt before. Almost like electric pulses were flowing all over my body whenever he touched me. Bert opened the door and sat down in the sexiest way I had ever seen. Putting one hand on the steering wheel, he turned to me, saying, "Did you enjoy the view?" and gave me a wink. I turned about five shades of red. Bert smiled and announced, "We've got reservations for seven o'clock at The Celestial Cafe. Then I'd like to show you my favorite spot. I'd like to call it My Happy Place."

"That sounds lovely. Megan said that restaurant is really nice and has great food." I added.

"It does have very good food. One of my favorites. In case you haven't noticed, a lot of the restaurants here have outer space-type names. Is that how it is in your dimension?" Bert curiously questioned.

"No, we had normal names. Like Texas Road-house, Dunkin' Donuts, and McDonald's. Just to name a few." answered I.

"Oh, we had those up until about 15 years ago. This restaurant is about 40 minutes away. Is that okay for you?" Bert asked.

"Oh, yes, that's fine. It will give me time to con-trol my nerves. I'm not sure if you can tell, but I'm real-ly nervous. Even though we've hung out, this is the first official date I've been on in about 10 years." I ad-mitted.

"I couldn't tell you were that nervous. You hide it well. If it makes you feel any better, I'm nervous too. It's been a while since I've been on a date myself."

As Bert drove, he would sporadically place a hand on my knee and gently caress my skin with his thumb. This singular action made every hair on my body stand on end, which in turn had me taking a deep breath. I never said anything to Bert, though, because I really enjoyed how it made me feel. We talked about everything on the drive, from my attack with Darren to the weather. I thoroughly enjoyed the time with him and didn't want it to end. What a relaxing drive this was.

"This is such a beautiful drive. I just love all the scenery." I commented.

"It is a beautiful drive down to the café. It's on the water, which is why it takes so long, but it is well worth the drive."

"Oh, awesome. I just love being on the water. I find looking out at the ocean or really any body of water to be very relaxing and soothing. In the other dimension, I would sometimes go down to the water when I needed to think."

Bert excitedly replied, "Oh, great then you will love my happy place I'm taking you to later. Look to your right. You will see the restaurant at the bottom of the hill."

"It's so beautiful." Up ahead I saw what looked like a wooden building painted navy blue with a shimmering crystal-like exterior and large windows showing off its elegant interior. I wasn't sure how they did it but the lights looked like stars in the sky. Just off the restaurant was a huge deck with a canopy.

*"Oh, I hope we can sit outside. It's such a beautiful night." I thought to myself.*

Bert parked his car in the back of the parking lot far away from any cars. "Sorry for the long walk, Faith. I just don't trust anybody."

"It's not a problem. It's a beautiful night for a walk."

Putting a hand on the door, Bert turned to me, "Stay there. I'll come around and get you."

"Oh, such a gentleman."

Bert winked then got out of the car and walked around to the passenger side of the car. I again followed Bert's every move. As Bert opened my door, he reached one hand out for me to take. Taking Bert's hand, I gracefully exited the car.

"Thank you, kind sir."

"You are welcome, beautiful."

Once I stood up, Bert grasped my other hand and fixed a gaze on mine. Time seemed to stand still as we stood there, locked in an intense stare. It was probably just a few seconds, but it felt like an eternity. Finally, Bert broke the trance, breaking the spell. "We should head in now."

I couldn't find the words, so I just shook my head yes. Letting go of my hands, Bert placed one arm around me, and we walked up to the restaurant. To my relief, this restaurant looked like a normal place from my dimension. Except for the name, there was nothing otherworldly about it. In fact, it was the fanciest place I had ever been. I stopped dead in my tracks. Bert looked at me with concern, "You okay?"

I turned to Bert, "Yes, I'm sorry. It's just really fancy. It surprised me."

"I wanted nothing but the best for you. At least for our first official date." Bert admitted.

"Awe, thank you." I smiled as we continued to walk. Once at the restaurant's front door, Bert didn't even have to open the door. A man in an all-black suit opened the door.

"Good evening, madam and sir."

Bert, in a perfect gentlemanly tone, answered back, " Good evening. We have reservations for two under Dawson at seven."

"Oh, yes, sir. Right this way."

The host led us inside. Once inside, I tried look-ing around without looking like a tourist. The place was surrounded with wall-to-wall windows. The ceiling was covered in lights.

*Oh, it's so pretty. I hope we can sit outside. I thought.*

The host interrupted my thoughts, "Sir, you re-served an outside table, is that correct?"

I turned to Bert and mouthed "Really?!?" Bert smiled big and shook his head yes. I got a big smile on my face. "Yes, that is correct."

"Right this way." The host replied.

We were led outside. The smell of sea air drifted up my nose as we walked outdoors. It was even more beautiful than I had thought it would be. The canopy was not like one I had ever seen before. It looked like the sky with lights twinkling like stars. There were round tables spread out so as not to seem too crowded. Our table was next to the railing overlooking the water.

Of course, it was dark so we couldn't see the water but only hear it. Which made it even better. There is something about the sound of waves that is so relaxing. A light warm breeze made it the perfect night to be outside. I just loved the outdoors, especially at night. Once at the table, the host pulled out the chair for me. After I was seated, only then did Bert sit down. The host passed us both menus and handed Bert the bar list.

"Your waitress, Olivia, will be with you shortly. Enjoy your evening."

As soon as the host left, Bert spoke, "So what do you think? I wanted to do something special for you and thought you'd love eating out here."

"Oh Bert, it's so beautiful. I love it. This is a perfect night too." I said beaming.

"It is a really pretty night. So how about a bottle of wine?" Bert asked.

"Wine sounds lovely."

Bert picked up the bar list and started looking while I looked at the menu. "Oh, what about Châteauneuf-du-Pape? It's a dry red wine."

"That would work. I was thinking about getting prime rib. I just love a good prime rib." I commented.

"Oh, prime rib sounds wonderful. And theirs is delicious. I think I'll join you." Bert added.

The waitress came over to their table. "Good evening, my name is Olivia. I'll be your server for this evening. What may I get you two to drink?"

Bert gestured to me first, "I'll have a glass of water." I told the waitress and looked at Bert as if to say, should I order the wine?

Olivia, the waitress, turned toward Bert, " And for you, sir."

"I'll also have a glass of water, and we'd like a bottle of Châteauneuf-du-Pape. We would both also like to order the prime rib dinner."

Olivia's eyes got wide. "Yes, sir, very good choices."

Once Olivia had left, I spoke up first, "I think she was both impressed and shocked. I bet she worried when we just ordered water."

"I think so too. It's a really nice bottle of wine. I guess she was impressed. Was it okay that I ordered for you? I figured since we talked about it, it would just be easier for me to order both right away?"

"That is perfectly fine by me. I don't mind the guy ordering if he knows what I want."

Olivia came back with their waters and wine. She uncorked the wine, then poured a little for Bert to taste before she poured two full glasses.

"That's good. Thanks," Bert told the waitress.

Olivia poured two glasses and gave the first to me. Once she set the remaining bottle on the table, she said, "Your dinner will be out shortly."

I picked up my glass and smelled the wine before tasting it. "It smells so good. I smell berries mixed with some sort of spices. Smells heavenly." I took a sip. Swirled it around in my mouth. Then took another sip. "Yep, It's really good."

"It's one of my favorites. I only get it on special occasions because it's a little expensive. I'm glad you like it." Bert said.

"Awe, you think this is a special occasion?" I blushed as I told Bert.

"Yes, I do. It's our first date. I've been wanting to take you out ever since I first met you."

I blushed again. "Honestly, I have too. I was so glad when you suggested meeting up again that first time. I was hoping I'd get to see you again."

Bert raised his glass to me. "To a wonderful evening with an incredible woman."

I smiled, clinking my glass with his. "To new beginnings."

Bert reached across the table and took hold of my hand. We sat in silence for a while, sipping on our wine. I glanced out at the water. I could not see it but only heard the waves. It was mesmerizing.

Bert broke the silence. "I love watching you. You look so content right now."

"I am. It's so calming listening to the waves. I needed this after these past few weeks. It's been crazy since I materialized here."

"That's what I thought. How have you been after all that? You've been through so much." Bert said with concern.

"I'm okay. I get nightmares sometimes that Darren is in my room attacking me. I even thought I saw him in my room in the middle of the night once, but I think I was just having a nightmare. I've pretty much come to terms with the fact that I'm here for good  and I will no longer see my kids again. I miss them, but I'm hoping one day I will see them again. Like maybe give birth to them again. That would be cool."

"I sure do hope that asshole wasn't in your room. Do you think he could get in?" Bert questioned.

"No, I'm very anal about making sure everything is locked up tight. Plus, I have that security camera on the front and back of my house. It hasn't picked up anything." I tried reassuring Bert.

"OK, that's good. I'm sorry about your previous life. I can't imagine having kids then losing them suddenly." Bert said sympathetically.

"I appreciate your concern. I have felt better since I met you. You have kept my mind off my problems."

Bert smiled, " It has been a pleasure getting to know you."

Just then, the waitress came over with our dinner. After placing them down, she asked, "Is there anything else you need?"

Bert turned to me, "No, I'm good. Thank you."

Bert then added, "So am I. Thank you. This looks wonderful."

"Enjoy," Olivia said as she noticed the whole time we had not taken our eyes off each other.

"We should eat while it's hot," Bert suggested.

"Yes, we should," I said, picking up the knife and fork. All of a sudden, I got really nervous to eat in front of Bert. My palms started getting sweaty, and my body was shaking a little bit.

"Faith, are you cold? You are shaking some."

"No, I am fine. Sorry. It's just..." I hesitated but decided what the hell, "I'm still so nervous around you. And eating in front of you is making me even more nervous."

"You had breakfast with me when I stayed at your house that one night."

"Yes, but we weren't sitting across from each other. We were side by side," I said laughing. "Saying it out loud makes me laugh. Sorry I'm being silly."

Bert reached over to touch my hand. "No, it's not silly if it's your feelings. Your feelings are always valid." Bert tried reassuring me.

After that little awkward bump in the road, I started relaxing and really enjoying the evening. We talked about everything     - from my old life to his childhood dreams of becoming a physicist. The food was delicious but I barely tasted it, too focused on Bert and how easily the conversation flowed between us.

"Are you enjoying your dinner?" Bert lovingly asked.

"I am," I answered, " It's probably the best prime rib I have ever had.  Even back home."

"Do you remember having a restaurant like this in your dimension?"

"Not this specific type of restaurant.  We had places on the water but not this fancy or nice. At least not that I have seen."3));1

The waitress, Olivia, comes over to survey their table.  "How are things going?   Would you all like some dessert?"

Bert raised a hand and gestured toward me. "No, I'm sorry. I don't think I could eat anything else.  I'm stuffed." I replied to the waitress.

Bert turned to Olivia, "We will just have the check, please." Bert was talking to Olivia but did not take his eyes off of me.

Bert's eyes had a way of boring into my soul. I felt  a warmth radiate all over my whole body down to the tips of my toes.  Before I knew it, Bert spoke up, "You ready to go, Beautiful?"

I looked surprised. "We need the check first."

Bert, with a smile on his face, laughed a little. "Honey, the waitress already came over, took my card, and brought it back. You were staring off into space for a while. You okay?"

I looked shocked. "Oh. Umm. Okay. I didn't notice her. I was just in my head, I guess." I started to blush.

Smiling at me, Bert met my eyes. Standing up, he offered me his hand. "Let's get out of here," Bert seductively said.

I wiped my sweaty palms on my dress before taking Bert's outstretched hand. Once I was safely standing, he placed a hand on the small of my back and guided me to the front of the restaurant. I thought we were going to the car, but when I started walking in that direction, Bert guided me toward the opposite direction.

"Sorry, Beautiful, we aren't going back to the car yet." I got a puzzled look on my face but didn't say anything. I trusted Bert.

We walked past the restaurant, down a small hill, and to a terrace that overlooked the bay. The night was warm with a gentle breeze, and the stars sparkled brightly in the sky. Bert stood behind me, wrapping his arms gently around my waist as I leaned back against him.

"Wow. This is a lovely view. I never noticed it when we were eating."

"That's why I love it here. It's down far enough that no one would know we were here." Bert declared with a mischievous voice.

If I didn't know any better, I would think I was in trouble, but I knew Bert better than that. We stared out at the water, listening to the waves. "This is so relaxing." I exclaimed.

"Yes, it really is. I thought you might like it. But I have one more surprise for you." Bert said. Bert took my hand and walked down the deck. The deck rounded a corner that I almost didn't notice. At the end was a set of stairs completely hidden from view.

"WOW, I wonder how many people know this is here," I asked hypothetically.

"Well, not many. The deck is hidden so well. And if you know the deck is here, you still have to come around the corner to see the stairs."

Bert suddenly stopped walking halfway down the stairs. He stopped me on one step and then moved down the step below. I wasn't quite sure what he was up to. Bert turned to look at me. "There's something I've been wanting to do all throughout dinner," he said. Bert was now eye to eye with me. He gently placed one hand on my cheek and stared intently into my eyes. "You really are beautiful," he said. He leaned in closer. My heart was pounding in my chest. Bert watched my hair blowing in the breeze. He took his other hand and gently moved my hair out of my face, tucking it behind my ear. All the while, still staring into my beautiful blue eyes. Leaning forward, he placed his soft lips on my trembling lips. Just one soft kiss was all I needed to feel weak in the knees. I felt myself start to wobble and put my hand on the railing to steady myself.

"You okay there, Faith? One little kiss, and you are about to faint. That's some power I've got." Bert teased with a wink.

I just shrugged. "Yeah, I don't know what that was about. I'd say low blood sugar, but we just ate."

Bert, still staring, leaned in again. Placing an arm around me this time, he slowly moved toward my lips. The kiss was slow at first. It started with just a peck, then when he couldn't stand it anymore, the kiss deepened. Bert gradually opened his lips and slid the tip of his tongue into my mouth.

Even with the wind blowing, I was getting hot. I could feel Bert's tongue exploring every inch of my mouth. I slowly probed Bert's mouth with my warm tongue. Finally, Bert abruptly stopped. I looked worried. "Did I do something wrong?"

"Oh, no, honey. I need to stop before this goes too far." Bert said truthfully. He took my hand and led me down the stairs. At the bottom of the stairs were stone pavers winding their way down a small hill to the sounds of the waves. "Let's walk down by the water." Bert instructed as we walked further into the dark.

As we were walking, I looked around at our surroundings. It was hard to see. The only light was coming from the restaurant up on the hill. I could just about make out benches under the deck.

"Oh, are those benches I see?"

"Yes. Indeed, they are." Bert answered.

"We should sit there. It's such a nice night. It would be great to just relax and enjoy it for a bit." I stuttered out, sounding a little nervous.

"No, there is a place for us to sit down closer to the water." Bert replied. "No need to worry. You sound a little nervous. I've been here loads of times. It's very peaceful at night,"

That did not ease my mind. "But is it safe?"

"Yes, totally. And besides, I'm with you." Bert reassured me.

Bert put his arm around me as we continued walking towards the water. "By the water, there is this really cool group of rocks that form a bench. I'm not sure if it's man-made or what, but I've been coming here for years. I've even been here during the day, and no one is ever around. I try to sneak down. I don't want to give away my favorite spot."

"That's a good idea. But now I know about it. Are there other people that you are acquainted with that may be coming down here?" I inquired.

"If you are asking if I have ever brought other women here, the answer is no. Until you, no one has been special enough." Bert admitted.

"OH" was all I could think of saying. What Bert said made me feel so wanted. It has been so long since a man has made me feel special. It looked like we were almost to the water. "So where is this rock bench you were talking about?"

"It just so happens, it's right over there." Bert said as he gently guided me to the bench. We sat down in unison. As if it was second nature, Bert placed his arm around me while I leaned against his chest. "It's like we were made for each other. You fit perfectly into me." I chuckled at his last comment, which made Bert laugh as well.

We were enjoying the night air as the conversation flowed freely. "It's so easy talking to Bert. I could stay here forever." I thought.

I turned to look up at Bert to express my appreciation for the evening. I didn't have a chance to speak because as soon as I opened my mouth, Bert bent down and gave me the biggest, longest, most passionate kiss yet. One minute I was sitting next to him on the bench, then the next I was sitting on his lap facing him. Bert lifted up my dress and started placing his hands on my bare back. My heart skipped a beat. I felt so comfortable around him, but I didn't want to rush things. Just when I was going to stop him, we both heard a loud bang.

# CHAPTER 13

In one swift move, I found myself sitting back on the bench. I didn't even remember Bert moving me.

"Bert…" I spoke up after a long pause. "….what was that noise?" I scarily asked.

Wide-eyed Bert was staring off into the distance. Without taking his eyes off whatever he was watching, he quietly said, " Look over there?" He wrapped his arm around me  and guided my gaze at what he saw.

"What's that? It almost looks like a shooting star but a lot bigger than a star." I noted.

"And it's moving this way fast. We should proba- bly get ready to go." Just as Bert spoke up, another object shot across the sky, this one descending much faster. "Oh shit. That one is going to hit someplace soon." Bert shouted as he stood and pulled me with him. We both sprinted toward the stairs when a deafen- ing boom echoed around us.

"Oh no, it must've hit somewhere close!" I wor- riedly shouted as we were running back to the deck.

We had just reached the stairs when yet another loud bang sounded. "Here under the deck! Quickly!" Bert yelled, wrapping his arms around me as he pulled us to safety.  Glancing out from under the deck, we saw fiery streaks raining from the sky.

"We need to get back to the car," Bert said, "but let's wait to see if this slows down first. I'm so sorry to put you through all this tonight. We should never have gone out."

"Bert, you have nothing to apologize for. Neither one of us had any idea this was going to happen. And honestly, I had a wonderful time. I didn't want it to end." I tried reassuring Bert.

"Oh sweetie, don't misunderstand. I had a fabulous time. Whatever this is, it interrupted something special." He leaned down and gave me a quick kiss. "OK, I don't hear anything now. Let's make our way up to my car. Slowly."

Bert took my hand and peered out before walking to the stairs.

As we were walking, Bert surveyed the area. By the water, nothing looked amiss. We made our way slowly up the stairs with apprehension. Once at the top of the stairs, we stopped dead in our tracks.

"What the hell...Oh no. My car." He muttered.

I placed a hand on his shoulder to lend support and he covered it with his own. "Be careful. We don't want to fall in. Follow me."

Right in front of us, where the parking lot had been, was a massive crater as wide as the Empire State Building is tall.

"Oh no…maybe your car is safe." I said trying to sound optimistic.

Like walking on a ledge, we made our way around the crater. Sweat trickled down my face. " I'm scared." I whispered. "I hope I don't fall."

"Don't worry, beautiful. I've got you." Bert said reassuringly, though he was clearly just as tense.

Just then, my foot slipped over the edge. I could see my life flash before my eyes. Panicking, I grabbed a hold of Bert's arm with my other hand. Without hesitation, he yanked me back, and we tumbled backward into a row of trees. I landed sideways on top of Bert.

"Are you okay?" Bert asked.

Noticing my right ankle was sore, I looked down. A red mark had formed on it. "Physically, I think I'm alright. My right ankle has a red mark on it where it hurts, but I can walk. I just saw my life flash before my eyes though. I didn't hurt you, did I?" I said as I tried getting up, but Bert held me down.

"No. You didn't hurt me. If we weren't literally running for our lives, I might have rather liked it." Bert admitted as his hands started to wander, until he heard a strange noise.

Bert's hands rubbing over me had my heart beating in ecstasy, which quickly changed to sheer terror when I heard the same noise Bert had.

Bert got to his feet, then helped me up. He crept over to the edge of the crater and carefully peered in.

"Wait, there is something down there," he told me. Reaching for his phone, Bert turned on the flash-light feature. Normally, Bert didn't need to grab his phone and turn the light on. All he needed to say was " flashlight," and the phone would materialize in his hands, but he wanted to be as quiet as possible. He quickly shined the light in the enormous hole.

What he saw scared him. Shining back at him was a massive metal structure of some kind. Bert instinctively jumped back.

Noticing Bert's reaction to what he saw, I could only assume it wasn't good. "Bert..." I calmly and quietly spoke, "...what did you see?"

He placed a finger over my lips signaling me to stay silent. Leaning over, I looked inside the crater and immediately jumped back.

Wide-eyed, I stared at Bert and mouthed "Something is moving."

Bert's expression changed. Grabbing my hand, we took off running toward his car. Praying to God the whole way that his car was still intact. As we ran, he was horrified. The parking lot was full of holes. What cars that were there had been damaged beyond repair. In the dark, we couldn't even tell if his car had survived.

"Oh no, Bert. This is awful. What're we going to do?" I worriedly asked.

"Let's just get to my car and assess the situation then," Bert tried sounding calm, but he really wasn't.

We had to dodge holes and debris we made our way to the car. Once we got closer to the restaurant, we were able to see how it withstood this attack.

"I'm glad to see the restaurant only has minor damage. No lights on. Maybe they turned them off for safety. " Bert said as he surveyed the area. "Oh, there's my car. Thank God. It looks in one piece." He excitedly told me.

"Good thing you parked at the end of the lot. Looks like that saved your car," I said, relieved. I was surprised Bert was still being a gentleman when he opened the car door first and helped me in. "Thank you. You okay?"

Bert looked surprised. "Yes. I'm okay. I'm more worried about you."

Taking a deep breath, I admitted, "I'm a little shaken up. I saw something move in that crater. It looked like a smaller version of the alien ship they showed on TV. And I swear I saw the whole thing shake."

"Yeah, I think we both saw that at the same time. I wasn't sure you noticed it. I just knew we needed to get away from it. I'm going to take you home. Hopefully, I'll be able to."

As soon as the car started, an alarm sounded. "What the hell?" We both said in unison.

"Good evening, sir. There is a mandatory curfew. You are supposed to be indoors and stay indoors until further notice. Haven't you seen the news?" The voice in the car almost sounded like it was scolding Bert.

He turned to me and shook his head. "We have been outside most of the night. We haven't heard the news."

"Oh, sir. Well, make sure you listen to it as soon as you go home. I'll take you there right away."

Bert saw the worried look on my face. " No. Not to my house. Take us to Faith's house."

The car voice spoke up , "Yes, sir. Right away."

Luckily, the car drove on autopilot. Bert was not in the mood to navigate through all the rubble in the parking lot. He could only imagine how bad the roads were going to be. "Maybe we should take the skyway. " He said to me. "Car, take the skyway. I think it'll be safer."

"Yes, sir. I will at our earliest convenience."

As the car navigated our way out, I noticed that the parking lot looked like a landmine. The autopilot expertly dodged the cars and potholes. Every time we drove past a car on fire, I held my breath. Hopefully, our car would not catch on fire too. I would feel better when we were home.

"Oh no, what if my home is destroyed?" I thought. My anxiety was starting to ramp up into a full-blown panic attack. "Bert, what am I going to do if my house is ruined?"

"Beautiful, don't worry about that. If that's the case, you will just come home with me. And if that's no good, we will bunk in with Megan." Bert tried calming me down. That got a chuckle out of me.

"Oh, she'd love that." I laughed.

The car turned out of Celestial Cafe's parking lot and onto the road. It didn't look too bad. "Just looks like a few potholes that are easy enough to dodge. Good thing since the skyway doesn't come out this far yet." Bert commented.

Driving past some small hills, Bert noticed another huge hole in the side of a hill that was just a few miles away from the restaurant. "Shit, look over there." He told me, pointing to the right.

"Damn, that's not good. How many of those little ships came down anyway? I thought Space Force was protecting us." I inquired.

"I guess they are doing everything they can. I just hope the men and women up there are okay." Bert added.

"Oh no, I didn't think of them. I feel bad." I mumbled.

"Don't feel bad. We've been a little busy trying not to get killed or seen." Bert reassured me. He let go of my hand and placed his hand on the back of my neck. His gentle stroking of my neck sent chills down my back. I found myself leaning into Bert's hand. A warm feeling radiating down to my toes. Even with everything going on, I could still feel loved and needed by this man. I turned to face Bert. I wasn't sure what, if anything, I was going to say, but I opened my mouth, and no words came out.

"Beautiful, you don't have to say anything. I think I am feeling the same way you are." Bert declared and stared longingly into my eyes.

"Sir, we are starting to reach the suburbs. Would you like to travel on the skyway?" the car voice asked.

"Yes, that would be better. Unless you see more danger up in the skies." Bert instructed.

"Yes, sir, I will be on the lookout." The car voice declared.

The roads didn't look bad at all, but being dark, you couldn't be too safe. Bert thought the skyway was a much better option. We only had a few potholes to swerve around and saw no signs of any major fires.

As the car started to ascend, I got nervous. I still was not used to flying cars. Luckily, we hadn't come across any issues driving home. No sight of the Department of Citizen Safety anywhere. Which was a relief. Being out during a curfew was cause for immediate detainment. Once in the air, I got up the nerve to look out at the roadway. I hated heights but was curious how bad it looked up here. The streetlights helped illuminate the damage.

"Damn, you can really see all the damage from up here. Look over there, another huge crater by that building," I observed.

Leaning over me to glance out my window, Bert inquired, "Shit, I wonder how the college and your building fared."

We both surveyed the area below. The potholes were barely noticeable, but we did see two huge craters on our way to my house. "It looks like those craters have something in them as well. Damn. They must be the alien craft. This can't be good," Bert commented.

"Yeah, I see it too. Oh wait a minute." I noticed something. "I see movement in the crater." I could see the alien craft start to vibrate, then out of nowhere appeared a tall, dark figure that I couldn't quite make out. "Hey, Bert. Do you see that? It looks like ..."

"An alien?!?" Bert blurted out.

The figure had two heads with strange-looking eyes, but it was hard to make out from up in the skyway. There was also something peculiar about the figure's hands or where the hands are supposed to be for humans.

"I'd laugh if I didn't think you were serious. I can't believe all this is happening." I started to breathe heavily as my heart started to race. Palms sweaty, I put a hand on Bert's knee.

"Baby, you're shaking. Are you okay?" Bert said as he turned around to face me.

With a shaky voice, I whispered, "I think I'm having a panic attack. I can't breathe." I started hyperventilating.

Bert looked really worried. In a calm voice, he tried sounding reassuring, "Faith, sweetie, we are almost to your house. Try taking a deep breath." He was gently rubbing my back as he softly talked to me.

While we focused on my hyperventilating, the car had entered my neighborhood. "Look, Faith, so far no huge crater sightings, and the streets are in good shape. There are just a few potholes. The houses look good as well." Bert talked smoothly while rubbing my back.

"Oh, thank God," I said with relief. "My house is in one piece. Which means my car is safe in the garage."

The car slowly started to descend right over my driveway. "We have reached your destination, sir."

"Thank you, car. I won't be needing you anymore tonight." Bert announced. "Stay there. I'll come around." He instructed me.

I watched Bert as he got out of the car and walked around. "He is such a gentleman. Good thing he's helping me. I don't think I could stand on my own right now," I thought.

Bert opened the passenger door for me. Reaching in, he grabbed a hold of my hand and helped me out of the car. As soon as I stood up, I could feel the earth spinning. Feeling wobbly, I almost fell over. Bert put an arm around me to hold me up against him. At the front door, I placed my hand on the keypad and unlocked the door with my palm. Once the door was shut and we were both inside, I was finally able to breathe again.

I took a couple of big, deep breaths. "I must have been holding my breath. I feel a lot better," I said.
"

Bert looked relieved as he surveyed me. "Your color is coming back. Let's go sit down in the living room."

"Oh, I need a drink. Let's go to the kitchen first," I informed Bert.

"Beautiful. I'll get you a drink. You need to sit. I don't want you passing out on me. Not tonight."

"OK. Thank you. You are so sweet. But I am feeling better," I reassured him.

Bert gently guided me into the living room. He made sure I was sitting down comfortably before heading into the kitchen. "Would you like water or wine?"

"I probably should have water, but I need wine. Red, please," I replied.

"Coming right up, ma'am," Bert said with a wink.

As he walked out, I noticed what a nice butt he had. *Oh boy. No time for that. Calm down, thinking to myself.*

Leaning my head against the back of the couch, I decided to close my eyes for a minute. Before I knew it, I was dozing off when all of a sudden a noise sounded. Jumping about a foot off the couch, I saw the monitor pop up. Bert came running in with a bottle of wine and two glasses.

"Thought I might have a glass also. And after that sound, it seems like I might need it," Bert explained to me as I smiled at him.

A red screen was on the monitor with huge white letters in the middle that read "**NEWS FLASH**."

Bert looked at me as he poured the wine. "This must be about what happened tonight," he inferred. I just shrugged and took the glass of wine. With wine in hand, we both leaned back on the couch and snuggled into each other to get comfortable.

A well-dressed female appeared on the TV monitor. In a sober voice, she began, "Good evening, city residents. As many of you may know, we were invaded tonight by the Cordelia Tribe. Space Fleet did everything they could to stop the invasion. As of right now, we have counted 115 of their spacecrafts that have landed. Unfortunately, it did cause some devastation in the process. There are huge building-sized craters with alien spacecraft inside. Please stay far away until we determine how much radiation they are emitting. Roads are riddled with potholes and debris. Some buildings have significant damage but should be able to be repaired. We are asking everyone to telework and stay indoors until further notice. If you do have to go out, which should be for emergencies only, please only use the skyway. As of right now, we do not know how many, if any, lives have been lost. Please stay safe, citizens. We will update you as more information becomes available." As the anchor woman was talking, they were showing pictures across the city and surrounding areas of the devastation. They even showed an up-close look at the alien spacecraft. It was a smaller replica of the bigger alien spacecraft that was on the news a week ago. Once the anchor woman stopped talking, another red screen flashed before their eyes, and the TV monitor shut off and disappeared.

I turned to Bert with a worried look on my face. "I know we just started dating, but would you be able to stay the night? This whole thing is scary, and I don't think I'll be able to sleep if I'm alone."

"Beautiful, I wasn't planning on going anywhere tonight. If it's okay, I may even stay here until all this blows over. Whenever that may be."

"Oh, that would be great." I felt a little weight re-lease from my shoulders. "But what about your work, clothes, and any personal things you may need?"

"Well, I don't think they'll have classes anytime soon. It's too dangerous right now. I do have my laptop in the car. Let me go get it. I can connect to my house computer system and have my things delivered via drone."

Wide-eyed, I enthusiastically replied, "Oh wow. That's cool. I sometimes forget this is a more futuristic dimension than mine."

"And sometimes I forget you haven't always been in my life. When I'm around you, it sure does feel like we've known each other our whole lives." Standing up, Bert was gazing deeply into my eyes. He placed a hand under my chin, gently raised my head, and gave me a small kiss on the lips. "I'll be right back."

I watched him go out the front door, then waved my hand in front of my face. "Damn, that man has a way of giving me all the feels. I'm all hot now." Noticing that our wine glasses were empty, I took the liberty of refilling them. Looking up when I heard the front door, Bert strolled in carrying his backpack.

"It's getting late. I'll just do this first thing in the morning. Since we can't go anywhere, I can always shower later on after I get my stuff."

"Sounds like a plan. I filled your glass for you." I handed Bert his glass. Grabbing his glass, he replied, "Thank you. You read my mind."

We snuggled up against each other on the couch, sipping our wine and talking about the events of the day. I was leaning on Bert's shoulder, almost falling asleep as I held my wine glass when my phone ringing snapped me out of my daze. "Oh, crap, that scared me." I muttered as I reached for the phone. Looking at the screen, I stated, "Oh, it's Megan." Answering it immediately, I yelled into it, "Hey girl, how are you doing after all the events of tonight?"

"I'm good. I've been home all night. I was calling to make sure you and Bert were okay. I knew you had a date tonight. I hope it didn't get ruined."

"No, it was great. We went to the Celestial Cafe on the water. We ate on their back deck. It was really romantic." I turned to Bert as I was talking and winked at him. "Then we walked on the beach and found some rocks to sit on. Shortly after that was when all hell broke loose."

"That's all the details I get. Come on. Where's the good stuff?"

"Megan, he's sitting right here."

"Oooohhh. The date isn't over yet. I see. Well, at least tell me if he kissed you."

"MEGAN!!!"

"Come on, girl. I'm not dating anyone right now. I need some juicy details."

I turned to Bert. He mouthed "Go on, do tell." Winked and blew me a kiss.

"OK. Fine. Yes, we kissed. Several times. Once before going into the restaurant. Then during dinner…."

"You kissed during dinner?"

"No, Megan. Calm down." I laughed. "During dinner, we kept making goo-goo eyes at each other." As I was describing the evening to Megan, I could feel Bert getting closer and closer to me on the couch. He started gently rubbing my back. I leaned into it as I continued. "He was a perfect gentleman during dinner. But afterwards, we couldn't wait to get out of there. Once a safe distance away, he grabbed me and kissed me like I've never been kissed before. It was really hot."

"Damn girl, I'm getting hot just thinking about it. I'm so happy for you. It's about time you found a good man."

"Oh, agreed." I was becoming increasingly distracted. Bert started nibbling my ear.  I tried pushing him away, but he wouldn't move.

"Alright, I can hear you are a little preoccupied. I'm glad you guys are safe. I'll talk to you tomorrow. I don't know what we are going to do about work on Monday." "

"Oh yeah. That's a good question.  I guess we'll hear later. Good night, Megan. Stay safe."

After I hung up from Megan, I turned to Bert. I was about to playfully slap him when he grabbed my face and pulled me into him. His fingers were entangled in my hair. He lowered his mouth on mine and passionately kissed me. After several minutes, he finally stopped .

"Hey, beautiful, you ready to go upstairs?"

I took a deep breath. *Oh boy. Time for a talk. I thought.*  "Bert, Sweetie, I'd love to go upstairs with you." He got up and reached out to help me up.  Once to my feet, I continued after placing a hand on his chest.

"But only for sleep. While I'd love to have sex with you. And oh boy, do I want to. I don't think it's a good idea. I rushed things in my last relationship, and I want to do things right this time. I've been hurt, and I'm trying to learn to trust again. I want to take things slowly if that's okay. But I'd love to fall asleep in your arms."

"Babe, I completely understand. I don't want to rush or pressure you into anything. But we would be making love, not just having sex. Just FYI. I can respect your boundaries. We can go at your pace. Oh and I'd love to cuddle with you." Bert leaned in to give me a gentle, soft kiss on the lips to let me know he's perfectly okay with this arrangement. Standing up, he reached for my hand, and we walked upstairs.

My bed never looked more inviting. I didn't realize how tired I was until I looked at my warm, comfy bed. "Hey, Bert, would you mind if I take a quick shower?"

"Not at all. Enjoy. I'll just make myself at home." He informed me as he sat down to take off his shoes.

I leaned down to give him a peck on the cheek, then hurried into the shower.

A little while later, I emerged feeling refreshed. Once I stepped into the bedroom, my eyes immediately started searching for Bert. I found him snuggled under my fluffy blanket, sound asleep.

"Poor thing must be so tired," I softly commented.

I quietly walked to the other side of the bed and
gently, without waking him, got under the covers with
him. Even though it wasn't that long since I was married in the other dimension, it still felt like forever ago
that I shared a bed with a man who had genuine feelings for me. Pulling the covers over my chilly body, I felt
a warm arm drag my body into his warm embrace.

*This feels so natural, I thought.*

With a deep, sleepy sigh, I drifted off to sleep in
the safety zone of Bert's arm.

# CHAPTER 14

A beam of sunlight streamed through the upstairs window, gently nudging me awake. I slowly stirred, raising my hand to shield my eyes from the brightness. The soft pitter-patter of the shower filled the room. Sitting up in bed, I decided to head downstairs to grab some coffee and breakfast while Bert was finishing up in the shower.

Grabbing the tray of food and drinks I requested from the monitor in the kitchen, I headed upstairs. No longer hearing running water, I assumed Bert was done in the shower. I knew that assumption was correct when I saw an exceedingly muscular body sitting on my bed in nothing but a towel.

"Oh, um, sorry. I brought up dinner. I mean breakfast. Juice, coffee, quiche, fruit, and danishes. I wasn't sure what you liked for breakfast."

"Well, that was nice of you. You didn't have to do that. I'm sorry I'm not dressed yet. I sent a message this morning to my house computer so my things should be arriving shortly."

"OH, that's good. And fast. You helped me with breakfast the other day, so I thought I'd return the favor."

I placed the tray on the bed and carefully sat beside Bert. We dug into breakfast together, comfortably enjoying the meal. With a mouthful of quiche, a knock on the window startled me so much I almost choked. Turning towards the noise, I noticed a drone hovering at the window with a large bag dangling beneath it.

"Oh, my stuff. Awesome." Bert enthusiastically commented.

"That thing scared me half to death," I admitted, catching my breath.

Bert started laughing. "I saw you jump a foot up in the air. This drone tracks where I am and delivers what I need."

With a shocked expression on my face, "Oh. I didn't know you had a drone. Actually, I didn't know the general public could buy them."

"They usually can't. I have mine through work. But I also use it personally as well." As we talked, he snatched his bag from the drone. He pushed a button and explained, "I just push this button to tell it to go back where it came from. I could also access it on my laptop, but this is easier. Now, if you will excuse me, I'm going to go to the bathroom and get dressed."

While Bert was in the bathroom, I cleaned up from breakfast and quickly got dressed. I didn't want to be half-naked when he came out of the bathroom. But that's exactly what happened when I was standing there in nothing but my bra and panties, Bert came out of the bathroom.

"Oh, damn, babe." Bert blurted out as he was gawking at me.

Blushing furiously, I quickly grabbed the robe that was on the bed. "Sorry. I thought I'd be dressed before you came out. I should have gone into my closet."

"No need to apologize. Nice view though." Bert tried reassuring me with a wink and a smile.

I turned ten shades of red, I muttered, "Down boy," and ducked into the closet for yoga pants and a crop top.

*Might as well be comfy today. We can't go anywhere.*

Stepping out into the bedroom, I looked over at Bert, still a little red-faced from earlier.

"Damn, babe, you look good."

"What? This?" I glanced down. "It's just my comfy lounge clothes."

"Even those look amazing on you." Bert complimented me as he walked over and gave me a slow, passionate kiss.

Blushing as usual, I asked, "So…what should we do today? We can't exactly go out. "

Bert gets a huge smile on his face, but before he could say anything, I quickly said, "No, not that." He smiles and nods back in my direction.

Trying to redirect the conversation, he suggests, "We could have a movie marathon. Do they have Star Wars in your dimension?"

"Oh. Thank God, yes!" I beamed. "I love Star Wars. My home office was Star Wars-themed."

"Seriously? I would have loved to see that. We don't have any fun décor like that here. The décor here is very sterile, I think. No personality."

Bert took my hand and led me downstairs. We spent the day wrapped in blankets, watching Star Wars movies and dozing off between them. It was the most relaxed I had felt in a long time.

*Was it too early to be falling in love with this man?*

# CHAPTER 15

Early the next morning, a loud banging noise woke me up.  It took me a minute to register where the noise was coming from. Glancing towards the window, I noticed the sun wasn't quite up yet. Boom boom boom.

*There it is again.*

Looking over at Bert, I noticed he wasn't stirring at all.

*Poor thing, he  must be exhausted from staying up late watching movies.*

Boom boom boom. That time I noticed it came from downstairs.

*Someone is banging on the door. Who the hell is that at this time of the morning?"*
I thought as I reached for my phone to check on the time.

*It's not even 6 a.m.*

Boom boom boom.

*Ugh, fine. I thought, aggravated.*

Getting quietly out of bed so as not to disturb Bert, I gingerly walked downstairs.   Placing a hand on the doorknob, I took a deep breath, then opened the front door.  Standing there with a wicked look in his eyes was the male chauvinist himself, my boss and the man who attacked me, Darren.  My heart skipped a beat.

"What the hell are you doing here? It's 5:45 in the morning."  I angrily shouted.

"Now, is that any way to talk to your boss? Damn woman. You look sexy as hell in that nightie."

I blushed. "Shit" I said to myself. I forgot what I was wearing.

Darren walked toward me slowly with hunger in his eyes.  He gave me no choice but to back up. The further he came toward me, the further I backed up until my butt hit the closet door.

"You aren't supposed to be here. We are all under a curfew."

"Oh Sweetie, that doesn't apply to me. After all, I'm in charge of the largest accounting firm in the state."

"I'm pretty sure the Cordelia Tribe won't give a rat's ass where you work when they try killing you. Now, please, why are you here?" I demanded, folding my arms around my body like a shield.

"Well, since you won't be in work, I needed to bring some things for you to work on."

"OK, but you could have sent them over with a drone."

"I can't have sensitive information floating up in the air for anyone to see." Darren placed a bag on the floor next to me as he placed one hand on the wall next to my head, and the other hand he was slowly moving down my hip. "Now that I delivered, we should go up-stairs so you can show me your bedroom."

With a shudder, I realized Darren did not know Bert was upstairs.

*How can I wake Bert up from down here? I tried, quickly thinking of how to get help.*

While looking around to find something close by that would make noise, I felt Darren's hand move my nightie up. I pushed Darren's hand away and yelled. "Darren, didn't you learn your lesson last time?"

"Oh, Sweetie. That boyfriend of yours was just an obstacle. I see it as a challenge. You obviously look like you want me. I can feel the heat radiating off you."

"That's because you are pissing me off. I, by no means, want any part of you. I need you to leave."

"I know you don't mean that." Darren's hands were pushing up in between my legs. I was struggling against him. He brushed my hair away from my face. As his finger traced my lips, I was able to bite down on his finger. As he screamed, I pushed his hands away and moved a foot away from him.

*Well, that should have woken Bert up.*

The sound of someone running upstairs vibrated in the quiet early morning hours. I turned to look at Darren. "You better get going," I demanded.

Darren had a surprised look on his face as Bert came charging down the stairs. " What the hell are you doing here?"

"Oh. Boyfriend is here. Calm down, I was just leaving. I had to drop off some work. We will be having a video conference first thing Monday morning. I expect you to be there. No excuses."

I noticed how Darren's mood drastically changed once Bert entered the room. "OK. See you." I said, while slamming the door in his face. I let out a big sigh and turned toward Bert. "Thanks. You showed up just in time."

"Beautiful, why didn't you wake me?"

"You were sleeping so soundly. I didn't want to wake you. If I had known it was him, I would have woken you up. Ugh. What an ass."

Bert was looking me over. "Did he hurt you?"

"No. I'm fine. He tried, but I bit his finger."

Bert burst out laughing, with me joining him. "That's funny. He deserved it. "

"He sure did. Did you sleep okay?"

"I did. Why was he here? No one is supposed to go outside right now."

"He seems to think that does not apply to him." I reached out for Bert's hand. "Let's go back up to bed. I'm still tired. Asshole woke me up." I took Bert's hand over my shoulder, guiding him upstairs. Walking up in front of him, I could feel his eyes burning a hole in my back. Suddenly, his hand gently swatted my butt.

"Hey," I laughed quickly, running up the stairs with Bert following closely behind.

Just inside my doorway, Bert playfully grabbed hold of me and gently threw me on the bed. Hovering over me, he stared deeply into my eyes. Slowly lowering his lips until they were mere inches away from mine, he gently kissed me.

"OK, beautiful, let's go back to bed."

# CHAPTER 16

A loud vibrating noise could be heard in the bedroom. I slowly stirred awake. I could feel a heavy arm pinning me to the bed. Looking over, I saw Bert fast asleep. Buzz buzz buzz.

*"Oh, that's my cell. Who is calling me at this hour? Why can't anyone let me sleep today?" I thought.*

Cautiously, I moved his arm so I could reach the phone. Grabbing the phone, I picked it up and noticed Megan had tried calling me 4 times.

"Oh crap," I blurted out a little louder than I meant to. Bert stirred. Gingerly getting out of bed, I reached for the phone and went into the office to call Megan back.

"Hey girl, sorry I didn't answer. We were sleeping. I didn't hear the phone. Everything okay?" I could hear Megan crying.

"No, my neighborhood was bombed by the Cordelia Tribe late last night. They hit my house. I can't stay here." Megan was, crying between sentences.

"Oh, Megan. I'm so sorry. We'll be over as soon as we can."

After hanging up with Megan, I went into the bedroom to wake Bert.  To my surprise, he was already awake.

"Hey baby, why did you get out of bed?  Come lay back down with me."

"Oh, Bert.  Poor Megan's house got bombed late last night.  She needs us to come and help."

"Oh shit. OK.  Give me a few minutes to get dressed."  Bert announced as he rose from the bed.  We quickly got ready then headed out to the car.

"I'll drive since my car is more accessible."

Getting in the car, we heard that familiar voice again. "Sir, there is a mandatory curfew which hasn't been lifted yet."

Annoyed, Bert responded, "Yes, we are aware. We need to help a friend. Head to Megan Lovelace's house.  Quickly."

"Yes, sir."

I turned toward Bert, "Oh, your car knows where Megan lives?"

"We have been friends for a long time.  I've been there before."

"Oh, that's true.  I keep on forgetting."

The car peeled out of the driveway and sped down the road.

"Sir, I think the skyway is the only way we can go."

"That's fine.  Just get us there."

I could feel the car swerving around potholes. Feeling nauseated and dizzy, I leaned back onto the headrest.  Closing my eyes, I tried taking a quick nap. The run-in with Darren earlier and now Megan…I was emotionally drained.  With my eyes closed, I could feel the car ascend onto the skyway.  Even though I have been in this dimension for several weeks, I will never be able to get used to flying cars.

The car jerked up and sideways suddenly.

Opening my eyes, I asked "What was that about?"

With an apologetic tone, Bert answered, "Sorry, Beautiful. You gotta look at this.  It's not any better up here either.  I wonder why we haven't heard about this?"

Sitting up, I gasped in astonishment as I witnessed what Bert had described. Alien ships were everywhere, unleashing a barrage of fireballs at the cars in the sky. The car's navigation system demonstrated remarkable skill, deftly dodging the fiery projectiles. Bert and I shared a collective gasp as a fireball hurtled straight towards our car.

"Watch out!" I yelled. Just then, the car took a nosedive to avoid getting hit. I felt myself being flung forward in my seat. Reaching my hand out, I stabilized myself on the door handle as my hair fell forward.

"Shit," Bert yelled as he threw an arm over me to hold me back.

"Sorry, sir and madam. Trying to keep you two safe," We heard the car admit.

"The car can apologize?" I asked.

"Yes, they thought it would be more personable if they programmed the AI with emotions. You okay, Faith?"

"Yes, I am. Just a little scared. I thought this way was supposed to be safe."

"I guess the government didn't anticipate them attacking us like this. I don't know why though. It seemed inevitable to me."

"Yeah, me too. I mean, they bombed areas on the ground. We fly cars, for goodness' sake. Of course, that would be the next place they go to attack."

"Exactly."

The car descended into Megan's neighborhood, and it was a sight of sheer destruction. Trees and bushes were all burned up, and houses were either crumbled to the ground, with their roofs smashed in, or had large holes in their sides. It was devastating. The further we drove into the neighborhood, the more my anxiety revved up.

"This is awful. Why are they doing this to us?"

"I have no idea. We definitely need to come up with a plan. It looks like we won't be able to stay in this area much longer."

Just when Bert was starting to talk about our future plans, we came upon Megan's house. The small two-story house had a huge hole blown out of the front façade. A person could see right into Megan's living room.

With a shocked voice, I announced, "Well, I guess she will be staying with us."

"She definitely needs a place to go."

As soon as Bert pulled into the driveway, we both hopped out and ran into the house. I called out as we opened the front door. "Megan, honey, OMG, are you okay?"

A sobbing Megan responded with a shaky voice, "I'm in the kitchen."

The kitchen still looked like it was in one piece. The woman standing at the counter, on the other hand, was a mess.

"Oh, sweetie. What can I do to help you?" I walked up to Megan and gave her a big hug. Megan held on for dear life, crying into my shoulder.

"It was awful. I was upstairs in bed. I heard loud explosions. There was a glowing red light flickering out my window, then all of a sudden, the house shook. I thought it was going to come tumbling down. I immediately jumped out of bed and ran down here." Megan became aware that she was standing in the kitchen in her silk camisole top and shorts. "Oh, crap. Sorry, Bert. I just realized."

Bert waved it off as if he didn't notice. Of course, that was the first thing he noticed.

Megan nervously asked, "Hey, can my dog and I stay with you, Faith? I didn't know where else I could go. I mean around here. My parents live a couple hundred miles away."

"Absolutely, can I do anything else for you?"

"I still need to get my things."

"OK, I'll go upstairs and grab some things for you." Leaving the kitchen, I quickly went upstairs to pack a few things for Megan. The upstairs looked normal with the exception of a few windows that were broken. Luckily, I know her well enough to know everything she'd want or need. I packed some clothes and toiletries in a bag. Grabbing the bag, I started to head downstairs. "*Oh,* the dog's bed." I blurted out. Bending down, I picked up the dog bed.

I placed the bag and dog bed by the front door, then walked toward the kitchen. I started going in but abruptly stopped when I saw Bert and Megan in a tight bear hug. By the looks of it, their pelvises were almost touching, and Bert was rubbing Megan's back while her head was buried into Bert's chest.

*What the hell?* I thought, a little concerned but tried to suppress the feeling. It didn't appear that they had seen me. I must have been staring at them for five minutes or more, and they had not moved.

*Time to end this. He's my man. Calm down, Faith. Megan just had an upsetting night. She needed support. Bert's a nice, caring guy. I thought.*

I saw them pull away, then stare into each other's eyes. They looked like they wanted to kiss but were fighting the urge.

*Oh hell, no. I'm not going to let that happen. I thought.*

Backing up a few feet, I yelled, "OK, guys. I've got Megan's things. Ready to leave?" I could hear quick footsteps as I walked into the kitchen.

Glancing at Bert and Megan, it was obvious something was off. "Hey, what's up?" I asked, looking at them both.

"I just can't stop crying. That was so scary. I heard a lot of noise outside. I didn't think it was them. Everything was supposed to have died down. I was coming down from my room and started walking into the living room when that blast happened."

Looking horrified, I questioned, "Oh, Megan, I'm so sorry. Here, I grabbed a lightweight jacket since you aren't wearing much." I said as I handed the jacket to Megan. "Did you get hurt?" Megan took the jacket as I spoke. Bert started toward Megan, then stopped. I gave Bert a puzzled look as if to say, *"What was that about?"*

"No, I'm fine. The wind from the explosion blew me backwards, but I landed on the carpet."

Bert looked at me, then at Megan. "OK, ladies, ready to go?"

Megan looked around her kitchen, then shook her head yes.

Bert picked up the bag and dog bed, then led the ladies out to the car. Once everyone, dog included, was safely inside, he started up the car. "Hold on tight. It's going to be a bumpy ride."

Megan looked confused. I added, "We had a little trouble getting here."

Once we got out of the obstacle course known as Megan's neighborhood, the car ascended onto the skyway. Looking down, I noticed the ground looked like a war zone. I was paying more attention to the ground scenery than I didn't notice what was going on in the sky. Suddenly, the car started weaving in and out of floating piles of fiery rubble. Above us were alien ships hovering, waiting to attack. Without Bert asking, the car was speeding as fast as it could back to my house. We needed to get to shelter - and fast. My body was suddenly full of adrenaline, at the ready if needed. Bert grabbed a hold of my hand. Looking in the backseat, I saw Megan clutching her dog for dear life.

Looking out the window, I made an observation, "Look, the DCS is manning all exits."

Bert placed a hand on my knee while looking in the backseat at Megan. "It appears so. Oh wait, look, they just stopped that car."

I looked worried, "Well, crap. What if they stop us from getting back to my house? I need to check on my house."

Rubbing my knee, Bert reassured me, "Beautiful, do you have your license?" I shook my head yes. "Then they will see we are local. It'll be fine."

The alien ships started to make a formation of some sort. Megan finally spoke up from the backseat. "Hey, guys, you see that? The ships are doing something suspicious."

"It looks like they are going into formation. Maybe a fight formation." Bert observed.

"Oh, they are. That can't be good." I responded. "And where are all these cars going? It looks like everyone is leaving the city. Should we be doing that? I really don't know where I would go though."

"Don't worry.  I have a family cabin in the mountains by a lake we all could go to." Bert explained.

"Oh, I forgot about your family cabin.  That's a great idea." Megan added.

*Of course, Megan would know about the cabin. All of a sudden, she was getting on my nerves.  I needed to calm down.Thinking to myself.*

"Yep, that sounds like a good idea.  Let's see how bad my neighborhood is, though."

Bert nodded, "Yes, of course."

"Oh, shit.  Guys, look.  The ships formed a bigger ship.  You can't even tell it's made up of smaller ships. What are they doing?" I observed

Megan gasped.  Bert just shook his head.

Sensing a panic attack starting, I tried taking slow, deep breaths and counting.  For whatever reason, focusing on counting something - really anything - helps to control my panic attacks.  In spite of that, I was still breathing heavily and shaking.

Bert turned to me with a concerned look on his face. "Beautiful, are you okay?  Another panic attack?"

"Yes, I am trying to control it, but it's not working". I started hyperventilating.

Megan leaned forward and started rubbing my neck and shoulders to help calm me down. "Thank you, Megan."

"Anything for you, Faith."

Abruptly, the alien ship sped off about a mile away and stopped without warning. In the center of the ship, a giant red beam about the size of a football field aimed right in the center of the city.

I blurted out, "Crap, that's city hall."

Out of nowhere, military aircraft sped by the skyway toward the direction of the alien ship. I had never seen so many military planes in one place. They all circled around the alien ship.

*That's not going to stop the aliens from firing at us, I thought this was a stupid idea but kept my comments to myself.*

We three shielded our eyes as a bright red light appeared all around us. Turning to the direction of the alien ship, I saw in the center of the bright red beam, an even more concentrated laser light leave the ship. No noise at first but a few seconds later, the laser hit a building in the center of the city. A loud explosion that rocked all the vehicles was heard for miles. Our car shook like we were in an earthquake. I felt my brain get rattled in my skull.

"Oh shit, that was the Capital Building," I observed.

"We need to get out of here. That explosion was too close for comfort," Bert worriedly commented.

Just then the car gravitated a hundred feet in the air and sped away from the commotion, propelling us back into our seats.

*OK, this is not helping the panic attack, I thought.*

We were back in my neighborhood in no time. It seemed like not all the houses were damaged. Some had holes in their roofs, while others had holes in their walls. We only saw one that was completely burnt to the ground. The trees were either covered in ashes or had singed branches. A few bushes were still smoking.

"Wow, it might have been a good idea to leave when we did. This is so sad." I declared.

Finally at my house, I breathed a sigh of relief when I saw my house was in one piece, but the shed, on the other hand, was a different story.

The car pulled into the driveway. As soon as it stopped, I jumped out and ran to the backyard.

"Faith, what are you doing? We should get inside." Bert called out to me, but I kept running. He took one look at Megan and ordered, "Stay here just in case something is wrong back there. At least I can keep you safe." Bert took off running after me.

I stopped dead in my tracks when I saw the shed. The whole top half was gone. It didn't look like it was burnt, though. Nothing about it made any sense. I felt a hand gently wrap around my waist.

"Sweetie, I'm so sorry. But at least it wasn't the house. You can replace the shed a lot cheaper than rebuilding a house."

Falling to the ground, I started crying. Bert bent down and took me in his arms. Burying my face in his neck, I sobbed for a good five minutes.

"Beautiful, we should go inside where we are safer."

Getting myself together, I let go of Bert and stood up. "I'm sorry. I saw the shed and lost it. This could have been my house. I would have lost every-thing. Some people did. Now, I feel guilty for feeling the way I did. This is just all too much."

Bert took my hand and guided me to the front door. Megan saw us coming around from the back and grabbed her things, following us to the door. "I saw your shed. I'm sorry, Faith."

Reaching my hand out to Megan, I apologized, "No, I'm sorry. You lost so much more than I did, yet I'm the one making a bigger deal of it than you."

"We all handle things in different ways. No need to apologize."

Us three with Megan's dog stepped inside the house. I took a deep breath and was so grateful to be home. What a day it had been.

I looked at the other two, "Are y'all hungry? I can get us something to eat. It's way past dinner and we haven't eaten breakfast or lunch."

Megan answered first, "Now that you mention it, I am starving."

Bert placed a gentle hand on me, "I'll go get us something. You two relax."

"Thanks, honey. You are too sweet." I replied

Megan turned to me, "You guys look like you are getting along well."

"We really are. It's been nice having him here. Getting to know him. I think I'm falling for him hard."

"I can see that. I think he feels the same way."

"I sure hope so." I couldn't help but think of that encounter between Megan and Bert as they were talking.

Bert waltzed in with a tray of food and drinks. "Ladies, here's some meat, cheese, and grapes for y'all. Plus wine and water. Gotta stay hydrated for whatever is coming. I have a late dinner, whichever way you look at it, coming your way. Enjoy this while that's being prepared."

I immediately took a long swig of wine. "Thanks, babe. You are so great."

Bert bent down and kissed my forehead. "So I've been told. Be back, lovelies." Off he went back into the kitchen.

We enjoyed wine and snacks. I tried keeping the conversation light. Too much heavy stuff has already happened.

"When this nightmare is all over, the two of us should go on a girls' trip. Maybe overseas to an all-inclusive resort."

"Faith, that's a great idea. Maybe to Italy. Visit a vineyard."

"Oh, I love that idea. We will have to plan it."

"OK, ladies. Dinner is ready," Bert called from the kitchen.

The two women strolled into the kitchen. Bert had set a candlelit dinner on the table.

"Something special for the most beautiful women in town." Bert winked at me. I knew he was trying to make Megan feel included, but deep down it really bothered me.

"Wow, Bert. This looks lovely. Thank you." I remarked.

"Thanks, I worked all day on it." Bert laughed as he placed plates of filet mignon and twice-baked potatoes on the table.

"I don't think I'll ever get used to the food being prepared behind the walls so quickly." I admitted.

"Well, that's not really where it is, but I get it. Have you been downstairs to see the mechanical room?" Bert asked.

"Yes, Megan took me down to see it when I first got here. In my dimension, I never did, so it's strange to have a basement here."

Megan spoke up, "Faith, you are a part of this dimension now. This is your home. Would you want to go back if you could?"

I thought about that for a minute. "You know, at first I thought I did. But now that I've met you two, no, I don't think I do. I am much better off here. Even though I don't have my kids...everything else is wonderful."

"Well, I for one am glad to hear that." Bert gave me a quick peck on the lips before sitting down to eat.

"Megan and I were just talking about a girls' trip when all this mess is over. Maybe to Italy."

"I think that's a great idea. Y'all should go to Veneto, Italy. It's in the northeastern part and it's beautiful. I went there after I graduated college," Bert explained to the women.

The conversation was flowing nicely between us as we ate. Bert really seemed to be enjoying himself sitting between 2 women.

*Don't even think about it. This is not going to happen. I thought as I diverted my attention to Bert.*

"We've all had a long day. I don't know about you guys, but I am getting tired. Anyone ready for bed?" I asked.

Bert gave me a wink, "I sure am."

"Now that you mention it, I am getting tired." Megan admitted.

The three of us cleaned up the kitchen, then headed to the stairs. Megan bent down to pick up her bag and the dog bed, but Bert stopped her.

"I'll get that for you," Bert said. Bert carried her things into the guest room.

"I'll get you towels, Megan. There are clean sheets on the bed. I keep it clean just in case. Can I get you anything else?" I asked.

"No, I should be good. Thanks," Megan said.

"OK. Hope you get a good night's sleep. I truly am sorry about your house," I said. I hugged Megan before Bert and I went off to bed.

It didn't take us long to get ready for bed. We were both exhausted, having not gotten a good night's sleep the night before. Bert climbed into bed first. Upon seeing me heading to the bed, he moved the comforter back for me while I climbed in. Before I laid down, he moved his arm so I could snuggle into his shoulder like it was second nature. Placing my hand on his chest, I started playing with his chest hairs.

All was quiet for a while then I spoke up. "I feel so bad for Megan. I wish there was something I could do for her."

"It's awful to lose a house like that. You are doing a lot for her. You gave her a place to stay. And don't forget - you lost your shed. She's not the only one suffering."

"True, but it was just a shed with gardening tools. It was nice you included her tonight." I wanted to ask about their encounter earlier, but I thought against it. Maybe this way, he'll say something.

"I didn't want her to feel left out. She was bawling when we got to her house. I tried comforting her, but I don't think it did any good."

"Oh, I'm sure it did. I thought I walked in on something earlier. There seemed like there was tension in the air, but I just thought it was because of everything going on."

"I just hugged her, maybe a little too tight. That's all. It was nothing. I think she might have gotten the wrong idea. I am sorry."

I felt my heart sink. I moved my hand from his chest. "Oh, I see."

Bert lifted my chin to look at him. "Beautiful, you are the only one for me. I don't want Megan. We have been friends for too long. She's like a sister to me."

"OK, I will try not to worry. It's just…I believe my husband - well, ex-husband, or what you call him now - was cheating on me."

"I'm sorry. It must be hard to live with a man when you know in your heart of hearts he is unfaithful. That's a weak man. But you have nothing to worry about."

Bert bent down and gave me a peck on the lips. Looking up at the heat in my eyes, he kissed me again with more intensity. Slowly slipping just the tip of his tongue into my mouth. My hand started rubbing the back of his head. Taking this as a sign, his tongue explored my mouth deeper.

I couldn't believe what was happening. One minute I was worried about losing Bert, then the next we were making out on my bed. This has been one crazy day for sure. He seemed to start to pull away, so I put a hand on his head so he would keep kissing me. I needed this right now to be reassured about our relationship. After several hours of doing more than just making out, we fell asleep in each other's arms, fully exhausted.

# CHAPTER 17

I was snoring my little heart out when a bright flash of light followed by a loud explosion woke us up. Jumping out of a sound sleep, I blurted out, "What the hell was that?" I looked at an exhausted Bert, and we both ran to make sure Megan was okay.

Running into the dark hallway, I ran right into Megan holding her dog. "Hey girl, are you okay?"

"Yeah, we're fine. What was that?"

Bert looked both of us women up and down to see for himself that we were okay. Then he demanded, "Stay here. I'm going down to investigate." He ran downstairs, taking two steps at a time. No sooner did he get down there than he yelled back, "Faith, you better come down here."

I looked at Megan. "Shit. That doesn't sound good." We took off running. At the bottom of the stairs, I stopped dead in my tracks. What I saw devastated me. The roof over the living room was gone, along with half the front façade wall, and the front lawn was on fire. I froze in fear, realizing we all could have died.

"Oh no. What am I going to do now?" I thought.

Bert must have seen the look of fear on my face and walked over to comfort me. "We'll figure this out. You aren't alone. People all over the city are dealing with the same thing. I'd say we could go to my place, but I live near the city too. We'll go to my family's lake cabin in the mountains. I'm hoping they're just

attacking the cities. Let's go get our things quickly."
Bert glanced at his watch. "Damn, it's only 3 a.m. So
much for a good night's sleep."

I refused to let myself think of what just
happened. I had no time for a meltdown or panic attack.
Following Bert upstairs, I was doing a mental checklist
of everything I needed. I might never be able to come
back home. Remaining speechless while packing, I felt
a hand on my back. Turning around, Bert was staring at
me.

"Sweetie, everything will work out okay. We
have each other, and that's all we need."

"I know. I just really liked this house. I can't
afford to rebuild it. Thank you for your support. Should
we go check out your house first?"

"No, I don't want to risk it. It's all replaceable
anyway. The most important thing is getting us to
safety."

We all walked to the driveway. Getting in the
passenger seat, I stopped. "Oh, I forgot. What about
my car? Should I drive it to your lake cabin?"

"No, I don't want you alone. I think we need to
stick together. You can go on your phone and navigate
it to come to the cabin on its own."

"Oh, that's neat. I keep forgetting about this
high-tech stuff."

Megan spoke up from the backseat. "It is cool.
Comes in handy." She spoke to me but was looking at
Bert. It was just a small glance, but it didn't get past me.

As the car's self-navigation drove through the obstacle course that was my neighborhood, the interior of the car remained quiet. Each of us was in our own mind. I was pondering how an incredible night had turned into a nightmare. Bert was concentrating on the drive and how to keep everyone safe. Megan kept stealing glances at Bert when she thought I wasn't looking, but I noticed it all. After all these years, Megan was starting to fall for Bert. She couldn't steal him away from me... could she?

The trio snapped out of it when the car came to a screeching halt.

Bert spoke up first. "What the hell? Next time, car, maybe a little gentler."

"Sorry, sir. A car fell out of the skyway right in front of us. I didn't have time to divert."

Bert looked at both women. "Y'all okay?"

I placed a hand on Bert's knee. "I'm okay."

Megan looked at Bert, then at my hand. With a frown, she answered, "Yeah, I'm okay."

At the next exit, the car veered up to the skyway. You'd think being in the air would make it safer, but it was more dangerous. There were vehicles on fire, burnt to a crisp, or abandoned. While there was no road to worry about, we were closer to the alien ships. The vehicles had to dodge lasers coming from the ships.

"Wow, it looks worse up here," Megan commented. "I'm surprised they let us drive up here so close to the aliens."

Just then, we passed an exit that had a DCS agent manning the ramp.

"Oh, there they are again. Now what are we going to do if they stop us this time?" I worriedly asked.

"Don't worry, Beautiful. I'll think of something if it comes up," Bert tried to reassure me.

"Oh, I didn't ask you—how far is your lake cabin?" I inquired.

"It's about three hours away," Megan blurted out without thinking. Bert gave her an evil eye.

"You've been there before?" I asked.

"Yeah... a long, long time ago." Once I turned back around, Megan mouthed "Sorry" to Bert.

Bert rolled his eyes at Megan. Putting an arm around me, he suggested, "Why don't y'all take a little nap? I'll keep an eye out and wake you when we get there."

"OK, honey. That's a good idea. I am so very tired." I leaned my head back on the headrest. As soon as my eyes closed, I sensed someone was staring at me. Opening my eyes, Bert leaned over and was mere inches from my face.

"I can't let my beauty fall asleep without a proper kiss." Bert placed his soft lips gently on mine, kissing tenderly at first, then slowly slipping the tip of his tongue into my mouth. Gently pulling away, he grabbed my hand and kissed the top of it. "Alright, sweetie. Get some rest. I'll wake y'all when we get there."

I glanced in the visor mirror and noticed Megan with a hurt expression on her face after witnessing that kiss.

*Sorry, girl. He's mine. After all, you did introduce us, I thought.*

# CHAPTER 18

Walking hand in hand on the beach with Bert, I felt more in love than with anything else in this world. The warm sun on my skin and the golden, powdery sand at my feet truly felt like heaven. Bert abruptly stopped me. Twirling me around to face him, he bent down and declared,

"You are my sun, moon, and stars. You have illuminated my life since entering it. I can't imagine how I got along without you. I love you with all my heart."

Pulling me close, he bent me backward and kissed my soft, moist lips. It was the most romantic thing I had ever experienced.

I was jolted awake by the tender touch of Bert's hand. Jumping about a foot off the seat, my heart started beating faster.

"Calm down, Beautiful. We're here."

"Oh," I sighed in disappointment. "It was just a dream. Damn."

From the backseat, Megan chimed in, "Wow, must have been some dream. I think I heard you moaning."

I turned to Bert. "Was I really?" He nodded. "Oh, oops. It was a good dream. Much better than reality. Nothing too spicy though, sorry, Megan."

"Well, at least you had a good dream. I had a nightmare that aliens were chasing us and trying to kill us."

"Damn, Megan. I hope that one doesn't come true."

The car drove up a long, winding road flanked by tall Italian cypress trees. At the end was a massive stone wall with a tall black gate. I looked puzzled. I thought we were going to his family's lake cabin. This didn't look like the entrance to a cabin.

Bert pulled up, and the gate dematerialized, allowing us in. Up ahead was the biggest house I had ever seen—it looked like a medieval castle, towers included. Bert stopped in front of the grand entrance.

"Here we are, ladies. By the look on your face, I take it you're impressed," he said.

"'Impressed' is one word for it. You never told me you were rich. And this is your version of a cabin? This is bigger than any cabin I had in mind."

"I'm not rich. My parents are. I've been on my own since I was 18. Calling it a 'cabin' is kind of a family joke."

"Well, good for you. A self-made man."

Megan piped up from the backseat. "Faith, you're going to love it. It's like a castle inside too."

I smiled, but it was forced. "I didn't realize you were so familiar with Bert's family's house."

Bert gave Megan a pointed look. "She's not that acquainted. She's only been here once."

We exited the car. Bert grabbed our bags and led us to the massive cathedral-style doors with wrought iron hardware. He ushered me in first, then stopped Megan.

He whispered to her, "What are you doing?"

"Nothing. I just wanted to let her know how gorgeous it is in here." Megan whispered back.

"It sounds like you're trying to make her jealous. I don't think she knows we were THAT involved."

"Well, maybe you should tell her. And that's not what I'm doing."

Meanwhile, I stood in the foyer, awe-struck. The stone floors, the grand mahogany staircase—I felt like I was in a movie. Turning around to talk to Bert, I noticed he was still outside, talking closely with Megan.

*Ugh. Now what?*

I took a deep breath and shouted, "WOW, Bert, this place is magnificent!"

He looked at Megan, rolled his eyes, and rushed inside. "Yes, it is something. I'll show you where we'll sleep. Megan, do you remember where the guest wing is?"

"No, sorry. I don't."

"Follow us. I'll show you."

The second floor was just as magnificent. Mahogany doors, stone floors, and a railing that overlooked the grand entry. Two long hallways stretched before us—one straight ahead, one to the right.

Bert pointed down the right corridor. "Megan, the guest rooms are down there. Choose whichever you'd like—they should all be ready."

"Thanks, Bert. See y'all later." Megan gave us one last look before disappearing.

"It's beautiful up here. I've never seen anything like it."

"This is only the second floor. The third is smaller—it's where my parents' master suite is. I'll show you later. The room I usually stay in is just up ahead."

We walked hand in hand, stopping in front of double doors.

"Here we are, my queen."

He opened them, revealing a massive room centered around a grand mahogany four-poster king-sized bed with a canopy. I just stood there, taking it all in.

Straight ahead was a bow window with a cushioned seat—perfect for stargazing. He placed my bag on a chaise.

"This is some room. I love it."

"My mom had expensive taste. I think the house is a little too much, but we're desperate."

I sat down on the bed. "Nice and comfy." I patted the bed beside me. "Come and relax."

Bert gave me a seductive look.

"That's not what I meant."

"Damn. But while we're on the subject…"

"Are we, though?"

"…we haven't had a chance to talk about last night."

"No, we haven't. All hell broke loose again."

"I worried you'd think it was too soon, but I let nature take its course. I didn't want to scare you off."

"At first, it felt too soon, but it also felt right. You haven't scared me off. But I am worried about your past with Megan. I didn't know y'all were that serious."

"Beautiful, you have nothing to worry about. It wasn't serious. We were young. I don't know what's gotten into her lately. Maybe it's fear of dying or being alone."

"I'm just glad I found my someone. Maybe that's why I ended up in this dimension. I didn't fit in where I was."

"You're my one and only." Bert leaned in and kissed me. It started soft, then deepened. I turned around to straddle him. He grabbed my waist and gently threw me onto the bed. I giggled.

He paused, looking at me for permission. I nodded enthusiastically.

Our first time had been amazing, but this? This was passionate and soul-deep.

An hour later, we were curled up under the plushest comforter I'd ever felt. He was snoring softly as I played with the hair on his chest.

"Should I tell him how I feel?" I wondered. "Is it too early?"

A knock at the door yanked us from the moment.

Bert jerked awake. "Ugh. Can't even get a few hours to ourselves."

He threw on a robe and opened the door in irritation. Megan stood there in a sheer robe.

"Megan, what are you doing?"

She looked down at her robe. "Oops. I was looking for Faith's room... but maybe I can keep you company?"

"You know damn well where her room is. And you know she's in here with me."

"Oh, hey Faith! Just wondering what we're doing tonight. Trying to pick an outfit. Can I come in?"

"No. Faith is in bed—naked. And it's not like we're going anywhere. Wear whatever you want."

Megan looked hurt. "Oh. Okay."

I called from the bed, "Hey Megan, I haven't decided what I'm wearing yet. Probably something comfy though."

She tried to peek in, but Bert blocked her. "Thanks, Faith. See y'all later."

He shut the door and turned around, only to see me propped on one elbow—sheet fallen. He grinned.

"Oh, we definitely have time for more fun."

I looked down. "Oops. Good thing she didn't walk in."

"I kind of wish she had. She knew what she was doing."

"That pisses me off. Should I talk to her?" Then a lightbulb went off. "Wait... is that why you suddenly wanted more fun?"

"What? No! I don't find her attractive at all. I said that because your hot self was half-naked on my bed."

Relieved, I smiled. He kissed me. "Let's shower and get ready for dinner."

"Together?"

"Didn't think of that, but sure. Why not?"

Forty-five minutes later, wrapped in towels, we lay tangled on the bed.

"Sweetie, we better get dressed for dinner. I'm ravenous now."

"Me too," I yawned. "All that exercise worked up an appetite."

We stepped out into the hall and ran into Megan.

"Hey," I said, trying to stay polite.

Bert was annoyed. "What are you doing over here?"

"I'm hungry. Just walking while I wait."

He didn't respond. We walked down to the dining room.

Megan leaned in. "Girl, I thought I'd have to save you. It got loud in there."

I blushed. "Sorry. Thought we were alone."

"You were inside your room, but I heard you. Almost opened the door until I realized."

"Oh boy. I've never experienced anything like it. Wow."

"I could tell. I'm jealous. You wouldn't want to share him, would you?"

I gave her a look. "Girl, you better be joking."

"Calm down. I am joking."

*Mental note: Be quieter. And talk to Bert about this.*

We entered a ballroom-sized dining room. A 30-person table dominated the space, but off to the side was a smaller, cozy table, already set with dinner.

"I took the liberty of ordering," Bert said, winking.

Oh damn. He heard everything.

"It looks amazing," I said, trying to change the subject.

"Anything would look good after the way we worked up an appetite," he said with another wink.

Clearly trying to get under Megan's skin. Hopefully, it worked.

We sat down to a four-course meal. The tension started to ease. We were starving—maybe that explained some of Megan's behavior. Or maybe not. Something about her felt… off.

"If she still had a thing for Bert, why set us up?" I wondered.

Then came the all-too-familiar noise. A loud beep. A screen dropped from the ceiling—bright red with **NEWS FLASH** in white letters.

A female news anchor appeared:
"Good evening, residents. As you know, we're under attack by the Cordelia Tribe. Some residents have ignored the confinement orders—and are now dead."

"Well damn. Don't beat around the bush," I muttered.

"And nope, not all dead," Bert said. "We made it to Megan's and here just fine."

Megan added, "I wouldn't say fine. We did run into trouble."

"But we're alive," Bert said. "And that's fine by me."

The anchor continued, "…The Space Fleet and Air Guard have tried to contain the threat, with little success. It appears only major cities are being targeted. For now, attacks have ceased. We urge you to evacuate the cities and head to mountain regions."

"Good thing we got here before the stampede," I said. I pictured it—chaos, people fleeing, skyways jammed. Sheer madness.

"What now?" I asked, worried.

"We stay here," Bert said, putting his arm around me. "And come up with a plan."

"What about work?" Megan asked.

"That obnoxious boss of ours saw the news. He dropped off work at my place," I grumbled. "Did he come to you?"

"No. Was he supposed to?"

"He made it sound like he was visiting everyone. Guess it was just me. Figures."

"You really need to report him," Bert said.

"Yeah, I'm beginning to think that," I snapped. "But right now, I'm just trying to survive. Maybe I'll never have to deal with him again."

After dinner, we headed upstairs. I needed Bert to myself. One of these days, I'd have to ask Megan why she set us up if she still had feelings for him.

"Night, you two. Don't do anything I wouldn't do," Megan called.

We ignored her.

At our bedroom door, Bert stopped me. "Hold on. Let me."

He scooped me into his arms and carried me over the threshold.

"Hey! I thought only newlyweds did this!"

"I'm starting a new tradition," he said, throwing me on the bed. "Now... what should we do tonight?"

After our third happy ending, we fell asleep curled in each other's arms. It was the best night's sleep I'd had in a long while.

Little did we know, our world was about to be turned upside down.

# CHAPTER 19

Curled up in a ball, with the plushest beige comforter I had ever been under pulled up to my neck, I could sense someone staring at me. I slowly opened my eyes to see Bert lying on his side, facing me.

"Good morning, my beauty," he said as he leaned in and gave me a kiss.

"Mmmm, good morning, sexy."

"How did you sleep?"

"Damn, Bert, this is the most comfortable bed I have ever slept in."

"Mom sure does love expensive things. But yes, it is very comfy. Would you like breakfast in bed?" Bert gestured toward a tray on the table in the sitting area of the bedroom. "I can bring it over so you don't have to get up. You look so comfortable."

"Yes, that would be lovely. What's on the agenda for today?"

"Staying alive," Bert answered sarcastically.

"OK, sounds good to me."

Carrying the breakfast tray of scones, fresh fruit, coffee, and freshly squeezed orange juice, Bert set it down on the bed. I sat up and immediately dug in.

"I didn't realize how hungry I was."

"You used up all your energy last night," Bert winked, making me blush.

We were enjoying a lighthearted conversation when a loud ring echoed throughout the house.

"What the hell? Someone's at the door. I wonder who that could be. No one knows we're here. Mom and Dad are in the UK, so it can't be them."

"Oh, crap. That can't be good then."

Bert got up and looked at me. "Stay here. I'll be right back."

"No. I don't know who that is. If you're in danger, I want to come with you. Otherwise, I'll worry about not knowing what happened to you."

Letting out a deep, exasperated sigh, Bert gulped, "OK, but you better put a robe on. I'm the only one who gets to see all your goodies."

Laughing, I grabbed one of Bert's robes from a hook by the door. Putting it on, I followed behind him. We hurried down the hall to the stairs as the bell rang again.

Aggravated, Bert said, "Someone's impatient."

I saw Megan running down the hall toward us. Bert didn't notice because he was too focused on getting to the door quickly to stop that god-awful noise. Megan ran right into Bert just as I was about to warn him of her fast approach.

"Damn, girl, slow down. It's my house. I've got this."

"Shit, sorry guys. It's Alena from work. I invited her    here."

"Damn it, Megan, why? This is not your house to willy-nilly invite whoever you want. I don't care if she is a friend of yours," Bert roared.

"I'm sorry. I didn't think you would mind. She had no place to go. Her apartment building was bombed."

"OK, but I'm not running a shelter here. No more people without my strict permission. Do you understand?"

"Yes. Again, I'm sorry. I should have asked. After all, you were nice enough to let me stay here."

Bert got to the door first as the two of us stood behind him. "And now I'm regretting that decision. Stay back, just in case it's not her." He carefully opened the door, more worried about looters than anything else. Standing there in the portico was a shaking Alena.

"Hello there. You must be Bert. I'm Alena," she introduced herself with a shaky voice.

Bert reached out to shake her hand. "Hi, come on in. I know this is all so scary for you. Here, let me take your bags."

"Oh, thank you. That's nice of you. I was in my apartment when it got bombed. I've been driving around trying to find someplace to go. Then I remembered Megan's number."

"I'm sorry. We didn't know you were coming until just now."

"Oh, I'm so sorry. I told Megan to make sure it was okay with you first." Alena shot an aggravated look at Megan.

"Sorry, girl. I knew he would say yes."

Bert looked annoyed. "Not your fault, Alena. You can stay here, but please run anything else by me. This house is not a shelter."

Megan nodded and took hold of Alena's arm. "Come on. I'll show you around." Megan bent down to pick up her bag and guided her up the stairs.

Bert turned to me. "That girl is really getting on my nerves." Taking my hand, he led me upstairs.

"And what are we going to do now?" I questioned.

"Get dressed," Bert said with a puzzled expression. "Get your mind out of the gutter."

"Well, we need to do something. After all, we're all stuck here. We should take advantage of your pool, play board games, or have a movie marathon."

"Those are all great ideas. We could do that. I also have an indoor bowling alley in the basement— and tennis courts outside. Although, I'm not sure if it's safe to be outdoors right now."

"I've always wanted to learn to play tennis. However, I agree with you. We should probably stay indoors."

\*\*\*\*\*\*\*\*\*\*\*\*\*\*\*\*\*\*\*\*\*\*\*\*\*\*\*\*\*\*\*\*\*\*\*\*\*\*\*\*\*\*\*\*\*\*\*\*\*\*\*\*\*\*\*\*\*\*\*\*\*\*\*\*\*\*

**Several weeks had passed** with no more news on the alien invasion front. The four of us kept occupied by either reading or taking advantage of the mansion's many amenities. I was having a great time just hanging out with my boyfriend and friends. Occasionally, I squeezed in some work too—but since no one in the area was working, there wasn't much to do. My boss, Darren, still made sure I logged in every day. That guy really was a gigantic asshole.

We were in the middle of a competitive game of bowling when my phone rang.

Annoyed, I picked up the phone. "Hello?!"

"Hello, Faith, it's Darren. I need you to come into work first thing tomorrow morning."

"Darren, no one is supposed to go outside. In case you haven't seen the news, we're under attack right now. We came up to my boyfriend's family lake cabin. I'm not even in the area."

"Well, I got a phone call from a very important client. This is an emergency."

"An accounting emergency? Really?!"

"Yes, really. See you tomorrow at 9 a.m. sharp." Darren hung up without giving me a chance to respond.

Aggravated, I threw my phone. "Ugh, that asshole. I have to go to work tomorrow. Some accounting emergency. Can you believe him?"

Bert's face turned three shades of red. "You've got to be kidding. That guy has some nerve. I don't want you going out. It's not safe."

"I'm sorry. I don't want to either, but he's insisting I come in tomorrow morning. By the way, I've seen these cars here move—I think I'll be okay."

"Okay, but I want you to call me when you get there."

"I sure will. I love that you're so worried about me."

"Of course, my love. Always. Now let's go to bed." Bert reached for my hand and guided me up to our room.

# CHAPTER 20

All snuggled up on Bert's shoulder, I couldn't imagine any place else I'd rather be. He leaned down and kissed me gently on the lips.

"Good morning, my love."

"Good morning." I was just about to pursue the kiss further when my alarm went off.

"Crap, I forgot—I've got to go to work."

Bert gave me one last kiss. "Why don't you hop in the shower, and I'll get your breakfast ready?"

"Sounds great. Thanks." I got up and headed into the bathroom while Bert made his way down to the kitchen.

I showered and got ready for work in record time. I chose a long maxi dress—the less revealing, the better, since I was going to see the boss today, which I was not looking forward to. It would be nice seeing my other coworkers, though. I missed them. Still, it was strange that Darren hadn't asked Megan to come into the office too. Maybe it was just for administrative staff.

As I opened the bathroom door, the delicious smell of breakfast hit me—both savory and sweet. I saw Bert had placed a tray on the little bistro table by the window.

"Oh, babe, this all smells amazing." I spotted quiche, cheese danishes, and freshly squeezed orange juice.

"I wasn't sure what you were in the mood for, so I brought both of your favorites. I'll get your coffee to go before you head out."

We sat and ate while talking about the absurdity of me going into the office at all. Thirty minutes later, Bert walked me to the garage. He handed me a to-go mug and opened the car door.

"You be careful out there. Call me as soon as you get to work."

"Will do, babe." I leaned in for a kiss.

Getting in the car, I took one last look at him and blew a kiss. As the car pulled out of the garage, I could see Bert watching me through the rearview mirror. A warm, tingling feeling rushed over my body. I was really falling hard for this man.

The drive into town was long and full of twists—literally. The roads were littered with rubble and potholes, making the ride bumpy and nauseating. Or maybe it was just the fact that I had to see Darren again. My stomach twisted into knots. I leaned my head back and tried to think about what Bert and I might do tonight when I got home.

The car came to a sudden halt. I opened my eyes to see the Lowe's Office Building. My nerves kicked in.

"Ma'am, we are at your destination," the car's voice announced.

"Thank you."

"I'll park in the garage."

"Thank you."

I grabbed my bag and headed inside. The lone security guard looked surprised to see me.

"Good morning, Faith. Darren's here, but I wasn't expecting anyone else."

"He insisted I come in today. Has anyone else from my department arrived yet?"

"Nope, haven't seen anyone. I didn't even know you were coming."

"Okay, thanks." I waved and headed up.

Once in my office, I immediately got to work, purposely avoiding Darren. When he came in mid-afternoon, I barely looked up.

"Good morning, Faith. Thanks for coming in. We've got a meeting in 30 minutes."

"Yeah, I saw your email. I'll be ready."

Without even a goodbye, Darren turned and left.

"Okay," I muttered, getting back to it. Then I called after him, "Hey, Darren!"

He stepped back in. "Yes?"

"When's everyone else coming?"

"Oh, it's just the two of us. Everyone else is video calling in. I just needed my one and only here to help."

Internally, I rolled my eyes. "Oh, okay."

He left again.

"Crap," I muttered, seeing I only had 15 minutes until the meeting. So much for leaving early—I had a backlog of work to catch up on after all that fun lately.

Soon, Darren peeked his head in again. "It's time. You ready?"

"Yes." I got up, and he let me pass before following too close behind. His hand touched the small of my back. I cringed. *Gross.*

To his credit, Darren acted totally professional during the meeting. I returned the energy. My coworkers on screen seemed surprised to see me there in person. The meeting went by quickly, thankfully. As soon as it was over, I grabbed my things to leave. But Darren followed me back to my office.

"I'm leaving," I told him flatly. "You don't need me here. I'll work from home."

Darren stood in the doorway. I pushed past him, but he grabbed my upper arm.

"We're not finished," he growled.

"Yes, we are," I snapped, and I kicked him hard in the groin.

"Bitch!" he cursed, doubling over.

Without waiting, I ran down the hall. My arm throbbed where he'd grabbed me—hard. I flew down the stairs, my feet barely touching the steps.

At the lobby, I sighed in relief. Empty. The security guard was gone. I summoned my car—

Suddenly, an arm yanked me backward.

"While you wasted time on the stairs," Darren sneered, "I took the elevator."

He dragged me into the nearest room—a men's bathroom.

"No one's here to save you now."

He shoved me against the wall and ripped open my shirt. I pushed back, but he punched me in the cheek and slammed my head into the tile wall. I fought hard, wriggling, pushing, scratching. He forced a kiss on me, shoved his tongue in my mouth. I bit down hard and kneed him again—hard.

Another punch to my face. My head hit the wall again.

As he bent over, groaning, I ran.

I burst out of the bathroom, across the lobby. I was nearly at the door when I heard footsteps pounding behind me. I turned—he was coming again.

I ran faster. The doors opened automatically. I was almost free—

He grabbed me again. I caught myself before falling.

Fueled by rage, I shoved him back, then kicked. He stumbled. Still falling, I shoved harder.

Outside now, I frantically looked for something to block the door—nothing. I turned back.

Darren was lying in sunlight, his face contorted in pain. Then—his eyes burst into flames.

"What the hell?!"

Flames spread across his face, neck, and body. His agonizing screams echoed around me.

"Justice. Thank you, God—if that was you," I whispered.

Drones buzzed overhead—two unmarked, one police, one medical. A black SUV screeched to a stop. Four men in radiation suits got out. Two circled Darren's burning remains. The other two rushed to me.

"Ma'am, are you okay?" the leader asked, gently touching my arm. "You've got visible injuries."

I was still stunned. "He attacked me. I was just trying to get away. I didn't know he would... burn like that. Am I in trouble?"

"No, ma'am. He'd be the one in trouble. We have zero tolerance for abusers."

"I still don't understand—what happened?"

"There are extremely high radiation levels in the sunlight. We think it's connected to the alien ships. The government is issuing suits now. You'll need to wear this." He handed me a black suitcase.

"Do I put this on now?"

"Yes, ma'am. Do you need a ride?"

"No, my car's in the garage. Will it be safe there?"

"Yes, the threat seems to be direct sunlight. But keep the suit on outside."

"Okay… thank you."

"Anytime, ma'am. Be safe. Do you want an escort to your car?"

"No, I'll be fine."

I walked to the elevator, asked for the garage level,  and leaned back, trying to slow my breathing. I was lightheaded, my palms sweating. A panic attack was building. I counted the tiles on the ceiling. Deep breaths.

Finally, the doors opened.

In the car, I felt like an elephant stuffed into the world's smallest vehicle. The radiation suit swallowed my petite frame.

"I guess if it keeps me alive, it's worth it."

I realized I had no idea how bad I looked. I pressed a button and a mirror appeared.

Yikes. My cheek was red, swollen, already bruising. A nasty gash cut below my cheekbone. Red marks lined my face and neck.

"Good afternoon, ma'am. Where are we headed?" the car asked.

"Back to the lake house."

"Right away. Estimated time: three hours or more."

"That's fine. I'm going to try and rest."

I leaned my head back, pain throbbing in my skull. "Great. A migraine."

I closed my eyes, trying to sleep. My last thought before drifting off was of Bert—my anchor, my calm in the storm.

# CHAPTER 21

Meanwhile, at the lake house, Bert was feeling uneasy about letting Faith go into work alone. It was strange that Megan didn't have to go in, but since Faith was in upper management, that was probably why.

He ate breakfast alone, wanting to avoid Megan as much as possible. Luckily, Alena kept her occupied.

Bert spent most of the morning swimming in the pool. Eventually, he stopped for lunch, then showered. He needed to be clean and ready for when Faith got home.

After his shower, he sat in the living room reading. It was so quiet he could hear a pin drop. From the kitchen, he heard Megan and Alena eating lunch and gossiping about workplace affairs involving married people. As he strained to listen, the TV monitor suddenly appeared, and the sharp **NEWS FLASH** rang through the air.

Megan and Alena came running into the living room.

Bert shot them an annoyed glance. "Didn't the monitor go on in there?"

Walking toward him, Megan replied, "Yes, but we wanted to watch it here with you."

Bert gestured toward the couches off to the side. Of course, Megan sat down next to him, and Alena sat beside her. Rolling his eyes, Bert turned his attention back to the monitor.

"Good afternoon, city residents. Earlier today, our drones discovered alarming footage that the DCS feels is necessary to show our citizens. This afternoon, a man and a woman were seen exiting the Lowe Office Building downtown. It is unclear why they were there. Telework is currently mandatory. Roll the video…"

A video appeared, showing the front façade of Faith's building. Darren stumbled out, followed closely by Faith.

Bert and Megan exchanged shocked expressions.

Bert spoke first, talking to the monitor. "Oh, sweetie…"

Megan tried to calm him. "Bert, I'm sure she's okay."

"They said 'alarming.' Just walking outside isn't alarming," Bert said, eyes fixed on the screen.

The news anchor continued, "…Keep watching. In just a second, the male steps into the light." The camera angle shifted from above Faith and Darren to a front-facing view of Darren. "We must warn you. This next part is disturbing to witness. Our government believes it's important to show everyone what could happen if you disobey executive orders."

The three of them watched intently.

The video showed the back of Darren's head. Suddenly, he stepped backward. The camera moved to reveal his face.

Bert growled, "Damn it. I don't want to see that asshole. I want to see my Faith."

Darren stood frozen, a terrified look on his face. His eyes widened—and then instantly burst into flames.

Alena screamed. Megan shrieked. Bert shouted, "NO!"

Alena burst into tears. "Sorry, guys. I've gotta get away from that. I'll be in my room."

"That's okay. We understand," Megan said as Alena fled the room crying.

The anchor continued, "Keep watching, citizens. It only gets worse."

Megan gasped. "Oh God. Is this what happened to Faith? Poor thing. I'm glad they didn't broadcast her all over the city."

"It's awful. I don't believe it. They didn't show her. She's okay," Bert said, as if saying it would make it true.

They turned back to the screen. After Darren's eyes ignited, his neck and shoulders were consumed in flame. It spread slowly, consuming the rest of him. Before long, there was nothing left but a pile of ashes.

Megan covered her mouth in horror. "That's a horrible way to die. Slow and painful. He was outside…

so was Faith…" She didn't finish, but the implication hung heavy in the air.

The anchorwoman returned. "As you can see, citizens, the government believes the alien ships are responsible for releasing high levels of radiation into the air. This is the only explanation for what you've just witnessed. The government now advises all residents to wear radiation suits when outdoors. If you disobey, you too could be engulfed in flames. We don't want to lose any more citizens. Radiation suits will be distributed to everyone, but please be patient. This will take time. Be safe. Signing off for now."

Bert just stared in the direction of the now-blank monitor. Megan scooted closer and wrapped her arm around him.

"I'm so sorry. She was a wonderful woman."

Bert turned to Megan in disgust. "We don't know that she's gone," he snapped.

Megan responded calmly, "Sweetie, if that happened to Darren just by being outside… more than likely it happened to Faith too."

Bert bent his head and started to cry. He usually never showed emotion, not unless it was someone he truly loved. This was different. His heart ached. It felt like he had lost his soulmate.

Megan gently guided his head onto her shoulder. "Here, let me comfort you." Instinctively, Bert wrapped his arm around her and cried into her shoulder.

From the corner of her eye, Megan saw movement. She turned to see Alena walking into the room. Alena stopped when she saw Bert crying. She opened her mouth in complete shock—she had never seen a man cry before. She looked to Megan for direction. Megan subtly nodded for her to leave.

After five minutes, Bert's cries slowed. He lifted his head and looked into Megan's eyes.

"I'm sorry. I shouldn't have lost it like that."

"It's okay. I'm here for you. I've never stopped caring about you."

In a moment of weakness, Bert leaned down and kissed Megan. It started as a soft peck... then deepened with intensity—desperate to feel anything besides the weight of grief crushing his chest. After a moment, he pulled away.

"I shouldn't have done that. Her body isn't even cold yet."

"She's gone, Bert. We could start fresh. We always had chemistry."

"The attraction was never the problem. You know that."

"I've apologized for what happened. It was a moment of weakness. That guy at the bar seduced me because you failed his kid brother—"

"Typical," Bert cut her off. "Turning it around on me. I was doing my job."

"I am truly sorry. Tell me how I can make it up to you." Megan gently turned Bert's face to hers and kissed him again. This time, she climbed into his lap and straddled him.

But all Bert could think about was Faith.

He wasn't kissing Megan. In his mind, he was with Faith.

He looked into her eyes—Faith's eyes, in his mind—and slowly unbuttoned Megan's shirt, sliding it off her shoulders.

He whispered Faith's name in his thoughts again and again, reliving their last time together.

# CHAPTER 22

The whole ride, all I could think about was being in the safety of Bert's arms.

"Ma'am, we are at the Lake House."

"Oh, thank goodness. This has been a long car ride in this monkey suit."

"Would you like me to park in the garage?"

"Yes, please. That would be great."

As we approached the six-car garage, the doors disappeared, allowing for a smooth transition into the interior. I was relieved when they closed behind us. I was *so* hot in the radiation suit. Shedding the uncomfortable weight, I made my way toward the house. Entering through the garage door, I stepped into the basement hallway. I'd only been down here to bowl or head to the garage. The bowling alley was just past the door, along with a nice-sized movie theater and a mini wine cellar.

"I really need to spend more time down here."

After wandering around, I figured I better head upstairs. Bert was probably wondering where I was.

*Actually, I thought, I'm surprised he hasn't texted or called me.*

I climbed the stairs and entered the kitchen. Quiet.

"Where is everybody?"

I passed through the dining room. Empty. I peeked into the saloon. Nope, not there either.

"Maybe he's in our room."

Starting toward the stairs, I stopped and decided to check the living room. Strolling in nonchalantly, I stopped dead in my tracks.

There it was. A devastating scene unfolding on the couch.

Megan was straddling Bert's lap, *topless*. He was kissing and fondling her, and her hand was between his legs doing God-knows-what. I froze. They were so into each other, they didn't notice me standing there. After several long seconds, I crossed my arms and cleared my throat.

"Don't let me standing here disturb you two."

Megan and Bert simultaneously turned their heads. Shock washed over Bert's face. He jumped up, knocking Megan to the floor.

"You're alive!" he shouted.

Surprised and furious, I scolded, "What?! Of course! I haven't been gone *that* long!"

"Sweetie, we saw you die."

Megan was still on the floor, topless, waiting for Bert to help her up. He ignored her and walked toward me. His eyes widened as he noticed the swollen, bruised cheek and contusion on my face.

"Oh, babe, what happened? Why are you in so much pain?" Bert reached out to gently touch my cheek, but I backed away.

Ignoring his questions, I followed with my own question, "What do you mean, you saw me die?"

"They had a news flash showing you and Darren outside. The camera zoomed in on him—his eyes and body burst into flames. We figured since you were outside too…"

"So you didn't waste *any* time getting into Megan's pants? So much for 'she's like a sister to me.' Must be a weird relationship you have with your sisters then. I see how you really felt about me."

I turned to Megan, who was still topless. "And I thought you were my friend. Put a shirt on."

Turning back to Bert, I asked, "If I hadn't walked in, would you have had sex with her?"

Bert glanced at Megan, then back at me. "I don't know. It did seem to be going in that direction. But please believe me, Faith, I don't have feelings for her. I was just… upset. I was thinking about *you* the whole time. I just wanted to feel *anything* other than this deep sadness."

"I told you I was learning to trust again, and this is what you do?" I yelled.

"Sweetie, we thought you had died."

I was furious. I felt like steam was pouring out of my ears. My face burned with rage.

"I can't look at you two right now. I'm going to take a shower. I already had a migraine before I got home, and now I feel like I'm going to be sick." I turned to leave, then stopped. "Oh, by the way—Darren attacked me today. That's what this is from." I pointed to my face. "If I'd known *this* was what I'd be coming home to, I might've just let him have his way. At least he *wanted* me."

I burst into tears and ran upstairs. Bert called after me, but I didn't stop. I slammed and locked the door behind me.

I sat on the bed, staring off into space, wondering what I was supposed to do now. I couldn't stay here with Bert and Megan... but where else could I go? Maybe I'd just move into another room. Time passed quickly as I spiraled.

About 30 minutes later, I heard hurried footsteps, followed by pounding on the door.

"Go away. I don't want to see you right now."

Bert's voice rang out with urgency. "Please, Faith. I'm so sorry. We thought you were dead. But right now, we're in danger. There's an alien ship above the house—we need to leave."

Reluctantly, I got up and glanced out the window. Sure enough, a massive silver hexagon ship hovered above the house.

"Crap," I muttered.

I opened the door slowly. Bert stood there, eyes full of sorrow, staring at my bruised, tear-streaked face.

"Oh, sweetie. I'm so sorry. I would *never* have kissed her if I'd thought you were alive. I kept hoping you were, but Megan... she convinced me otherwise. After seeing Darren burst into flames, I—"

"I *should* have known Megan had something to do with it. But we can talk about this later. Right now, we need to hurry." I pointed out the window.

Bert grabbed our bags, took my hand, and led me downstairs. Just outside our room, I paused.

"What about radiation suits?"

"I called my contact at the university. They're delivering four suits—and one for Megan's dog—any minute now."

"I already have one."

"I figured, but I wasn't sure about its condition. Better to have a backup."

"That's sweet. They make radiation suits for dogs?"

Bert nodded. "Yeah. Pets are family too, so they made ones for dogs and cats."

"How are we all going to fit in your car?"

"My parents have a Land Rover in the garage. We'll take that. I'm sorry—it'll be awkward with Megan. But Alena can keep her busy."

"We could always just leave her here."

Bert gave me a look. I sighed. "Fine. I'll just pretend she's not even there."

We made our way to the garage. Megan and Alena were already there. A large package sat near the garage door.

"Our radiation suits—perfect timing," Bert said, opening the box and handing them out. The spare went in the trunk. We all began suiting up in silence.

Alena broke it first. "This thing is already hot, and I haven't even put the hood on."

"It really sucks when you're in a car for hours," I added. "I wish it was safe to take the hood off in there."

"We can't?" Alena asked.

Bert explained, "No. Cars pull in outside air. Even with filters, there's still some risk."

"Yeah, that makes sense," Alena said.

Once everyone was suited up—including Megan's dog—Megan casually positioned herself by the front passenger door. Bert walked over with me, nudged Megan aside, and opened the door.

"Here you go, beautiful," he said.

I looked right at Megan and sweetly whispered, "Thanks, babe," as I gave him a soft smile.

I wasn't going to let Megan think she'd gotten to me. Bert and I would talk about that later.

Once everyone was inside, the garage doors opened and the car's voice spoke.

"Sir, where would you like to go today?"

"The university, please."

As the Land Rover pulled away from the house, a sudden red flash lit up behind us. I turned around just in time to see the alien ship firing on the lake house.

"Honey, I'm so sorry," I whispered.

"Yeah," Bert said quietly. "That sucks. I'm just glad we got out of there before it blew."

# CHAPTER 23

The Land Rover was a good choice because we sure did have obstacles to go over and around. Luckily, the roadway was empty due to everyone using the skyway, which made no sense to me. The trouble was more in the air than on the ground.

We had only been at the lake house for a few weeks, but as we drove further inland, the surroundings were astonishing. The city buildings were either reduced to piles of rubble or missing their upper halves. Some were still on fire. It looked like a war zone—well, I guess it was a war zone.

Everyone in the car was speechless. I was the first to speak. "This is so devastatingly horrible. What do they want? How much longer can we put up with this?"

Bert, trying to sound positive, said, "Good questions. Hopefully, the government is trying to figure out the why of it all. We'll keep going as long as we have to. I'm just glad we're together. I'd be so worried if you were alone." He looked over at me as he spoke.

Megan finally chimed in from the backseat. "They obviously want to do away with the human race. But the why is the question."

"Well, based on how they're attacking us, that part is clear. I'm just going to try and keep us safe," Bert noted.

"That's sweet of you," Megan jabbered.

Bert snapped, "Don't get any ideas. I'm only trying to protect you because you're with us." Then, turning to a terrified Alena, he asked, "Alena, are you okay?"

"No, not really. I'm scared. I'm not ready to die. I wanted to get married first."

I reached around to comfort her. "We're all scared. Safety in numbers, right?"

"Yeah… safety in numbers," Alena said with a shy, nervous smile.

The Land Rover kept scaling piles of rubble left from buildings and roads. Up ahead, I could see a hexagon-shaped alien craft suddenly halt in front of a line of cars. A door on one side of the ship opened.

"Oh no, watch out. That ship looks suspicious," I said, worried.

Bert nodded, eyes scanning for somewhere to hide. "Yeah, that's not good. We need to find cover."

Just then, a laser blast fired from the ship. At the same time, several vehicles nosedived from the sky toward the road.

"Watch out!" I yelled as a car hurtled toward us.

Bert swerved the Land Rover, avoiding the vehicle just in time. "Idiot," he muttered as he sped up, dodging falling cars. "I'm going to the university. There's an old fallout shelter in my building. Hopefully, we can get in there," he said, punching the coordinates into the car's computer.

I took a deep breath to calm down. "I hope it's not full."

"It won't be. That shelter's just for my building. There are shelters all over campus. We just never thought we'd actually need them."

Dusk had fallen, making obstacles harder to see. The car hit pothole after pothole, bouncing everyone around. Periodically, we saw distant explosions—some in the air, some on the ground.

Suddenly, the car screeched to a stop.

"What was that?" Bert asked.

"Sorry, sir," the car's voice responded. "Someone jumped in front of the vehicle."

The headlights illuminated a young woman holding something.

"Bert, I think she has a baby. We need to help her," I said.

"No way. There isn't room, and she's not wearing a radiation suit. Seems fishy to me. Maybe it's not even a real baby—could be a setup," Megan snapped.

"She's a young mother. Stay here—I'll go see what's going on," Bert instructed, squeezing my knee before getting out.

The three of us watched as Bert was lit up in the headlights walking toward the woman.

"She's crying. Poor thing," Alena observed.

"She does look worried," I added.

We watched Bert speak to her. She pointed behind her down the road. Bert gently put his arm around her and led her to the car. Alena shifted over to make room.

Bert opened the door. "This is Michelle and her baby, Isaac. We'll be giving her a ride. I'll get you that extra radiation suit," he said before heading to the trunk.

Under the car's interior light, I could see a huge red mark on Michelle's cheek. "Michelle, are you okay? I see your cheek hurts." I was starting to see the benefit of visually recognizing people's injuries.

Michelle spoke in a soft, nervous voice. "My boyfriend hit me hard when he kicked us out of the car."

Alena gently placed a hand on Michelle's shoulder. "I'm sorry. You're safe now."

Bert returned and got back in. "OK—let's get to the university."

"Yes, sir," the car responded.

"So how is it you're not in a radiation suit? Shouldn't you be a pile of dust right now?" Megan hissed.

"Megan, that's not nice," I snapped.

"Sorry. Inquiring minds want to know," she shrugged.

Michelle answered, "That's okay. I had one, but when my boyfriend kicked us out, he took off with it. He wants to sell it. He's such a lowlife. I'm just glad he waited until dark."

Megan eyed her. "Interesting. Why didn't you have one on earlier?"

"We were at home. We left just thirty minutes ago. He didn't want me wearing one. We didn't have one for the baby, so he figured if something happened to one of us, it should happen to both of us," Michelle said.

"That guy sounds like a real piece of work," Bert muttered.

"You're better off without him. I'm glad we drove by when we did," I added.

As we neared the university, Bert's chest tightened. His home away from home was in ruins. The massive brick entrance had collapsed. Buildings were flattened. Trees scorched. Vehicles burned. Tires melted into pavement.

Bert let out a groan of despair followed by several choice curse words.

"Oh, babe. I'm so sorry. This is awful. From the looks of it, we might not be able to get into the shelter," I said softly.

"We'll get in. The entrance isn't through the building."

The roads were a mess. Bert's building looked as bad as the rest—roof gone, top floor windows shattered. He parked at the curb. We all stepped out and looked over at the lake—peaceful despite everything.

Bert came over and put his arm around me, kissing the top of my head. "When this is over, we can start our lives together. Maybe even move in."

I turned to him. "Sweetie, I need time to trust again after what happened with Megan. Even though she manipulated you when you were vulnerable, it was hard to see. I can't unsee it." I could feel Megan listening, but I didn't care. Alena, thankfully, gave us privacy.

"That's fair," Bert said.

We grabbed our bags and followed Bert. "The shelter entrance is over here," he said, pointing toward an open field behind the building.

All I saw were scorched trees and dirt. But Bert walked up to a low brick corner and pushed it. A square tube structure rose from the ground.

"This is how we get in," he said.

The tube was spacious enough for all five of us—and baby Isaac. Once inside, Bert shut the door and the lift began descending. First, we passed thick dirt walls, then concrete, then a hallway lit up below. When the tube landed, we stepped onto cold concrete. The air smelled stale. The walls were stark white.

"Wow, this place is bigger than I thought," I said, suddenly self-conscious. "Everyone's going to see the red marks on my face and neck. Great first impression," I thought.

"All shelters connect underground," Bert explained. "Each building has its own, independently sealed. Ours is up here to the left."

A hatch door closed over the elevator shaft behind us.

"We can take off the suits now. There's a spot inside to hang them up," Bert said, and we all removed our helmets.

He led us to a vault-like door. "Stand back. I need to punch in a code and scan my eye."

Bert entered a six-digit code, and a robotic scanner emerged, flashing green. A vacuum seal released, and the door slid open to reveal a 20x20 cement room with a row of hooks along one wall.

"This is just the entry room. We hang suits here, then move into the main area." He ushered us inside. A green laser flashed as each of us entered.

After securing the door, he unlocked another, even bigger door. Inside stood four people, their faces lighting up when they saw Bert.

A man extended his hand. "Hey dude, we thought you were a goner. Your neighborhood's demolished."

"Well, damn. I've been with my girlfriend," Bert replied, pulling me forward. "This is Faith."

"Hi, Faith. I'm Travis. Nice to meet you. And I know Megan"

"Hey there, Trav," Megan interrupted. "How's it going?"

"Hey, Megan. Who's the cutie behind you?"

"Oh, that's our friend and co-worker Alena. She's a gardening whiz," I offered.

"Really? Clara could use your help," he said, gesturing to a tall brunette.

"Hi, I'm head of the Horticulture Department," Clara said. "We don't have many skilled gardeners. I'd love your help."

"I'd love to help," Alena said. "Gardening is my zen."

"Great. Come with me," Clara said, leading her out.

"And this is Michelle and baby Isaac," I added.

"Sorry, we're not well-equipped for babies," Travis said.

"That's okay. He sleeps with me, and I breastfeed," Michelle reassured him.

Travis blushed. "Oh. Okay."

Bert laughed. "Don't worry, Trav. It's not like she's going to whip her boobs out in front of you."

Michelle grinned. "I know how to be discreet."

"This is Violet," Travis continued, pointing to a petite woman with long black hair. "And that's David."

"Nice to meet you," I said politely.

"You're cute," Megan said to David.

Bert rolled his eyes at me.

"Come on, I'll show you where you'll sleep," Travis said. "We've got about 50 people here now. Space for 200. Plenty of room."

I exhaled. "Well, at least no one's mentioned my face. So far, they seem nice."

We followed Travis down the corridor.

As we walked, I asked Bert, "Hey, it looked like they were waiting for us. How did they know we were coming?"

"Oh, there's a sensor near the brick outside. It alerts the shelter when someone's arriving," he explained.

The first room we entered off the hallway was the kitchen. It was way bigger than I expected, equipped with commercial-sized appliances.

I looked around, impressed. "This is an incredible kitchen. I wasn't expecting it to be this big."

"That was Bert's idea when we renovated," Travis replied. "We're set up to be here for a while if needed."

I gave Bert a pat on the back—he deserved it.

Just past the kitchen were two huge rooms. One was the pantry, filled with shelves stacked with canned goods and non-perishables. The other looked like a storage room filled with cleaning supplies, medical gear, and everything else you'd expect in a long-term shelter. Down the hall was a small office with typical furniture, followed by a larger health aide office, complete with six beds, a desk, and even a portable x-ray machine.

I felt a little flicker of excitement—I was an X-ray technologist in the other dimension.

"I could totally use that," I thought. "I should say something… but not right now."

At the end of the hall, we entered a massive communal area. It reminded me of the cafeteria in the Lowe Building, complete with fake trees, plants, and even artificial grass to bring a sense of calm. There were long rows of tables and chairs, couches, bookshelves stacked with games and books—it was cozy, almost peaceful.

Beyond that was the dorm—well, what passed for a dorm. A massive open room lined with triple-stacked bunk beds, like something off a naval ship.

Megan finally broke her silence. "I feel like I just stepped onto a battleship. Is this the best y'all could do? No privacy?"

Bert didn't miss a beat. "No, there's no privacy. This is about surviving. But if you want to try your luck outside, you know where the door is."

Megan rolled her eyes but said nothing more.

We passed through the dorm and into a small hallway. On the right was a giant bathroom—one for everyone. No separate men's or women's sections. One wall had about fifteen showers, the opposite wall had around twenty-five toilets, and sinks lined the center.

At the end of the hallway was the gardening room, filled with upright towers and raised beds. As we entered, I saw Alena already elbow-deep in dirt with Clara by her side.

Alena looked up, beaming. "Hey guys! Isn't this place awesome? I'm in heaven."

I smiled and waved. "Hey girl. I'm glad you're able to help out here. This shelter really is amazing."

Turning to Travis and Bert, who were talking quietly, I asked, "So, are all the shelters laid out like this?"

Travis started to answer, but Bert jumped in. "Sorry, man—you can take it from here."

Bert gave him a nod. "All good. Yes, they're all laid out the same. We figured that would make them easier to manage. Travis and I were on the committee that renovated them all. We just finished about six months ago."

"Interesting timing, wouldn't you say?" Travis added.

"Yeah," Bert replied. "Makes you wonder if someone knew something."

"Now that you're here," Travis said, "do you have time for a quick meeting?"

"Yeah, I sure do." Bert turned to me and planted a kiss on my lips. "Why don't you go get settled? I'll meet up with you later."

"Sure thing, sweetie. See you soon."

Once Bert and Travis left, I turned toward the dorm. "Coming with me, Michelle?"

"Yeah, I'll walk with you. I need to feed Isaac."

Megan hurried after us. "Hey, I'm coming too."

I didn't respond. Honestly, I didn't want to deal with her. I'd hoped I could ignore her down here—but clearly, Megan wasn't going to make that easy.

When we reached the dorm, I noticed that each bunk had neatly folded blankets and pillows.

"That's nice of them. I didn't notice that before," I said to Michelle.

"Yeah, that was sweet. Travis is a great guy," Megan replied.

Michelle looked curious. "So how do you know him, Megan? Did you two date?"

I bit back a laugh. Clearly, Michelle already suspected the answer.

"No, I met him when I dated Bert," Megan said, shooting me a smug look.

I gave her a fake smile.

"Oh, you dated Bert too? Interesting. How do you feel about your friend dating him?" Michelle asked innocently.

"I introduced them," Megan said, still smug. "So I'm fine with it. I wanted her to be with a great guy."

"That's sweet. I don't think I could do that," Michelle said, then excused herself to feed Isaac.

I chose an empty bunk and got to work making the bed. Exhausted, I claimed the bottom bunk, but I was open to switching if Bert wanted to share the top. I laid down and closed my eyes, hoping to rest—but ten minutes later, I felt someone watching me.

Opening my eyes, I turned my head—and there was Megan, sitting on the opposite bunk, staring.

Letting out a frustrated sigh, I asked, "Megan, is that the bunk you chose? Out of all the empty ones, why this one?"

"I wanted to be near my bestie."

"Really?" I sat up. "Megan, have you even noticed I haven't spoken to you since we left the lake house?"

"Yes, I noticed. But I thought you were just tired from your ordeal. How's your face feeling?"

"It hurts. I have a massive headache. And yeah, I'm tired—but that's not why. You tried to sleep with my boyfriend!" I snapped.

Everyone in the dorm turned to look, mouths hanging open.

I offered an embarrassed "Sorry," then turned back to Megan. "You are absolutely clueless. I thought you were my friend."

Megan didn't look remorseful at all. "We thought you were dead. I am sorry."

"And you waited a whole hour to jump his bones? What kind of friend does that? Why even set us up if you still had feelings for him?"

"I didn't. But… you made him more appealing, I guess. He never looked at me like that before."

"And he never will," I said sharply. "He clearly has feelings for me. It's going to take time for me to move past what you did—but for now, would you please move bunks?"

Megan looked down, finally seeming a little ashamed. "I understand. Yes, I can."

She gathered her things and moved to the farthest bunk she could find.

I rolled over and pulled a thick army-green blanket over my head. My pillow was soft—surprisingly comfortable for a bunker—and I drifted off quickly. For a moment, I almost forgot we were hiding underground from a war being waged above us.

But as I fell asleep, an image kept flashing through my mind—Darren bursting into flames.

I had caused his death.

Granted, he deserved it… but still.

I was the cause of another human's death.

Could I live with that?

# CHAPTER 24

I was startled awake, jumping a foot off the bed. A gentle hand rubbed my shoulder.

"Sorry, sweetie, I didn't mean to startle you. They're about to serve dinner. I don't want you to miss it. It'll be the only food given until tomorrow morning," Bert calmly explained to my sleepy self.

"OK, honey. I should eat something—it may make me feel better." I sat up and instantly felt dizzy. Placing a hand on my forehead, I leaned back against the wall.

With concern in his voice, Bert said, "You okay? Maybe you should see the nurse."

"Maybe. I'll see how I feel after we eat. I had a nightmare about Darren going up in flames. I caused his death."

Bert gently rubbed my back. "Oh, sweetie, you are not the cause. It couldn't have happened to a better guy."

Shaking my head, I admitted, "But I am. When he was attacking me, I pushed and then kicked him. He fell backward into the sunlight. If I hadn't done that, he would still be alive. I caused his death."

In a soft, reassuring voice, Bert tried to soothe me. "And if he were alive, he'd still be able to attack you. It's his own fault he's dead, not yours. He did it to himself by coming after you."

"Yeah, I guess. Let's go eat. I'm hungry," I said, though I wasn't entirely convinced that his death wasn't somehow my fault.

Carefully getting up from the bed, I reached out, placing a hand on Bert for support. As I looked around the dorm, Bert noticed.

"Megan's not here, if that's who you're looking for," he informed me.

We talked while walking to dinner, and Bert caught me up on everything I'd missed while sleeping.

"Oh really? Where is she? Please tell me she left the shelter," I asked.

"Sorry. No such luck. Everyone needs to help around here. She's helping in the kitchen," Bert replied.

"OK, good for her. What should I do?"

"Nothing right now. You need to heal. You still look like a mess. We'll reevaluate in a week."

Bert guided me into the communal area, which was abuzz with people eating and talking. He walked me over to the kitchen window. There were rows of metal trays with a meager portion of canned meat, vegetables, and peaches. A small metal cup of water accompanied each tray. I didn't mask the look of disgust on my face.

Bert commented, "I know it's not much, but we're limited down here. It's just enough to keep us nourished."

He picked up trays for both of us and led us to a table where the same people I'd met earlier were sitting.

Violet was the first to speak up. "Hey, guys. Faith, how are you feeling? Bert filled us in on what happened. That sounds awful."

I looked around at everyone. They all seemed genuinely interested in my story. I hadn't planned to talk about it, but my face gave it away.

After explaining everything in detail, I added, "The attack was awful, but watching my attacker burst into flames and die right in front of me was a new level of horrifying. I remember wishing him dead, but I didn't really mean it. I'm not just physically hurt—mentally too. My body is still sore, but I feel better after my nap."

Violet tried easing my mind. "It's not your fault he died. He was just an asshole who got what he deserved. If he hadn't been messing around, he wouldn't have died."

"Wow, that must've been scary," Clara added.

"Sorry you had to deal with all that," Travis said.

I was touched. They truly seemed to care. "Thanks, guys. He had been stalking and harassing me for far too long. I'm just relieved it's over."

While we were eating, a couple approached our table. Travis greeted them graciously. "Hey, Craig. Hey, Steph."

"Hey, guys," Steph replied enthusiastically. "We just thought we'd come over and introduce ourselves to your new friends."

I noticed Craig wore dark sunglasses, and Steph seemed to be escorting him.

Bert was first to respond. "Hey there, I'm Bert. This is my girlfriend, Faith."

Steph looked excited. "Oh, you're Bert! I've heard a lot about you since we arrived."

Bert glanced at Travis. "All good things, I hope."

Travis nodded. "Of course. I told them you were a huge part of making this place livable and ready for emergency use."

"It's not that big of a deal, but yes, I did a lot for this shelter. I'm the designated lead for this one. I'm a physics professor at the university," Bert explained.

Craig spoke up for the first time. He reached out to shake Bert's hand, but his arm went too far left. Steph gently guided it. "Sorry—I'm still adjusting to seeing without eyes," he laughed.

Bert shook his hand, then I reached out as well. "I'm so sorry to hear about your eyesight. If you don't mind me asking—how did it happen?"

Craig replied, "Not at all. Maybe someone will learn something from me. I was doing yard work when the radiation spike hit. I felt like I was being burned alive. I ran into the garage, but by then, my eyes were already on fire. Steph was already there and dumped a bucket of water on me. My hair grew back, but… no more eyes."

"I'm so sorry you had to deal with that. That's awful. But you were lucky. I've seen firsthand what prolonged exposure can do," I told them.

"Yes, we heard about your ordeal. I'm sorry too," Steph said.

Inwardly horrified, I thought, *Jeez, does the whole shelter know about my attack?*

"Steph here is the nurse on duty. She can examine you if you'd like," Travis added.

"OK. I'm starting to feel a little better. If I feel bad again, I'll let you take a look," I replied.

Steph nodded. "Sounds like a plan."

"So... want to see my eye sockets?" Craig asked cheerfully.

Steph playfully punched him. "He loves freaking people out with how they look now."

"Sure. I'm a bit curious," I admitted.

Craig removed his sunglasses. "It's not as bad as it looks."

Where his eyes once were, now only two charcoal-like hollows remained. I tried not to stare too long, but inside I was horrified. What a reminder for both of them.

I accidentally spoke my thought aloud: "Does it hurt?"

Craig shook his head. "Not anymore. It burned for a couple of days, but my lovely wife had some miracle medicine."

"Well, that's good. I thought we were the first to experience high radiation exposure, but I guess not."

"I was afraid to say anything at first. I didn't want to become a test subject. But Steph talked me into going to the hospital. Someone there contacted the authorities without my permission."

"I'm sorry they did that without asking—but I'm glad they did. Maybe that's why they sent drones and vehicles my way. If not, I might've shared your fate—or worse."

Suddenly, loud music blared from the center of the communal room. A large box dropped from the ceiling. Four monitors lit up with a red screen: **NEWS FLASH**

"Great, now what?" Clara muttered.

Travis added, "This is never good."

A news anchor appeared onscreen—disheveled and clearly under stress.

"Good evening, city residents. I hope this message finds you safe and sheltered. It is with great sadness I report that earlier today, the Capital Building was bombed. Our mayor was killed instantly. Many others were injured…"

Gasps rippled throughout the room. People whispered in disbelief. I turned to Bert with fear in my eyes. He gently rubbed my back as the broadcast continued.

"…This event has occurred in other major cities. We are attempting to contact a representativ from the Cordelia Tribe for a peaceful resolution. Please continue to wear radiation suits when going outside."

The screen cut to footage of people walking outside, confidently ignoring protocol. Then—without warning—they burst into flames. Their bodies crumpled into ash.

"As you can see," the anchor continued, "this is what happens when warnings are ignored. Until next time, stay safe."

The monitors vanished into the ceiling.

Everyone at our table sat in stunned silence.

Bert leaned into me. "Should I say something?"

"Probably, but what could you say? We can't change anything down here."

"Yeah… good point."

Violet spoke softly. "Poor Mayor Collins. I hope she went fast."

Travis reassured her. "I'm sure she did. A bomb would've been instantaneous."

"It's just all so sad," Clara added.

I turned to Bert. "What are we going to do now?"

He shook his head. "We'll stay down here like they asked—and continue to make the best of a bad situation."

**And that's what we did.** We continued on like living underground was normal. Everyone in the shelter had a job to do—no freeloaders.

Megan worked in the kitchen, and surprisingly, she was great at it. I never knew she could cook, but she actually enjoyed it. I, having medical training in my other dimension, helped out in the health office. Of course, no one but Bert and Megan knew I was from another dimension—and that secret stayed between us.

Alena was her cheerful self, thriving in the garden. Michelle, because of her baby, helped care for the little ones.

Life moved forward in the shelter. Day by day. Not knowing when—or if—tomorrow would come.

# CHAPTER 25

It had been six months since we were shut in the shelter. I, while anxious at first, had grown to like my life underground. I became known as the *First Lady* because Bert, my boyfriend, was the leader of the shelter. He occasionally went to meet with other shelter heads. I didn't really know what they discussed—just assumed it was about how things were going in their respective shelters.

I was busy organizing medical supplies when Bert came into the medical office.

"Hey, sweetie. You never visit during my work hours. What's up?" I said cheerfully.

Bert leaned in and kissed me hello. "Hey, honey. Can I talk to you for a second?" he said, sounding concerned.

I noticed the worried look on his face. "Sure thing.  Hey, Steph, I'll be right back."

Steph turned around from her desk where she was working on patient charts. "No problem. Take your time."

Bert escorted me to his office. As we walked, I asked, "Honey, you're worrying me. What's this about?"

Gently placing a hand on my lower back, he guided me to his desk. He closed the door and turned to face me.

"I wanted to talk to you privately. A few of the other shelter leads and I have been instructed to go above ground. Apparently, the government needs some scientists, and since I'm the head of the physics department, they've called me in."

My mouth dropped open. "No. I need you. They can't have you. Why can't they ask someone else?"

"Faith, sweetie, we tried to convince them not to send us. That's what all the meetings have been for. We've done everything we can remotely. They're trying to solve the radiation issue. The government has formed a task force, and I'm part of it. I'll be safe. Travis is in charge until I get back. He has orders to protect you if need be."

I rushed to him and wrapped my arms around his neck, starting to cry. "Now I'm really scared. I can't lose you."

"You won't lose me. We're going to a secure underground location. I'll be safe."

"Will I be able to call you?"

"Not every day, but I'll do what I can."

"Okay. When do you leave?" I asked sadly.

"Now. They want us there as soon as possible. I told them I wouldn't leave until I talked to you first."

"That soon? Damn it."

"Yeah. They want things back to normal as soon as possible—well, except for the little alien infestation. They're still working on that one."

"Do you know anything about it?"

"Not really. They want to fix the radiation problem first, then set up a meeting with an alien representative."

"Okay. I get the urgency. But I still don't like it. Can I walk you to the exit chamber?"

"That would be nice."

Bert grabbed my hand and slowly started guiding me toward the office door. Then he suddenly stopped.

"Wait a minute," he blurted out.

A worried look crossed my face. "What's wrong, honey?"

"I forgot something."

He pulled me into a tight embrace, placing his hands gently on my cheeks.

"I've never felt this way about anyone before. You've changed my life for the better. You are my world. I will be back as soon as I can."

Without warning, his soft lips crashed into mine. The kiss was slow and passionate at first, but quickly grew more intense. Bert was memorizing every inch of my lips—and I was doing the same. We didn't know when he'd be back. After several minutes of hot and heavy kisses, we had to break apart.

"Faith, I'd love to continue this, but I have to go. I'll truly miss you."

Bert looked into my eyes for a long moment. I thought for a second he might say those three little words I'd been longing to hear—but he didn't. I wanted to say them myself but was afraid my feelings wouldn't be returned. I was pretty sure he felt the same way, but I didn't want to risk a fight right before he left.

"Bert, I'll miss you so much. It's going to be weird staying here without you. Please call as soon as you can."

He placed his hand on the doorknob, then stopped again. "Just one more quick one," he said, gently kissing me again.

To our surprise, there was an audience when he opened the door. Travis, Steph, Craig, and Clara were standing outside, waiting.

Craig immediately spoke up. "I see y'all were saying your goodbyes," he giggled. "You see what I did there?" He laughed. "I can't see. But my hearing's sharp—I heard some tongue action going on."

Steph placed a hand on Craig's shoulder. "Craig, honey, you're embarrassing them. They're blushing." Everyone started laughing.

"Okay, guys. Thanks for coming to see me off. I appreciate it, but right now, I do have to go." Bert took my hand and led me to the exit chamber. The others followed.

"Travis," Bert said, "please keep an eye on my girl."

My heart fluttered when he said *my girl*. This was a man I could marry. He was going off, and God only knows when he'd be back. Just thinking about it made me cry again. Bert turned to me.

"Sweetie, don't cry. I'll be fine. I'll be back as soon as I can."

Through the tears, I could barely speak. "Okay."

At the chamber entrance, we all gathered around to wish him farewell. He hugged everyone, stopping at me last.

"Sweetie, you need to stay out here. I'll call you as soon as I can."

Bert hugged me tightly, then bent down to gently kiss me goodbye. He slowly let go of my hand as he stepped into the room.

I stood outside, peering through the small window at the top of the door. I watched as Bert put on his radiation suit. Before placing his helmet on, he looked at me one last time and blew a kiss. I smiled through teary eyes. He turned to the exit door, gave me one final look, and walked out.

I stood there staring at the door for what must've been five solid minutes. I don't know what I was waiting for. He was gone. His mission was too important.

I felt a warm hand on my shoulder.

"Faith, honey, you can't stay here the whole time he's gone. Why don't you come back to the health office? We've got supplies to inventory before the forage team goes out," Steph said gently.

Steph and I had become best friends over the last few months, and I was thankful for that now. I felt lost without Bert. Snapping out of my trance, I said, "Oh. Yes. Good idea."

We returned to the health office and got back to work, going over supplies for the next forage run. The day passed quickly. Keeping busy helped, but I still dreaded bedtime. Bert and I had fallen asleep snuggled next to each other every night. Now I was climbing into that bed alone. It hit me hard.

I reluctantly crawled into bed and hugged my pillow, pretending it was him. Eventually, I drifted off to sleep thinking of my one and only love.

I was jerked awake in the wee hours of the morning. Turning over, I saw Travis standing beside my bed in the dim light.

"Hey, Faith. You have a phone call," he whispered.

I immediately jumped out of bed, nearly knocking him over. "Oh! Sorry. Finally!"

"Faith, slow down. He'll wait."

"So, it is Bert. How did he sound?"

"Tired. He had a long day of traveling. You can take it in our office."

Travis guided me to his and Bert's shared office.

All the shelters had one of those old bag phones from the previous century. Primitive—but reliable. Sitting at Bert's desk, I picked up the receiver.

"Hey, honey. How are you?" I said cheerfully.

"Hey, baby. Better now that I hear your voice. Sorry it took so long. We had a long journey. Unfortunately, I can't tell you where I am."

"I figured. I'm just glad you're okay. I miss you so much. It was weird going to bed without you."

"I know. I didn't realize how much I got used to cuddling up with you," Bert admitted.

We talked for five more minutes about nothing in particular. I hung on every word, knowing I might have to replay this conversation in my mind for days. After we hung up, I sat at his desk, daydreaming about the day he'd return.

Eventually, I got up and headed out. Travis was waiting.

"Hey, Faith. You okay?" he asked gently.

"Yeah. It was great to hear his voice. I miss him so much. I think I'll try going back to bed now. I couldn't sleep knowing he was out there somewhere. But now that I've heard from him, I'm suddenly exhausted."

Travis hugged me. He slowly pulled away and looked into my eyes.

"I get it. I'll walk you back."

We walked to the dorm in silence. At the door, he stopped.

"I've got work to do, so I'll let you go on from here. Hope you get some more rest." He hugged me again, this time tighter and longer. Then he held the door but didn't open it.

"Hey, Faith. One last thing before you go to bed?"

"Sure. What's up?" I asked nervously.

"It's been great being your so-called bodyguard while Bert's away. And… I find myself starting to have feelings for you."

"Oh." I took a step back.

Travis stepped closer. "I'm going to ask Steph to step in for me. Because right now, I really want to kiss you."

I was speechless. "Oh," was all I could say.

I kept my eyes on him as he reached for the door. But he didn't open it.

"Everything in my bones is telling me to kiss you," he said, just inches from my lips.

I placed a hand on his chest and stepped back. "Travis, I'm flattered, but… I love Bert." My mouth dropped as the words slipped out. "Wait—I do. I love Bert. I need to tell him. Can you call him back?"

I turned to run to the office, but Travis gently stopped me.

"Faith, that's great. I didn't know you loved him. But no, I can't call him back—I don't have the number for where he is. And I'm sorry for trying to kiss you. Let me get the door."

He opened the door for me.

I walked into the dark dorm room, unaware that Megan's bunk had a clear view of the doorway. She saw everything that happened between Travis and me—and tucked it away for potential blackmail.

I climbed into bed, oblivious to Megan's gaze tracking my every move. We hadn't talked since the first day in the shelter. I treated her like a complete stranger. And almost eight months later, it still bothered her.

All she did was try to steal my man.

*It's not like I killed someone, Megan thought bitterly.*

# CHAPTER 26

I kept busy but was secretly marking down the days Bert was gone on the frame of my bunk bed. It had been a month since he last called. I was getting worried. Travis told me not to, but the silence weighed heavily on me. Since our uncomfortable encounter a month ago, Travis and I had kept our distance—we only talked to each other when others were around.

At breakfast, I was in a particularly good mood. I didn't know why, other than the fact that Steph gave me an inactive pill to help me sleep. We'd been rationing them since we weren't sure how long we'd be down here, but it gave me the best night's sleep I'd had since Bert left.

We were all sitting together—Steph and her husband Craig, Michelle and her baby, Clara, and Alena—deep in conversation about what local restaurant made the best pies. None of us had eaten one in almost a year, but the debate was heated and nostalgic. Then the dreaded News Flash music rang out in the room.

Everyone went silent, turning toward the monitors that dropped down from the ceiling. The familiar red screen with "**NEWS FLASH**" in bold letters appeared.

A woman news anchor came on screen. "Good morning, city residents. I hope this finds everyone safe and sound. I have an important news brief. There was an explosion as a group of world-renowned scientists were working on a solution to our radiation problem."

My heart sank.

My friends all looked toward me. Steph tried to comfort me as tears welled in my eyes. I turned toward her, panic in my voice.

"What if he's...?" I couldn't even finish the sentence.

"Don't jump to conclusions, Faith," Steph said gently. "Let's just see what she says."

I nodded, shaky and nervous, and turned back to the screen.

"The good news is they nearly figured out a solution to our little problem. The bad news is, unfortunately, there is one casualty, and several more are injured. I cannot reveal the identity of the individual who courageously lost their life, as we are still working to contact their loved ones."

Right then, the door to the communal room opened, and Travis walked in.

My stomach dropped. He could have just been coming for breakfast—but he was headed straight for me.

Everyone was watching him.

He bent down beside me and whispered, "Faith, I need you to come with me. Steph, you should probably come too."

I jumped to my feet. Steph stood as well, placing a hand on Craig's shoulder. He gently squeezed it in return.

As we followed Travis out, the room exploded with whispers. I knew what everyone was thinking.

Was Bert the one?

My heart was pounding. It felt like it would explode before we even reached the door. The hallway felt longer than ever. Steph walked silently beside me, probably afraid to speak until she knew something certain.

When we finally reached Travis and Bert's office. *Is this even still Bert's office? I silently thought.*

Travis placed his hand on the doorknob and looked at me, expression unreadable. Then, wordlessly, he opened the door.

I stepped inside, my head bowed, not ready for what I might see.

Then I heard someone clear their throat.

Looking up, I gasped.

There, leaning against the desk, stood Bert— alive, battered, and beautiful.

His hair was a mess. His clothes were dirty— maybe the same ones he wore when he left. There was a red mark on his forehead, but I didn't care. I ran to him, flinging my arms around his neck.

"Oh my god, you're alive! We just heard the news report. I thought it was you when Travis came to get me!"

"Gentle, please," Bert said softly, wincing.

"You're hurt," I said, pulling back. "Steph! Come quick!"

Bert grabbed my hand. "Just a minute, y'all," he called toward the door. Then turning to me, he said, "Faith, I've missed you so much. I'm hurt, but I'll live. My counterpart... he wasn't so lucky."

I stared at him, heart pounding.

"We were working on a device to interrupt the alien signal and hopefully reduce the radiation levels," Bert continued. "Just when we thought it was working, it exploded. He was right next to it. Gone instantly. I was across the room and got thrown back. I think my arm is broken. And I'm pretty sure I have a concussion."

He gently pulled me into his arms. We stood there, just holding each other. Then he pulled back and pressed a long, deep kiss to my lips.

"OK, y'all can stop eavesdropping now," Bert called out.

Steph and Travis burst into the room. They both gently hugged Bert.

"We were all so worried about you," Travis said. "Poor Faith was about to lose her mind."

Steph moved into nurse mode. "How are you feeling? Let me look at that arm."

Bert peeled off his shirt, revealing a nasty red mark and a deep bruise.

"I've got a horrible headache and I'm nauseated," he said. "And my arm feels like it's being ripped out of its socket. It hurts right here."

Steph nodded. "Let's go to the medical office. I'll scan your head and arm."

We all headed down the hall. In the medical office, I grabbed the scanner while Steph got pain meds. Bert lay back on the exam table.

"Your head checks out. Brain looks normal," Steph said.

"Oh, so I do have a brain?" Bert joked.

Steph rolled her eyes and moved the scanner down his arm. When she reached the humeral neck, the scanner beeped loudly.

"What does that mean?" Bert asked.

"You've fractured your humeral neck," she explained.

"Great. Now what?"

"You'll be in a sling, on pain meds every four hours. No lifting anything."

"I'll make sure he behaves," I said with a wink.

Bert grinned. "Oh, you will, huh? And what happens if I misbehave?"

"I'll think of something," I replied, winking again.

"If you two are done flirting," Steph said, amused, "I'd like to get this sling on him now."

I glanced over at Travis. He looked... uncomfortable. I mouthed, "Sorry."

Travis shrugged and said, "Looks like you two have it handled. I'm gonna grab some breakfast. Want me to make an announcement that you're back, Bert? With that news flash, everyone thinks it was you."

"That's probably a good idea," Bert said. "So I don't get swarmed later."

After Travis left, Bert turned to me. "I hope he was good to you while I was gone."

"He and Steph took great care of me," I replied. "But there's one thing no one could take care of for you."

"Oh, I hope not!" Bert laughed. "But... was it Steph that stepped in when I asked Travis?"

Steph nodded. "He said he had some things to take care of and wouldn't be able to keep a close eye. Since I work with Faith, he asked me to take over."

"I'm glad. Thank you," Bert said sincerely.

Steph finished fitting him with the sling. "All set. No lifting."

"I'll behave," Bert said, turning to me. "Have you eaten?"

"No. Let's get you something first."

We went to the communal room. As soon as we walked in, it went dead silent. All heads turned.

Whispers filled the air.

"Oh, it's Bert."

"Thank God Bert's not dead."

"I'm sure Faith is excited."

Everyone ran over to greet him, careful with their hugs.

"OK, y'all. I appreciate all the love, but I'm starving," Bert said, laughing.

"Go sit down, sweetie," I said. "I'll get your breakfast."

"Sounds like a plan."

Bert made his way to our usual table and sat next to Travis, catching up on gossip.

"Thanks for keeping an eye on Faith," Bert told him. "It helped me not worry so much. How's she been?"

"She's doing great," Travis replied. "Strong woman. If it still bothers her, she's not showing it. Maybe she'll open up to you."

"I hope so. Anything big happen while I was gone?"

"Two newcomers. An older couple. Their home was bombed, so they came here. The wife used to teach at the university. She's helping with the kids, and he's working maintenance."

"That's great. We can use the help."

Just then, Bert looked up and smiled. "Here comes my hero now."

I smiled back. "I'm hardly a hero. Just a woman trying to keep her man from starving."

Only a hero could figure out how to keep our world from imploding.

# CHAPTER 27

As Bert was finishing his breakfast, the monitors dropped from the ceiling. The familiar music sounded as the red screen popped on, reading the words: **NEWS FLASH**.

"Oh no. Now what?" Bert said apprehensively, glancing at the worried expression on my face.

"Good morning, city residents. I know we just spoke earlier this morning, but I have an important update about our unwelcome guests. It appears they caught wind of our efforts to fix the radiation issue, and they have agreed to a meeting. The government, with help from the military, has assembled a negotiation team that has been learning their language. I will now show you a clip of their negotiator speaking with ours. Play the clip."

An image of an open field appeared on the screen, with a beach in the far-off distance. After a few seconds, our negotiator, flanked by a small group of people, walked into the center of the frame. Movement was visible at the far left of the screen. The negotiator for the Cordelia Tribe approached our group.

This was the first time anyone had seen what they looked like.

Their skin was very similar to ours. They stood at least a foot taller than our people, with long arms and legs. Each alien had two heads, both with triangular-shaped eyes and noses. They also had three hands—two on the left and one on the right.

Whispers rippled through the communal room.

"Look at them."

"Wow."

"They're kind of beautiful."

I was sure that last voice was Megan's. I just shook my head and ignored the comment. Turning to Bert, I murmured, "Hey, they look just like what we saw in that crater. So we weren't losing our minds."

"It appears not," Bert whispered back.

The Cordelia Tribe spokesman, in a rough, broken accent, said "Hello" in English. Both mouths on their two heads moved in sync, but the voice came out monotone—as if only one was truly speaking.

Our negotiator replied with a greeting in their language. To us, it just sounded like a series of odd, gurgling noises.

"I guess that's hello in their language," I whispered to Bert.

"Guess so. It's weird."

"It was a nice gesture, though—both greeting each other in their native tongue," I added.

The two figures shook hands and continued speaking in the Cordelia Tribe's language. Though no one could understand the conversation, it appeared peaceful.

The news anchor returned. "As you can see, the talks were peaceful—but what the Cordelia Tribe wants is not so peaceful for us. Apparently, their home planet is dying. They've been searching for a new one. After exploring many possibilities, our planet is the only one suitable for them. Initially, they wanted to join us peacefully; however, our government perceived their arrival as an attack, which turned them hostile.

The radiation issue was a side effect of their ships occupying our skies. While we have now learned what they want, no peaceful solution has yet been reached. More negotiation meetings will follow. For now, we are signing off. Have a safe day."

The communal room erupted into multiple conversations at once. Everyone was confused and worried.

I turned to Bert. "What does that mean? Are we just supposed to live with them now?"

"I don't know," he replied. "I guess we'll have to wait and see. For now, we should just keep going about our lives as normally as we can down here."

"Sounds like a plan. Aside from you leaving me for a bit—and the whole reason why we're down here— I kinda like our lives here. Everyone's gotten so close. And Megan's been great about not bothering us," I added.

Peace talks were finally on the table, but so was the fate of our planet—and something told me this was only the calm before the next storm.

# CHAPTER 28

Life continued on in the shelter. I was busier than I ever imagined in the medical office. From a flu outbreak to food poisoning—which I loved to blame on Megan's cooking—typical colds, sleeping problems, and broken bones, there was never a dull moment. No one thought we'd be down here for a year, and the lack of sun exposure caused many of these health issues.

Bert was busy trying to solve the sunlight problem by getting artificial lighting into the shelters. After several meetings with the other shelter heads, they were able to replace the lights in the communal rooms with solar simulators. Most of the men in the shelter pitched in to help install them. Before long, everyone started feeling better—physically and mentally.

Alena absolutely loved working in the garden area. She was always coming up with new ideas to improve and speed up the harvest of fresh vegetables.

Michelle was having a blast taking care of the children. She even started a class for the school-aged kids. Her baby had just celebrated his first birthday. Michelle was upset at first because they were stuck in the shelter, but Bert and I helped throw him a birthday party. It was exactly what everyone needed to lift their spirits.

The party gave Bert an idea.

"Hey, Faith, this party was a blast. Look at how much fun everyone's having. What do you say we have a monthly birthday party for everyone?"

"Sweetie, that's a wonderful idea. Let's do it."

In the blink of an eye, a year had passed. We had celebrated three months of birthdays. With the solar simulators installed and the monthly celebrations in full swing, everyone's morale had skyrocketed. There were definitely happy vibes all around.

At dinner one night, I turned to Bert. "Hey, honey, I'm a little worried. It's been so great down here lately. Almost too good to be true. You know what I mean?"

Bert nodded. "Yep, I do. I'm just waiting for the shoe to drop. But I have faith we'll be alright."

But everything was not fine.

While dinner was still going on, the monitor dropped from the ceiling.

"Oh boy. This isn't good. I jinxed us," Bert mumbled.

The flickering red screen appeared, reading: **NEWS FLASH**, followed by the anchor woman coming on screen. She looked exhausted, with a red mark and a bandage around her head.

"Good evening, city residents. It has been an eventful day. Our negotiations with the Cordelia Tribe have hit a brick wall. They are insisting on taking over our land as well as our government. We offered to share both, but their leaders did not like our counteroffer. They've resumed their attacks and plan to take our planet by force if necessary..."

A video played, showing every major city with a spaceship hovering over city halls. A rain of fire fell from the center of each ship, melting everything in its path.

"...So far, it's only been the major cities, but we suspect the fire will spread everywhere before long. As of now, we are confident everyone in the shelters is safe. Unfortunately, not everyone made it into shelters. We've lost thousands of citizens, with many more injured. We're praying for the safety of our remaining citizens. Signing off for now. Good luck, and Godspeed."

The silence in the room was deafening as everyone tried to grasp what they had just heard. Life as we knew it was over. Our world aboveground was no longer the majestic place it once was.

I was shaking and starting to hyperventilate.

"Sweetie, take slow, deep breaths. We're safe down here. Didn't you hear them?" Bert calmly tried to reassure me.

"But they don't know that for sure," I said. "We could die down here."

"Faith, sweetie, you need to calm down. I don't want a riot. Regardless of what happens, we're together. I'm not going anywhere now."

Bert leaned in, placed a hand on my back, and gently kissed me. Then he pulled me into a warm embrace. I always felt so secure in Bert's arms. His hugs made everything better.

Everything—except possibly losing my life because of an alien invasion.

I escaped a narcissistic husband only to find myself in a world under alien attack. Just my luck.

# CHAPTER 29

I wasn't the only one having a panic attack. Several of the residents were panicking. I quickly excused myself from the dining area and headed to the medical office. Steph saw me come in and immediately handed me a bottle of water.

"I'm not gonna lie, I'm kinda freaking out too," she admitted.

"I know. I feel like I'm going to have a full-blown meltdown. The thought of being down here forever... I mean, I thought the idea of Bert being gone was bad enough, but now, this... This is so much worse."

Steph sat down next to me and placed her hand on mine. "We have to stay strong. If not for ourselves, then for everyone else. They look up to us. You're the First Lady, remember?"

I chuckled through the tears welling in my eyes. "Yeah, a title I never asked for."

"But you wear it well," she smiled.

Suddenly, the door burst open. It was Travis.

"Hey, Faith, Bert's looking for you."

I stood quickly. "Is everything okay?"

"He wants to talk in private," Travis said, stepping aside.

My heart pounded harder with each step toward Bert's office. I opened the door to find him pacing back and forth, clearly in deep thought. When he saw me, he stopped and walked over.

"I've been thinking," he began. "We may have to stay down here longer than expected. Possibly a few more years... if not longer."

I swallowed hard. "How will we survive that long?"

"I've already started drafting a sustainability plan. We've got the solar simulators. Alena's expanding the gardens. If we can stretch the supplies and keep morale high, we'll make it."

"You think we'll make it?" I asked quietly.

"I know we will," he said with conviction. "But I need your help. The people need reassurance. I was thinking... maybe we hold a community meeting? Let everyone air their concerns. Maybe even give them something hopeful to hold on to."

I nodded. "I'll do whatever you need."

He pulled me in and held me tight. "Thank you. I don't know what I'd do without you."

As much as I wanted to melt in that moment, I knew we had work to do. A lot of it.

That evening, Bert called for a shelter-wide meeting. Chairs were set up in rows in the communal room. The kids sat up front on the floor, while adults filled in the rest of the space.

Bert stood at the front with me by his side.

"Thank you all for coming," he began. "I know the news has shaken everyone. But I want to remind you—we are safe here. We are prepared. And we are not alone."

The room remained silent.

"We've survived almost a year underground already. Together. And together, we'll survive whatever comes next. We've made incredible progress—solar simulators, food production, education for our children, birthdays, celebrations. We've built more than just a shelter. We've built a community."

There were a few nods and murmurs of agreement.

"We will not be forgotten. When it's safe, we will return to the surface. Until then, we continue to live— not just survive. We celebrate each other. We protect each other. And we do it together."

The room broke into soft applause.

I stepped forward. "And if anyone needs to talk, the medical office is always open. We're here for you— not just physically, but emotionally too. Don't suffer in silence."

More nods. A few people stood and offered thanks or asked questions. The energy in the room shifted—less fear, more unity.

Afterward, Bert and I stood in the hallway outside the communal room.

"That went better than I expected," I whispered.

He smiled. "That's because you were there."

"No," I said softly. "It's because we were there. Together."

He leaned down, his forehead resting against mine. "Whatever happens out there... I'm not going anywhere. This is our home. These are our people."

And for the first time since the invasion began, I believed we might actually be okay.

# CHAPTER 30

People were busy at their designated work areas when a loud bang echoed through the shelter. The ceiling shook. Lights flickered. I looked at Steph, heart pounding.

Steph shook her head. "Go check on him. I've gotta check on Craig anyway. I know you feel like I do—if anything happens, I want to be with my man when it does."

"Thank you, Steph. Yes, I want to be with Bert if we're about to be attacked. Stay safe." I hugged her and then ran down the hall to Bert and Travis's office.

I burst in without knocking—normally I'd be polite enough to, but the situation was too urgent. "Babe—" I started to say, but the words caught in my throat.

There stood Megan. She was in Bert's arms.

"Megan? What are you doing here?"

She turned toward me with a smug smile. "I just thought Bert should know what happened while he was away. I got scared when the ceiling shook, so I ran in here to hug him—so he could protect me. Completely innocent. Not unlike your little situation with Travis."

I blinked, stunned. "What are you talking about, Megan? More lies, I see."

"Oh, no, Faith. I *saw* you two that night. Not lies. I just figured Bert deserved to know, since you clearly weren't going to tell him."

"There's nothing to tell. Travis escorted me when Bert called and then walked me to the dorm. That's it. Anyway, now's not the time," I said firmly.

Bert spoke up, his voice laced with irritation. "I agree. Megan, go see where you can help. Check the kitchen and pantry for damage."

Though he was talking to her, his eyes never left mine.

Megan smirked. "Sure. I'll leave you two alone. Looks like you've got some talking to do." She waved at me mockingly and walked out.

As soon as the door shut, Bert turned to me. "Faith, is there something you want to tell me?"

"No—nothing happened. Travis was a perfect gentleman. He hugged me, then left. He did say he was developing feelings for me, and that's why Steph took over as my bodyguard. I told him I—"

I froze.

"You told him what?" Bert asked, a trace of anger in his voice.

"I told him... I told him I loved *you*. And that I had no feelings for him whatsoever." I realized that was the first time I'd said it out loud. My nerves kicked in. What if Bert didn't feel the same way? My heart started racing.

"Bert, don't you see? Megan's trying to get us to fight. She wants you for herself."

I was still standing near the door when Bert strode over and cupped both of my cheeks in his hands. His face was just inches from mine.

"I love you more than life itself," he said—and then kissed me with such intensity I nearly melted into him. He turned me and gently pressed me back against the desk as we kissed deeply. But after a moment, he broke away, breathless.

"I'm sorry. We don't have time for this. I've got to make sure everyone's safe."

"Yes. We've got work to do. I need to check for injuries."

Suddenly, another loud bang shook the ceiling. I stumbled backward—right into Bert's arms—as I tried to open the office door.

"Are they bombing the campus?" I croaked.

"Looks like it," Bert said grimly. "We've got cameras set up. I'll pull up the feed."

He walked over to his desk and powered up the old laptop. They hadn't installed newer tech in the shelter, figuring it wouldn't be needed. Bert pulled up the surveillance feed. There were aerial shots and views of each building.

What we saw was devastating.

Everything was flattened. The campus was in ruins. Fireballs burst from the belly of the spaceship, raining down like molten marbles, destroying everything in their path.

"Bert, what about the elevator control panel?"

"Let me check..." He moved the cursor around. "Oh no. Well, that's where it *used* to be."

"Damn," I muttered.

Bert zoomed the view out. Laser beams were obliterating anything left standing. The ceiling above us rumbled louder with each strike. Without a word, Bert reached around and pulled me close, shielding me instinctively.

Then, we saw it—a laser beam locked on to the entrance of our shelter elevator.

We both froze, eyes wide.

"How secure is that entrance?" I asked, trying to stay calm.

"It's pretty secure. But I don't know how long it'll hold if they keep at it."

"We need to tell everyone."

"Let me talk to Travis first."

Just then, Travis burst into the room. "Hey, guys. I think we've got a problem. I'm guessing you heard all that?"

Bert nodded. "Yeah, we saw the feed. Fireballs. Laser beams. Everything's gone. And the worst part..."

"There's a *worse* part?" Travis said incredulously.

"Yeah. They're targeting the shelter entrance."

"Shit. That vault is strong, but if they keep at it…" Travis trailed off, shaking his head.

"I agree. I think we need to tell everyone," Bert said.

"People already heard the explosions and felt the shaking. They know something's wrong," Travis added. "Most of them are already in the communal room."

"Okay, let's go. Faith, stand with us. I want Megan to see that you and I are solid."

"Of course. I'll always be by your side." I squeezed his hand.

We headed to the communal room. The moment we entered, silence fell over the crowd. Everyone turned toward us. We walked to the front by the kitchen. Bert held my hand on one side; Travis stood on the other.

I spotted Megan sitting in the front row and gave her a bright smile. A silent message: *He's still mine.*

Bert cleared his throat. "Good afternoon, everyone. I'm sure you've heard the noises and felt the shaking. With help from my fiancée, Faith—"

Wait. *Fiancée?* Did I hear that right?

I tried not to react, but I caught the shocked look on Megan's face. She wasn't happy. Not one bit.

Bert continued, "…We pulled up the security footage. The campus is under attack. Fireballs. Laser beams. It's all gone. We appear to be safe *for now.*"

The crowd stirred—some shouting, some crying.

"I understand you're scared," Bert said. "But panicking won't help us. There's nowhere else to go. We need to band together."

When he finished, he leaned toward Travis and whispered, "Anything to add?"

Travis nodded. "We'll get through this if we stick together."

Suddenly, an angry voice rose from the back. "Band together, my ass! You're saying we might *die* down here. I'd rather take my chances outside than be buried alive."

It was Vinnie. He stormed toward the door.

"Vinnie," Travis called out, "if you go up there, you'll *definitely* die. Down here, we've got a *chance*."

Vinnie looked around, then left the room without another word.

Travis moved to follow, but Bert stopped him. "Let him go. He lost his wife in the first attacks. He's been struggling ever since. People are free to leave— even if it breaks our hearts."

Travis just nodded. "It's sad."

Bert addressed the group again. "That's all for now. If anything changes, we'll keep you posted. For now, continue your chores. Stay busy. Stay alert."

As the crowd slowly dispersed, Bert, Travis, and I walked out together. When we reached the office, Bert turned to Travis.

"Would you wait inside for a minute?"

"Sure thing, buddy." Travis gave Bert's shoulder a pat and went inside.

Then Bert looked at me, gently pressing me back against the wall. "Thanks for standing by me. I needed that. And I hope I didn't shock you too much when I called you my fiancée. We've been through a lot... but if we survive this, I want to make you my wife."

He kissed me deeply.

"I would love nothing more than to be your wife," I whispered. "Everything went fine. Except for Vinnie. That poor man... I hope he survives."

"Yeah. Aside from that, it went better than I expected. And Faith, I *will* keep you safe. Whatever it takes."

"I know you will." I stood on my tiptoes and whispered, "I love you more than words could say." I kissed him softly. "Now, I'm heading to the medical office. I need to see if Steph needs help."

"I'll see you at dinner. I'm going to talk to Travis about backup plans in case things get worse."

He gave me one last kiss—and a playful smack on the butt—as I walked away. I smiled, despite everything.

I just hoped Bert and Travis could come up with a plan. These people were my family now, and I wanted *all* of them to stay safe.

# CHAPTER 31

At dinner, I was sitting with all our friends, enjoying the measly amount of food that was provided. Looking around, I realized I didn't need anything else but these people who had become my family. Steph and Craig were a great couple. I could only hope Bert and I would become as great as them. Alena, Clara, Michelle and her little one, and Travis—I was one lucky lady. A tap on my shoulder snapped me out of my thoughts and made me jump a foot off the seat.

"Hey, it's just me. Sorry. Didn't mean to scare you," Bert said quietly.

"Oh, hey there. Are you just getting done working?" I asked.

"Yep. I was meeting with the other shelter heads, trying to figure out what to do. There's a storage unit with a fire proof vault door a little further down, away from the main entrance. We may be able to fit in there. A group is already taking everything out to make room for as many of us as possible. It's not ideal, but it's something."

"Well, it's a plan. It'll work if need be." I tried to sound reassuring, but I was worried. There's no way that storage unit is big enough.

The group continued eating, trying to keep the conversation light and cheery. But the constant banging of fireballs could be heard above in the distance. People were visibly concerned, flinching every time a noise echoed through the walls.

With a terrified look on my face, I turned to Bert. "Sweetie, should we go into the storage unit?"

"Not yet. I don't want to go in too early—this could go on a while, and we can't live in there. Besides, I don't think there's enough room for everyone," he replied quietly.

"Let's hope we won't need it," I said, mostly to reassure myself.

Dinner continued, but the heavy cloud of fear hung over all of us. Then, suddenly, a thunderous clang echoed throughout the shelter. Wide-eyed, I looked at Bert and our friends. Bert and Travis immediately jumped up and ran out of the communal area.

Turning to Steph, I said, "That didn't sound good."

"No, it didn't," Steph replied, grabbing Craig's hand. "Don't let go of my hand. Just in case."

Craig gently rubbed her hand. "I'm never letting go. Where my queen goes, I go."

About ten minutes later, Bert and Travis ran back in. Bert rushed to me and whispered, "It's not good. Stay with me, please."

Worried, I nodded.

Bert stood next to our table and raised his voice. "Good evening. Can I get everyone's attention, please? The ceiling of our elevator was just blown off. We are now open to the elements. While the shelter is still intact, it's not as secure as the storage unit, which has a vault door."

Chaos erupted. People shouted over each other, panic quickly taking over. Travis, frustrated, yelled at the top of his lungs, "HEY! Quiet! If you want to hear what we're planning, shut up!"

He nodded to Bert.

"Thanks, my man. As I was saying—we're going to start evacuating, one table at a time. Our only problem is, there's not enough room for everyone. All the shelters are asking for ten volunteers to stay behind. I'll be the first volunteer for our shelter."

Bert looked down at me. "Well, I'm not going anywhere without you. I'll stay."

Steph looked at Craig. They had a silent conversation with just a squeeze of their hands and a look in their eyes.

"I'm not going anywhere without my bestie. Craig and I will stay behind as well," Steph said.

"That's four. Thanks, guys," Bert replied.

Alena and Clara both stood. "We'll stay too."

Michelle spoke up. "This isn't a life I would choose for my son. Isaac and I are staying."

Bert looked concerned. "Are you sure, Michelle?"

She nodded.

Travis looked from Michelle to Bert. "Well, I'm staying too. I'm not leaving my main man."

Bert nodded in thanks. "That's nine. We just need one more. Any volunteers?"

Megan stood up. I looked over at her, immediately concerned.

"I'll stay. It's the least I can do after all the trouble I caused," she said.

Bert looked at me, then back at Megan. "Thank you. That's all of our volunteers. Now, I'll be calling each table one by one. When called, please put on your radiation suit and exit to the left of the shelter. You'll see someone directing you from there. Thank you all, and stay safe. The table closest to the door may go first."

Bert continued calling tables until everyone but the volunteers were left. Megan was still sitting alone, looking a little nervous.

I called to her, "Megan, why don't you come down here?"

She walked over slowly. "Hey, Faith. I really am sorry for everything I put you through. We may die, and if I had a man, I sure wouldn't want him sleeping with one of my friends right after I died. I mean, give my body a chance to get cold. I was so wrong."

I was a little taken aback. Did she actually mean it?

"Thank you for seeing that. But we don't know what our fate will be. We could all still be fine."

The others had been quietly watching our exchange. It was clear they hadn't known everything that had gone on between Megan, Bert, and me.

Sensing the tension, Steph jumped in to change the subject. "So, Bert, what do we do now?"

"Now we wait. There's not much else we *can* do. We don't even know if the aliens are planning anything more."

Craig chimed in. "Would they go through all this trouble if they weren't planning to kill us?"

"Craig makes a good point," I said.

Megan stood up and walked to the shelf holding the games. "Well, we can either sit here and feel sorry for ourselves or play some card games," she said, grabbing a couple of decks. "I even found a Braille deck."

"In that case, I'm in," Craig said enthusiastically.

Megan laid out the cards. "I've got one more surprise—but Bert, you can't get mad. It's just us now."

Bert looked uneasy. "Megan, what now?"

She disappeared into the kitchen and came back with a box of ten bottles. She was beaming.

"I've been making wine. These are the only bottles I've got. Since we might die soon, I say we drink them."

Clara jumped up. "Megan, you're a godsend. Oh, how I've missed wine. Don't we need glasses?"

"Why? Let's live a little," I said cheerfully, grabbing a bottle and opening it.

"This was a much-needed surprise. Thanks, Megan," Bert added.

We drank, played cards, and laughed for hours. For a moment, I almost forgot our lives were hanging by a thread.

But then, an explosion shook the shelter. A flash of orangish-red light flickered from under the door.

"Hey guys," I said, pointing. "There's a light coming from the door. It's flashing."

"Shit. That's not good," Michelle said, pulling Isaac closer.

"It looks like fire," Bert observed. "And it's coming this way."

"But how? We're underground," Alena asked.

"We *are*, but the elevator shaft is exposed. They blew off the ceiling—it's a straight shot down here now," Bert explained.

"So what, we just sit here and wait to die?" Megan asked.

"Do you have another idea? We don't exactly have anywhere else to go," I replied.

"Yeah, you've got a point. I guess I've had a good life. Let's finish this wine while we wait to die," Megan said, her voice soft.

The ten of us passed the bottles back and forth until they were all gone.

After all, we might not live long enough to get a hangover.

# CHAPTER 32

Hearing flowing liquid, the ten remaining behind turned to look toward the doorway from the communal area to the main hallway.

"It's coming this way!" I shouted.

I grabbed hold of Bert's hand. All ten of us decided to join hands so no one was left alone. The sound of crackling, flowing fire filled the air. As if in unison, everyone began shaking with fear.

Isaac clung tightly to his mother's neck. Michelle, in a shaky voice, said, "You guys have become my family over this last year. I love you all. But maybe I should've gone into the storage unit. It's too late now."

"I'm just glad we aren't alone," Steph said.

The fire crackled louder, engulfing everything in its path.

Looking over her shoulder, Megan screamed, "It's here."

The flowing fire filled the hall as it made its way toward the group. Distant screams echoed throughout the shelter. It sounded like they were coming from the storage unit. The stench of chemicals and burnt flesh surrounded us. Michelle's eyes widened. It seemed like she would have died either way.

I turned to Bert and said, "I love you."

Bert responded, "I love you too, babe."

Red-hot fire overtook everything in the room.

I was waiting for the excruciating pain I knew would come—but it never did. Instead, I just felt warm, tingly, and a bit dizzy.

*What's going on?* I thought. *I should be burning alive. I wonder if the others are experiencing the same thing.*

I looked over at Bert. Through the flames, it was hard to make out his facial expressions, but he didn't look like he was in pain. I looked to Steph, who was on my other side. She didn't look in pain either. I tried listening for screams, but all I heard was the crackling of fire.

Suddenly, the fire backed away from us and, almost with a crawl-like motion, retreated the way it came.

I looked around and saw that we were all okay. No scorch marks. No burns. Even baby Isaac looked untouched.

I slowly turned toward Bert and, afraid, reluctantly said, "Um… do y'all know what just happened?"

Megan said, "That was weird, right? It seems we're all okay."

"Yeah, weird. I don't know what to make of all that. But we *heard* screams—like people were being burned alive," Craig commented.

Bert stood up. "Y'all stay here. Travis, can you come with me? We're going to investigate."

"Sure thing," Travis said, standing.

I watched them leave, feeling deeply uneasy.

"Is everyone okay?" I asked. Michelle was checking on Isaac.

"Isaac and I are okay. Good thing I wasn't in that storage unit. I just don't understand why *we* were saved," Michelle confessed.

I noticed Alena crying, with Clara gently comforting her.

"Alena, are you hurt?" I asked.

Between sobs, she said, "No. Not hurt. I'm glad we didn't die… which makes me sad for the ones that did."

Steph was checking on Craig. "Craig and I are okay. Does anyone need medical attention?" Everyone shook their heads no.

About thirty minutes later, Bert and Travis returned. Bert took a deep breath.

"Well… we're the only ones left. The storage unit door was blown off its hinges. It looked like everyone curled up together before they died. We checked the other shelters too. It's all the same. Such a sad sight."

I started crying. "Then why *us*?"

A loud popping noise sounded, and suddenly, the same two-headed Cordelia Tribe alien from the negotiations appeared in front of us.

"Because you each have something we need," the alien said in a heavy accent.

Bert spoke up. "Just us ten?"

"Just the ten of you from this place. There are more around the world. The fire that rained down purified everything. What remains is what's useful to us. Don't worry—we won't hurt you. We only wish to live in peace with your kind. You will have a happy life, free of war, pain, hunger, and sadness. I will be in touch. Oh, and feel free to leave the shelter. The radiation levels have normalized."

As suddenly as he appeared, he vanished.

We all sat in stunned silence, staring at each other.

I looked around and blurted out, "So… that's what they look like in person."

"I think he was kind of cute. That *was* a male, right?" Megan asked.

Everyone laughed.

Steph said, "Yeah, he was cute. Sorry, Craig—you're still my number one." She leaned in and kissed him.

"Y'all want to go outside?" Bert asked.

We all jumped up and ran to the exit room, then abruptly stopped.

"Do we wear the radiation suits?" I asked.

"Sweetie, he said the levels were back to normal. I don't think so," Bert replied.

Bert walked up to the exit door, hovering over the keypad. "Y'all ready?"

All nine of us—including baby Isaac—nodded.

The door opened after Bert keyed in the code, and he led us into the hallway. We looked down toward the storage unit. The door was hanging off its hinges. It looked dark inside. No one dared go down and look.

Megan looked up at what was left of the elevator shaft. "Since this is obviously broken, how do we get above ground?"

Bert stepped up to a panel, keyed in another code, and an access hatch in the ceiling opened. A ladder unfolded from above. Sunlight shined down through the opening.

"This is how," Bert said. "We climb up."

We all reluctantly climbed the ladder. As each of us reached the top, we had to squint at the sheer brightness.

I was expecting to see a war zone.

But that wasn't what we saw at all.

The scorched earth was gone. There was no smell of burnt flesh, no charred grass or trees. Instead, the air was fresh and clean. The rumble of destruction was gone. No burned-out vehicles, no broken roads.

I looked up. The Skyway wasn't even there anymore.

In place of all that destruction were lush green trees, bushes, and grass. Birds chirped happily, in rhythm with the warm breeze.

"The fire *did* purify everything. It doesn't even look like there was a war," I said.

We stood in awe, arm in arm.

Bert said, "This is the start of our new lives. Let's make it better than ever before."

I looked over at him just as he said, "Now, this is a nice place to start a family with Faith."

I looked surprised, but happy.

"So… you want to start a family with me?" I asked.

Bert had a puzzled look on his face. "What did you say?"

"You just said this is a nice place to start a family," I replied.

Confused, Bert said, "No, I didn't say that. I *thought* that."

"But I *heard* you say it."

Steph added, "Faith, sweetie, none of us heard Bert say that."

Then I heard Steph say, *Do you hear this?*

I looked at Steph. "Of course I heard that."

Everyone looked at me like I was going crazy.

"Steph didn't say anything," Megan said.

"Faith, I *thought* that in my mind," Steph clarified.

"What? But I heard it clear as day!"

"Faith, I think you can read minds," Alena said.

"What? I've never been able to do that before," I said, stunned.

"Maybe that strange fire did something to you," Bert suggested. "That alien did say we each have something they need."

"Oh… well, did it do anything to you guys?" I asked.

They all shook their heads.

"Why just me?"

"Maybe in time we'll get powers too," Bert said. "Remember, he said we all have something they need. We'll see. But for now, I think we need to enjoy the fact that—for whatever reason—we're alive. Let's enjoy the beauty in front of us and live for the now."

The alien had mentioned purification, which reminded me of the storm that occurred a year ago— how it had purified my life. It swept away the darkness and negativity from my existence.

I was grateful for the life I had. Aliens may have invaded our planet, but with this wonderful man by my side, we would not only survive—we would thrive.

I just had to be teleported into another dimension to find my place in this world… with my soulmate.


Stay tuned to see if Bert and Faith thrive in Their New Earth.

www.ingramcontent.com/pod-product-compliance
Lightning Source LLC
Chambersburg PA
CBHW030246120726
47903CB00005B/1640